D1211433

A Drop of Magic

The Magicsmith - Book 1

by

L. R. Braden

Bell Bridge Books

Bell Bridge Books
PO BOX 300921
Memphis, TN 38130
Print ISBN: 978-1-61194-941-4

Bell Bridge Books is an Imprint of BelleBooks, Inc.

We at BelleBooks enjoy hearing from readers.
Visit our websites
BelleBooks.com
BellBridgeBooks.com
ImaJinnBooks.com

10 9 8 7 6 5 4 3 2 1

Cover design: Debra Dixon
Interior design: Hank Smith
Photo/Art credits:
Shop background (manipulated) © Chesterf | Dreamstime.com
Woman (manipulated) © Viorel Sima | Dreamstime.com

:Lmde:01:

For my mother, who read to me early and often, and my husband, who makes all things possible.

Chapter 1

METAL DUST CLUNG to the sweat on my arms, glittering like shining scales. Even with the studio door propped open behind me, the uncommonly warm October air did little to temper the heat of the forge. A shower of sparks erupted as I plunged the carbon steel rod back into the annealing embers and dragged an arm across my forehead, taking care to avoid the bulky, blackened welding glove. I'd probably still end up with sooty streaks decorating my otherwise pale face. I always did.

Lost in the beat of my old MP3 player, I started belting out the lyrics of Robert DeLong's *Don't Wait Up* as I prepared the next rod. Then a touch settled—light and tentative—on my arm, and the bottom fell out of my stomach.

Tongs clutched in one hand, hammer in the other, I spun.

"Whoa, whoa." His lips formed the words, though I couldn't hear them over the music blaring through my headphones.

An inch shorter than I was, wearing jeans and a polo shirt, I had no reason to think the man was anything but human. But then, who could tell these days? He took a step back, hands raised, either to show he meant no harm or to ward off the blow he thought was coming.

Behind him, near the open door, stood a second man. He wore a rumpled brown suit that matched his hair and eyes. Average height, average build, average looks. Nothing remarkable about him.

Moving to put the anvil between us, I set the hammer down and pulled off my headphones, but kept a white-knuckled grip on the tongs. The higher-than-average number of violent crimes this summer had me on edge—along with everyone else—though none of the violence had come so far as my neck of the woods. It seemed unlikely a murderer would get my attention before attacking, but my heart raced a mile a minute as I faced the strangers. "Who are you?"

The man nearest me lowered his arms. "We announced ourselves, but it seems you didn't hear."

I scowled at his attempt to put the blame back on me. This was my studio, and they were uninvited guests.

"My apologies." This came from Mr. Unremarkable. The monotone of his voice matched his appearance, revealing nothing. "You may call me Smith. My associate is Neil. Am I addressing Alyssandra Blackwood?"

A muscle under my right eye twitched. Most people only knew me as Alex. Alyssandra hadn't existed anywhere but legal documents since I was twelve and traded the name in for something stronger, more practical.

"We've come to purchase an item from you, an engraved silver box."

My shoulders dropped as the tension in them eased a little. Customers didn't often stop by the studio unannounced, but it wasn't unheard of. People sometimes got my address from the Souled Art Gallery in Boulder where I showed my work, or from previous customers, and came to commission pieces. Most were courteous enough to call ahead. "I'm booked on orders right now. I could maybe get to it next month."

"You misunderstand. We are looking for an object already in your possession."

"Oh. Well, sorry to disappoint, but I don't have an item like that in stock."

"We know the box came your way. If you hand it over, we can make it worth your while." Neil had the slick, sleazy tone of a used car salesman.

Curious though I was about this box, and why they thought I had it, I'd had enough of the conversation. Even if they weren't killers, they gave me the creeps. I shook my head. "You were misinformed."

"Ms. Blackwood," Smith said. "Be reasonable. We're willing to pay handsomely, and considering the other parties involved, you're not likely to get a better offer. Surely it isn't worth the risk?"

My breath caught as the thinly veiled threat hit me like a punch in the gut.

"You need to leave, now." My voice trembled slightly. The studio only had one door, and they were between it and me. I was trapped. Shifting my stance, I tightened my grip on the tongs, willing them not to shake.

Smith raised his hands in a placating manner. "I think we've gotten off on the wrong foot. You might not even realize you have the item we seek. It would look quite common, like a jewelry box."

"I told you, I haven't got anything like that. Now get out of here before I call the cops." It was a bluff, of course, I'd left my cell phone in the house. Even if I could call, the police would never arrive in time to help. That was the downside of living so far from town. I was on my own.

"Enough of this." Neil stepped around the anvil and reached for my arm.

Time slowed.

I didn't like to fight, I avoided confrontations when I could, but if he thought I was going to roll over, he was wrong. With a guttural howl, I twisted my wrist out of Neil's grip and swung the tongs into his face. His skin split apart like newspaper peeling back from a fire, scorched black and crinkled around the edges. An unearthly shriek filled the studio, and I stumbled back, shocked at the damage I'd done.

Neil shimmered and seemed to melt. His skin became transparent, and a network of blue veins crawled beneath its surface. His nose spread and sank into his face, leaving two flared slits. Below that, the mouth emitting that horrible sound elongated until the gaping, needle-lined hole grew so large I could have put my whole fist in without scraping my knuckles. When he reached up to cover his face, his fingers had nearly doubled in length, the webbing between them connecting all the way to the tips. His fingernails stretched and thickened to claws. The creature before me was straight out of a horror movie, and I added my own scream to the cacophony.

Wielding my tongs like a baseball bat, I backed away from the writhing shape which had been the man Neil seconds before. Even at the best of times, my stomach cramped when someone mentioned the fae. Seeing one in the flesh was like having a bucket of ice water dumped on my head. I shivered from head to toe, and fought the urge to throw up.

Smith crossed the space between himself and Neil in two steps and pulled Neil's arms down to expose the hideous gash burned across his cheek. My stomach lurched at what I'd done. White glinted where bone showed beneath charred flesh. The eye above had swelled shut and was rapidly turning a sickly greenish color. Smith placed one palm against Neil's forehead, and the horrible wail abruptly cut off as Neil sagged in Smith's arms.

"It seems we were mistaken." Smith spoke as he had before, without inflection or emotion. Nothing to show surprise or concern that he was holding an unconscious, injured faerie in his arms. "Good day, Ms. Blackwood."

My mind went blank as I fumbled for words.

Smith took my stupefied silence in stride. Hefting Neil without visible effort, he gave a small parting nod and carried his companion out of the studio.

I remained where I was until the sound of car doors closing and the crunch of gravel told me I was alone. Then, still clutching my tongs, I inched to the door and took a deep breath of the outside air. The driveway was empty, no cars in sight. No faerie goons either. My knees gave out under the weight of the panic I'd been keeping in check, and I sank to the ground, tongs still clutched in my shaking hands. The tea I'd had for breakfast felt like acid in my stomach, threatening to come back up.

A gray tabby with yellow-green eyes peeked around the corner of the shed with a questioning, "Meow?" Cat had appeared on my doorstep a few months back, begging for scraps, and I'd made the mistake of giving him some. He'd come around every day since. Despite the fact he'd already stuck around longer than most of the guys in my life, I'd steadfastly refused to name him.

"Fat lot of good you were."

Lifting his nose, Cat swished his tail and stalked away.

It was silly to take my anxiety out on Cat, but it was easier than dealing with the panic and adrenaline threatening to overwhelm me. Anything to distract from the flesh seared to the tongs in my shaking hands.

I couldn't imagine forging more, so with a wary eye on the door I dampened the coals and stored my tools, each in its marked place on my pegboard. The gooey tongs went on a shelf, I'd throw them in an acid bath later.

The oversized shed I used for a studio was a short walk from the ranch-style house on the seven acres of Colorado mountainside I called home. Shutting the door on Cat's meows for handouts, I poured a glass of water with trembling hands and guzzled it down to steady my nerves.

My first instinct was to call Uncle Sol. Not really my uncle, he was the closest thing I had to family since an accident took my mother and left me orphaned at seventeen. It wasn't just for comfort that I thought of him, though. Few people outside the PTF—Paranatural Task Force—

had seen a fae without glamour since the end of the Faerie Wars a decade before, and those who did were required to report it.

Like many officers from the war, Sol joined the PTF to help police the fae after the peace treaties were signed. They kept the registries of all the fae and halfers who ventured off the reservations, as well as the few magic-wielding human practitioners not on the leash of the Church. They also investigated reports of paranatural activity, magic misuse, and the possible existence of other creatures, like vampires, aliens, and ghosts, though only the fae and practitioners had ever been substantiated.

I wasn't sure exactly what Sol's job with the PTF was, just that he was a pretty big muckety-muck whose work was classified. His assignments often took him out of the country and off the radar, and he'd left for another such mission last month. He'd be incommunicado for at least another week, which meant I'd have to call the local PTF office just like anyone else.

Pushing back the unruly auburn hair that had escaped my ponytail yet again, I picked up my cell phone. The voice mail icon blinked in the corner.

I'd completely forgotten about Aiden's call the night before.

After a hectic afternoon installing my work at the gallery and four hours schmoozing with people whose clothes cost more than my car, I'd wanted nothing more than to fall into bed. Aiden was a dear friend, but it was hard to compete with a soft mattress at the end of a long day, and sleep ultimately won out over what was sure to be one of his classic "the world is out to get me" paranoid tirades.

I hesitated, staring at the icon, but conversations with Aiden tended to drag on, and I had my own mess to sort out at the moment.

Most cities had a PTF office, but Nederland was too small to warrant its own staff, so I punched in the number for the Boulder branch. First, I suffered through the standard automated menu—press one if you think you may be paranatural, two if you want to report someone you think may be paranatural, etc. Then there was the call center secretary, whose job seemed to be to test how long people would stay on hold. I drummed my fingers against the counter as my irritation grew with every transfer, hold music grating in my ear. Finally, I found my way to an actual agent.

"Ben O'Connell here," the gruff voice said. "You have an incident to report?"

"Yes. Two guys threatened me, and at least one was a faerie."

"What makes you think that?" His condescending tone put me on edge, like he didn't think I was qualified to identify a fae without the special training he'd undoubtedly had.

"For starters, his face melted when I hit him with my iron tongs."

"You what?" I jerked the phone from my ear in pain. When I brought it back he was mid-rant. ". . . how dangerous it is to confront a fae?"

"It's not like I meant to," I snapped defensively. "He grabbed me and I reacted. Besides, I didn't know he was a fae before that."

"Fine." He sounded only mildly placated. "What happened next?"

"I guess his glamour broke, because he stopped looking like a person."

"Yes, iron will have that effect." I could practically see him nodding. "What did he look like without his glamour?"

"About six and a half feet tall, see-through skin, webbed hands, no nose, and a huge mouth full of teeth like needles."

"A sea fae then. What about the other?"

"He looked human, but he didn't seem surprised when his friend changed. If he wasn't a fae himself, he at least knew the other guy was."

"Can you describe him?"

I tried to remember specifics about Smith's features, but he appeared in my mind only as the vague impression of a man. "He had brown hair and eyes, and he was wearing a brown suit."

"Did you get their names?"

"Yeah, but I doubt they were real. The fae was Neil, and the second guy called himself Smith."

"Did they say what they wanted?"

"They were looking for an engraved silver box."

"Do you have this box?"

"Nope. I've got no clue what they were talking about, or why they thought I had it."

"All right, Ms. Blackwood. Thank you for bringing this to our attention. If your visitors are registered we should be able to track them down through their visas. There aren't many sea fae in this area."

As part of the peace treaty that gave the fae sovereignty over their reservations, the powers-that-be also negotiated visas that restricted and recorded fae presence on human lands. The fae reservations were nations unto themselves where the human government had no jurisdiction, and humans were strictly prohibited from entering. In exchange, any fae who wanted to leave the reservation had to register with the PTF and apply for a visa that monitored the length and purpose of their stay. Considering their actions, I held little hope my visitors had followed the rules.

"In either case, we'll try to locate them and bring them in for questioning. Then we'll contact you with any findings deemed safe for release from your case file."

I grimaced at the bureaucratic parlance that boiled down to *don't hold your breath.*

"If you have any further contact with them, report it immediately."

"I will." I pressed the disconnect button and glared at the phone. If only Uncle Sol had been available.

I was still holding the phone when a knock at the door made me jump. My heart rate went into overdrive. Neil couldn't have recovered already, but Smith? Pocketing the phone, I crossed to the front window and peeked out. A short, round woman with dark skin and darker hair stood on my porch.

I breathed out, but my shoulders refused to relax. There was a reason I lived miles from the nearest town. It was rare for me to get a single visitor in a week, which was just the way I liked it. This was nothing short of an invasion.

I pulled the door open enough to speak, but left the chain in place. "Can I help you?"

The woman straightened as though she could make up for the difference in our height with sheer will. "Ms. Blackwood?"

"Yes."

"I'm Detective Garcia." She indicated a polished badge on her belt." I work for the Lakewood Police Department."

I narrowed my eyes, frowning. "What can I do for you, Detective?"

She gestured to the cracked door that separated us. "May I come in?"

Clenching my teeth, I slipped the chain off the door and stepped back. "What's this about?"

"I just need to ask you some questions." She pushed past me and paced straight to my dinged-up dining table.

I made a detour to the attached kitchen, where I poured a mug of coffee from the half-empty pot left from that morning and zapped it in the microwave. "Want a drink?"

"No, thank you." She pulled out a seat facing me, her back to the wall, and plucked a small notebook and pen from her pocket.

I sat across from her, clutching my warm mug in both hands. My knee jumped like a jackhammer under the table. "So what's this about?"

"I'm part of a special task force investigating a number of possibly connected deaths."

My stomach turned to lead. Had the police finally found a connection between all the recent murders? But. . . . "What's that got to do with me?"

Garcia watched me with an unreadable face. "Are you familiar with a man named Aiden Daye?"

The pressure in my gut spread to my lungs. I didn't like where this was going. "He's a friend. We went to college together. Why?"

"I'm sorry to have to tell you this, but Mr. Daye is dead."

The mug slipped from my fingers. I was only dimly aware of coffee spilling across the table and dripping to the floor. My vision began to swim. I crossed my arms over my stomach and rocked in time to the throbbing in my ears until I remembered how to breathe.

"He was killed in his home last night." Garcia's voice sounded distant, as though she were at the far end of a tunnel.

I slammed invisible chains over the door behind which my emotions pounded. A cold hollowness enveloped me, and I welcomed it like an old friend. I hid in that emptiness like a child in a blanket, waiting for the monsters to pass.

"When did you last hear from him?"

I remembered his picture flashing across my screen and the voice mail I'd put off listening to. "Oh my god!"

"What?" Garcia perched at the edge of her seat, looking as though she wanted to vault the table and wring her answers out of me.

"He called me last night, but I was tired. . . . I didn't answer." My voice caught on the implication. Could it be my fault he was dead, because I'd been too wrapped up in my own life to answer the damn phone? My message may well have been the last words of a dying man. Fumbling the phone out of my pocket with shaking fingers, I accessed my voice mail and put it on speaker.

"Alex?" Aiden's characteristically tense voice was pitched low, carrying my name through the receiver in a hoarse whisper. "Damn it! What's the point of having a cell phone if you don't pick up? Listen, I think someone's watching me. I've got this feeling, ya know? Anyway, you should pick up the present for your grandfather as soon as you can. Okay, well, I'll talk to you tomorrow."

As the message cut off, Garcia and I stared in silence at the phone in my hand, processing words cast back to us by a ghost.

Garcia recovered first. "Do you have any idea who might have been following him?"

I shook my head. "Aiden always said stuff like that. He always thought someone was out to get him. When we were in college, he thought people were planting devices in his room to spy on him. He wouldn't let anyone into his house until he'd run a background check. He was paranoid."

"Maybe he had reason to be. Did he ever mention who might be out to get him, or why?"

"No. His paranoia seemed totally illogical. Just a weird quirk. When we asked him about it, he'd get all secretive and say it wasn't safe to talk."

"You never saw any evidence that he was being targeted?"

"Like I said, I thought he was just being paranoid. But that part about picking up a present for my grandfather . . ."

"What about it?"

"I don't have a grandfather. I haven't got *any* relatives. Aiden knows, er, knew that."

"Could it be a misdirect to confuse whoever he thought was watching?"

I shook my head. "I don't know. If he was trying to confuse someone he did a good job, because I have no idea what he was talking about."

Garcia pulled a digital recorder out of her pocket. "I'd like to make a copy of that message."

"Of course." I played the message again, choking up at the end. Turning away, I scrubbed at the pressure building in my eyes and tried to push away the conviction that if I'd only answered the phone that night I might have prevented my friend's murder. "Can you tell me what happened?"

"Home invasion. We don't know what, if anything, was taken, but the house was tossed." Garcia paused before adding, "Your friend put up a fight."

I pictured Aiden fighting for his life and clenched my fists. Why hadn't he just run? But then, that was just like him, fighting even when he knew he couldn't win.

"We haven't released the name or details yet," Garcia said. "So please keep this to yourself for the time being."

Without thinking, I blurted, "I have to tell David." Then added, "He was Aiden's only real friend besides me."

Garcia flipped to a back page in her notebook. "Would this be David Nolan?"

"Yes."

"I'm planning to speak with him later today. I'd appreciate it if you'd wait until tomorrow to talk to him." Garcia's tone made it clear that "appreciate" really meant "insist," and I wasn't going to like the outcome if I didn't comply.

It pissed me off, but I could understand the reasoning.

"You and Mr. Nolan were the only emergency contacts listed with Mr. Daye's employer. Do you know if he had any living relatives?"

I shook my head, a cavern opening up in my chest. "He didn't."

She nodded and made a quick stroke in her notes. The finality of the motion made me cringe.

"When will his body be released?"

Garcia's eyes softened. "You'll need to contact the coroner's office for that information."

I didn't need to know, not really. Aiden had a standing order at a crematorium. David and I had teased him mercilessly when he told us about it. Now? Well . . . I rubbed at the pressure behind my sternum, trying to ease my breath. All I had to do was scatter the ashes when they arrived.

Flipping her notepad closed, Garcia pushed back from the table. "Thank you for your help, Ms. Blackwood."

I held up a hand to stop her as a thought struck me. "A couple fae came to my studio this morning looking for a box they seemed convinced I had. Do you think it could have to do with Aiden? If he meant for me to pick something up . . ."

Garcia sat back down. "What happened, exactly?"

"They were looking for a silver box. When I said I didn't have it, one of them tried to grab me, and I hit him with the iron tongs I was holding. His glamour broke, and he passed out. The second guy seemed to believe I didn't have what they were looking for, and they left."

"Hmm. If they were killers you'd probably be in the morgue, but the timing is suspicious. I'll check with the PTF, look for a connection. What agent did you speak with?"

"O'Connell, O'Conner, something like that. He's in the Boulder office."

"Thank you, Ms. Blackwood." Garcia held out a business card. "If you think of anything else, call me."

I took the card, swallowing a lump in my throat. "Please find who did this to my friend."

She nodded. "I intend to."

Cat was still on the porch when I opened the door for Garcia. For a moment, I considered letting him in just to have another heartbeat nearby. Then Garcia's SUV started down the drive, and I closed the door on the offer of comfort in those big green eyes.

Crossing the living room, I picked up one of the framed pictures on my stone mantle. It showed David, Aiden, and me making silly, drunken faces on a spring break beach in Mexico. The dull ache in my chest sharpened, growing deeper. When I'd started college, I'd been alone. No parents, no relatives, no friends. A lifetime of moving had left me with few real connections and no delusions about lasting relationships. David changed that when he sat next to me in freshman lit and struck up a conversation despite my best efforts. Two months later he introduced me to his eccentric roommate, Aiden, and the three of us became inseparable. With Aiden gone, it felt like a piece of my heart was missing.

I stared at the photo until a growling stomach reminded me I was still alive. Hobbled by the order not to contact David until the following day, I found some leftovers in the fridge, ate them cold, and turned in for an early night, all the while clinging to the dim hope that a good night's sleep would bring a better tomorrow.

Chapter 2

FROM THE MOUTH *of the valley, a warm wind blows the scent of decay into my face, whipping my hair into a tangled curtain. I stand alone on a field of death. Corpses of fallen soldiers litter the ground as far as the eye can see, and every face is my father's, staring at me with blank eyes. I clench my jaw against the familiar pangs of anger and loss that threaten to break free of the prison in which I locked them so long ago.*

Rows of humans in shining armor stand under the banner of the Church's Sorcerer Troop on the hill to my right. A horn sounds. Hazy red sunlight glints off metal as they begin their descent into the valley. To my left, the faerie hoards scream their battle cry. From monsters that make my blood run cold, to angels whose beauty bring tears to my eyes, the faerie army begins its advance.

"It isn't safe."

I turn toward the voice. "Aiden?"

He nods, staring into me with one dark, heavy-lidded eye. A shock of straight, black hair covers the other.

"What are you doing here?"

"Keeping my promise."

Promise?

Aiden pushes back his hair, revealing a swollen eye. His ocher skin is bruised purplish-black, and blood oozes from a gash in his cheek. When he smiles his lopsided smile, his teeth are stained red from the split in his lip. He looks just like he did the night he saved me. The night he promised he would always be there for me.

"They're coming for you," he says.

"Who?"

"Everyone."

Waves of darkness crash in from either side, crushing me between them.

My eyes snapped open.

Heart hammering against my ribs, strings of sweat-drenched hair plastered to my clammy skin, I untangled myself from the twisted sheets and focused on slowing my breath.

Aiden's battered face dredged up a memory I hadn't thought of in years. Sophomore year, when I was dumb and naive, and I'd had way too much to drink, I left a party with some jock I barely knew. By the time I realized my mistake, I was in the middle of nowhere with a man twice my size.

I shivered at the memory of meaty hands pawing me, a warm tongue probing my lips.

Aiden had tried to stop me at the party, told me I was drinking too much, but I'd ignored him. Not just ignored him. I'd chased him off, accused him of ruining my fun. But on that god-forsaken hillside, it was twerpy little Aiden who yanked open the door of that jock's Firebird.

He got his ass kicked that night, but he saved me. That was the night he promised he'd always be there for me, no matter what.

The ache in my chest made a mockery of that promise, and it was my own damn fault. Once again, I'd been stupid and selfish, and Aiden had paid the price. I'd been too wrapped up in my own damn life to answer the phone. One simple act that could have changed everything. Now Aiden's face had joined those of my father and mother to haunt my dreams.

I wiped a trail of tears off my cheek.

The clock on the nightstand read 5:23 a.m. The early hour, coupled with a long night of jumping at every snapping branch and creak of the house for fear some homicidal maniac had come to murder me, left cobwebs clinging to my thoughts. I rubbed the grit from my eyes and cringed at the rancid flavor in my mouth. I needed more sleep, but that dream had robbed me of any desire to close my eyes again. Besides, I was scheduled to open at the bookstore.

I draped an arm over my forehead and sighed. Maybe I should quit my day job. With my art doing so well, I didn't need it.

But I couldn't do that to Maggie. She was more than just my bibliophile boss, she was a friend. As roommates in college, we'd gotten into and out of more trouble together than I cared to remember. I couldn't leave her hanging.

Plus, working at the bookstore kept me from becoming too much of a crazy shut-in.

Shaking off the disturbing dream, I stretched to my full extension, feet dangling off the end of the bed while my palms pressed flat against the headboard.

I shuffled to the kitchen in slippers and a t-shirt, switching lights on as I went, until I reached the coffee maker I'd treated myself to last Christmas. It didn't do anything fancy, like cappuccinos with swirly patterns in the foam and whatnot, but the built-in timer meant coffee was ready and waiting when I stumbled over to pour myself a mug of steaming black caffeine. I downed half the cup in a single gulp, topped it off, and carried a bagel slathered with cream cheese to the bar that separated my kitchen and living room.

Chewing a bite of bagel, I contemplated my phone. I'd missed a call from David shortly after passing out last night. Guess that meant the cops were done with him. He probably wasn't awake yet, but Aiden's death hung over me like a black cloud, threatening to drown me in sorrow.

"Alex?" He picked up faster than expected. "Are you okay?"

"I'm fine. I just . . ." I bit my lip. "Did the police talk to you?"

"Yeah. I can't believe Aiden's gone. I wasn't able to sleep at all last night. How're you holding up?"

"I'm managing. Not sure it's really hit me yet. I was hoping we could get together today. I work till four, but I could come over after. Maybe order Chinese and watch a Kung Fu movie in Aiden's honor?" Aiden, David, and I had a tradition of renting old martial arts movies and mercilessly tearing them apart until our sides split. It seemed as fitting a way as any to say goodbye.

"Sounds great, Alex. I'll meet you at my place around four-thirty."

"Perfect." I just had to survive my shift without falling apart.

MAGPIE BOOKS WAS tucked between a deli and a health club just off Arapahoe in Boulder. The drive took half an hour along the winding canyon road that traced the curves of Boulder Creek, and despite waking early, I was pushing the clock as usual. The eastern sky was just starting to lighten when my rusty blue Jeep shuddered to a stop behind the bookstore.

Emma Yamada, my opening counterpart, loitered by the back door in calf-high black boots, striped rainbow leggings, a short black skirt, tie-dyed tank top, and black fishnet sleeves. Magpie didn't have much of a dress code, so long as all the important bits were covered, but my outfit of jeans and a t-shirt was downright professional compared to her drunken punk rainbow.

Tired and depressed though I was, her unapologetic fashion brought a smile to my lips as I waved in greeting. "Hey girl, been waiting long?"

Emma shook her head and pushed off the wall, her many piercings flashing as they caught the early morning light. "Did you hear? There's been another one!"

My smile faltered. "Yeah, I heard."

She was practically bouncing with the news. Small shops like Magpie were breeding grounds for local gossip, and nothing sparked more interest than a murder. Well, almost nothing. The idea that the fae might have broken the peace treaty was spreading like wild fire.

"It was all over the news this morning. People are up in arms, claiming the faeries want to start another war, but that's just crazy."

"You don't think the killer is a faerie?"

She shrugged. "It's possible, but they could just as easily be human. Besides, why would the faeries want a war?"

"Why would anyone?" I countered.

"Good point."

Like me, Emma lost her father to the Faerie Wars. Unlike me, there'd been enough left of hers for a funeral. While I tried not to let anger cloud my judgment about the fae, Emma actually succeeded. In fact, she seemed enamored by them.

"They haven't identified the victim yet, but it apparently happened Friday night. Oh! Speaking of which, how did your show opening go?"

Bless Emma's short attention span. Gleefully clinging to the new topic, I reaffixed my smile. "It was good. Lots of rich people in fancy suits that wanted to shake hands with an artist."

"Don't knock it. They're paying your way so you can do what you love, right?"

"Yeah. It just feels so. . . . I dunno, like I'm outta place. Like any minute they're gonna realize I don't belong there and kick me out of my own damn party."

"As if James would ever let you leave. I bet he was lookin' hot. That man is fine."

I gave a noncommittal grunt. Fine didn't begin to cover James Abernathy, owner and curator of the prestigious Souled Art Gallery where I showed my work. When he'd first appeared on my doorstep with an offer of patronage, I'd been dumbstruck by more than just the opportunity he represented.

Emma gave me a knowing look. "I've said it before, you two should hook up."

I rolled my eyes. That was the problem with being a single woman pushing thirty—everyone thought they were entitled to an opinion about my love life, or lack thereof. But I'd given up the illusion of lasting relationships when I was sixteen, after the fifth time I'd come home from school to find all my worldly possessions stacked in boxes by the front door. A few moments of pleasure weren't worth the inevitable pain when it all fell apart.

I shook my head. The last thing I needed was that kind of emotional complication. I'd finally managed a level of stability in my life, and I was damn well gonna keep it. Pushing the thought away, I focused on helping Emma carry in the fresh-baked goods provided by her mother's bakery. Emma would sell them at the bookstore's café, where she worked her coffee magic.

A few minutes later, the mouth-watering smells of fresh-baked pastries and brewing coffee filled the store. Emma slid a latte across the counter and winked. "Just the way you like it."

I took a long sip and sighed with pleasure. Now *that* was coffee.

Smiling, I tipped my chin toward Emma's hair. "I like the new look. Big plans for Halloween?"

Emma's hair was almost as versatile as her wardrobe, changing with her moods. Last week's bob of blue and green stripes had been replaced by short spikes dyed black and orange with two purple tendrils that framed her face.

"I promised to take my sister trick-or-treating so mom could do a promotion at the bakery, but I'm headed to a party after that. You wanna come?"

I shuddered. Bad enough I had to make small talk with strangers to promote my work, I couldn't imagine doing it for fun.

"Thanks, but I've got plans." Plans that included curling up with a blanket and a good book and not having to interact with other people.

Emma frowned. "You're never gonna find a guy if you stay cooped up all the time."

"And I'm okay with that." Drink in hand, I walked over to collect the day's periodicals, glanced at the Post's page one headline, and nearly dropped my coffee.

Lakewood Murder: Violence escalates as police search for connections.

I tried to set the paper down but couldn't get my fingers to unclench. Gruesome articles were a dime a dozen in our violent world, but they'd always had the surreal quality of distance. A sense that they could never touch my life. The twisting pain in my chest proved that wrong.

Glancing up to confirm Emma was busy with her own work, I took the crumpled paper to the back room and read the media's take on Aiden's death.

Police have yet to release the identity of a man found brutally murdered in a Lakewood residence late Friday night, but sources say he was the victim of a home invasion. With eight similar deaths in the Denver area since early summer, this year is looking to be one of the deadliest in a decade.

Despite forming a special task force to look into possible links between these murders, local authorities have refused to comment on whether or not they believe the deaths to be the work of a serial killer. Meanwhile, local Purity representative Danielle Williams was all too happy to offer an alternative theory.

"What can you expect with one of the largest faerie reservations so close? The fae don't care about human lives. They killed from the shadows for years before the massacres of the war, it's no great stretch to believe they'd—"

I crushed the paper between my fists, disgusted that Aiden's death had been used as a jumping off point for a Purity speech. Still, the article reiterated Emma's earlier comments. Even after a decade of peace, there was a lot of hostility toward the fae. Many people were willing to believe the worst of them, with or without proof.

I had as much reason to hate the fae as anyone, and for a while, I had. A long time passed before I realized my father's blind hatred took him from me as much as the faeries. I'd never really forgiven them, but it turned my stomach to see Aiden's death used as a soap box for people to air their prejudices. Didn't they realize they were only making matters worse?

Smoothing the paper out, I put it away, checked for new releases, and stocked the displays to settle my nerves before opening.

Since most of our regulars were nearby office workers who got their morning java fix at our café, Sunday morning traffic was pretty light. The bookstore, on the other hand, did more business when people were off, so sales evened out. Nothing appeared out of the ordinary, but the hairs on the back of my arms and neck tingled. I couldn't shake the feeling I was being watched.

I rubbed my hands over goosebump arms. Was this how Aiden felt before he died?

Of the handful of people who'd come in when I opened, there were only three I didn't recognize—a man and woman browsing the health and wellness section together, the bulge under her shirt making it obvious they were expecting, and a man sitting alone in the café. Every time I looked at the man I could swear he'd been staring at me the moment before, but he was either engrossed in his magazine, sipping his coffee, or watching pedestrians pass the window.

Peering through gaps in the shelves as I straightened books, I sized him up. Mid-twenties with a pale complexion, sandy brown hair, and dark eyes. Average height, he had a lanky build that bordered on thin. He didn't *seem* like much of a threat, but with a homicidal maniac on the loose, who could be sure?

He sat at the little table, slowly flipping the pages of his magazine and nursing a macchiato that had long since gone cold. People came and went around him, but he just sat there sipping and flipping, and I suspected, watching me. Though I never caught him in the act.

Maybe I was just being paranoid.

At twelve on the dot, Jake strolled through the door. A lanky teenager with dishwater hair, Jake worked at the bookstore to pay his way through college. It was a match made in heaven since Maggie didn't mind him doing homework when business was slow, and Jake needed money bad enough to pick up every shift kicked his way. Extra useful now that we were short an employee.

"How's it going, Alex?"

I shrugged and lied, "Can't complain."

Walking up to the counter, Jake glanced around at the bare walls. "Wasn't your friend supposed to set up today?"

My friend, Sophie, was a local painter and illustrator I'd met at an artists' retreat a few years back. She was scheduled for Magpie's next "local artist" display.

"She should be here any—"

The front door jingled again, and Sophie stumbled through with a portfolio under each arm. "A little help here?"

"Go ahead," Jake said. "I've got this."

Trotting to the door, I took half of Sophie's load. "Glad you could make it."

She sniffed. "*Some* of us don't use our status as artists to be flaky."

"It was one time, get over it."

She waved the comment away. "You're gonna love these. Remember that trip we took to Utah in July? I worked off those sketches to make some really terrific landscapes."

Sophie and I often took inspirational hikes, gathering sketches and studies from nature to incorporate in our work. We usually stuck to day hikes near my property, but we'd spent three nights in the Canyonlands of Utah, taking in its unique scenery.

She started pulling out pictures and lining them up against a shelf.

While she spoke, the guy who'd creeped me out all morning pushed back from his table.

A cold tremor rippled through my muscles.

Dropping his cup in the trash, he strode toward me.

My heartbeat drowned out Sophie's words as she prattled on about some botched date with an accountant she'd met online. I couldn't tear my eyes away from the even steps of the stranger's dusty brown boots as they closed the distance between us.

Then they passed, and the bells on the door chimed.

My shoulders sagged and I breathed a sigh of relief. I was just being paranoid after all.

"Well?" Sophie crossed her arms, one high-heeled foot tapping.

"What?"

"Really, Alex, you're hopeless." She gestured to the paintings. She had every reason to be proud.

"Soph, these are incredible!"

Sophie ducked her head and blushed. It was pretty rare to see Sophie without words, and it didn't last long.

We made a circuit of the store, discussing the best placements, then went back to collect the paintings and start hanging. As I reached for the first one, however, Sophie grabbed my arm and spun me back toward her.

"Do you know that guy reading the paper?" she demanded.

"What?" I peeked over her shoulder, panicked I'd somehow overlooked the stranger from that morning, but it was only Marc, one of our regulars.

"Do you know him?" She prompted. "He's certainly attractive, and he looks well-off."

I slapped a mental palm to my forehead. Unlike me, Sophie actually lost sleep at the thought of being single at thirty. Since she was twenty-nine and counting, she was currently speed dating. I'd lost track of the number of first dates she'd been on in the past few months.

"With that stellar assessment, you know about as much as I do. His name is Marcus Howard, and he owns a nearby investment firm. He's a pretty private guy. At least, he's not one of those customers who shoots his mouth off about every little detail of their boring-ass lives like some we get in here."

I'd also discovered Marc and I were neighbors of sorts. He claimed to live just above Nederland on a large piece of mountain property, but I'd never seen him in the small town. When I told him where I lived and asked for more specifics, he changed the subject. I'd never brought it up again and neither had he. Since he didn't seem to want guests, I didn't pass that info along.

"That's not very useful," she complained in a whining whisper. "Do you at least know if he's single?"

I shrugged. "He doesn't wear a ring, and I've never seen anyone with him."

"All right." She straightened up and patted her hair. "How do I look?"

"Desperate?"

"Some friend you are," she huffed. "I'm going to introduce myself."

Sophie picked up a painting and marched off, hips swaggering a figure eight. One of the display spaces was just to the side of Marc's chair. She pardoned and demurred, then stretched awkwardly over the end table to lift the painting onto its hanger. This raised the bottom of her shirt enough that I could almost see her bra and Marc, sitting below her, saw a lot more than that.

As soon as her painting was out of danger, Sophie "lost" her balance and tumbled into Marc's lap. I clapped a hand over my mouth to keep from laughing.

"Oh my," she exclaimed. "Please excuse me!"

Marc's eyebrows disappeared beneath his coppery locks as he lurched up, easily lifting Sophie with him, and set her back on her feet. "Are you all right?"

"Yes. I really am sorry, though. Let me make it up to you. Can I buy you lunch?"

"No, thank you." He pulled at his tie like he was loosening a noose. "I should be getting back."

"What a pity," she pouted. "Well, if you change your mind, give me a call." She offered a card, which he quickly tucked away in his pocket.

"Excuse me." Marc gave a little half-bow and marched over to where I leaned against a bookshelf, watching the show.

"Sorry, your paper got a little crumpled," he said brusquely as he pushed it into my hands.

This time, I couldn't stop the laugh that bubbled out.

"It isn't funny," he said, but the twinkle in his hazel eyes exposed the lie.

"I'm sorry." I giggled again. "You're right. It really wasn't that funny."

"Bah." He waved his arms in exasperation.

I called, "Have a good day," to his retreating back, and admired the view as he walked away.

Sophie was looming when I turned to face her. "Is that really your idea of an introduction?"

Sophie tried to keep her expression disapproving, but the muscles in her face twitched, pulling the corners of her mouth up. "A real friend would have arranged a proper introduction."

"Sorry, Soph," I chuckled, "but thanks."

"For what?"

"I really needed a laugh. You're the best." On impulse, I reached out and gave her a hug.

She stiffened for a second, then returned the embrace. "I am a terrific friend."

"You are."

"That was pretty ridiculous, wasn't it? He practically ran out of here."

"Did you see his face when you landed in his lap?" I was giggling again.

"He turned almost purple. I thought he was going to have a stroke." She gave in and started laughing too, causing a couple browsing nearby to stare at us.

"I did discover something I'll bet you didn't know." She winked at me. "He wears boxers, and he's well-endowed."

I nearly choked. "Oh, Sophie, you didn't!"

"How could I pass up an opportunity like that? Besides, it was a perfectly natural accident."

"Sure it was," I gasped. "Just like your little tumble."

It took ten minutes to pull ourselves together after the conversation devolved into body part comparisons, but we managed to hang the rest of Sophie's paintings without incident. When Jake inquired what was so funny, having missed the entire exchange with his face buried in a book, it took three tries to get the story out. His face drained of color then flushed red in quick succession. With a look that said he would never understand women, he dove back into his studies.

On a whim, I asked Sophie, "What are you doing tomorrow night? The moon is close to full, and I'd love to get some studies of the boulder field in the moonlight."

The boulder field two miles above my house was one of Sophie's favorite places to hike. It had a beautiful meadow, aspens, pines, plenty of rocks, even a small creek. An artist could sketch for hours and never draw the same scene twice.

"That sounds great! I can be at your place by eight."

"Awesome. Have fun till then."

She winked at me, "I always do."

The rest of my shift flew by, and at 4:05 I was out the door.

"Ms. Blackwood?" The sandy-haired stalker from the café stepped into the alley behind Magpie Books.

Chapter 3

THE DOOR LATCHED behind me, cutting off my escape. My Jeep was ten feet away.

Keeping my eyes on the stranger, I inched across the parking lot, digging blindly for my keys. "Who are you?"

He crumpled a candy wrapper and tossed it over his shoulder, licking the last flecks of melted chocolate from his fingers before answering. "My name is Malakai. I was a friend of Aiden's."

I squinted, trying to place his features. Aiden hadn't been close to many people. "I don't remember meeting you." It came out as more of an accusation than I meant, but suspicion seemed like a reasonable response to a guy ambushing me in the alley.

Malakai raised his hands, placating. "It would be more accurate to say I was a relative of his. You and I have never met."

"What do you want?"

"That is a very complicated question with a lengthy answer. I'd prefer to discuss it in private."

I glanced around the empty alley and raised an eyebrow. "This is too crowded for you?"

"It is too public. If you'll come with me—"

I barked a laugh. "As if I'd go anywhere with a total stranger. If you have something to say, spit it out." I was halfway to my Jeep, keys in hand, and feeling much braver.

"Fine," he sighed. "I have information about Aiden's death."

"So tell the cops."

"My situation is . . . complicated. That's why I've come to you. I'm conducting my own investigation, and I'd like your help."

"Are you some kind of PI?"

He bowed deeply, one arm tucked behind his back, the other extended along his front leg. It would have been appropriate for the grand hall of a castle, but in the dirty alley wearing jeans and a sweatshirt, he looked ridiculous. In a perfectly even voice he announced, "I am a knight, and I need your help to complete my mission."

I didn't mean to laugh. I couldn't help it. The guy was clearly insane.

"You don't believe me?"

I smirked. "That you're a knight?"

"It's the truth."

"Do you ride a horse and carry a sword?"

"Sometimes."

"Oooookay. So what's this mission you're on?"

"As I said, I'm investigating Aiden's death and I need your help."

"What kind of help?"

"How much do you know about your mother's family?"

I blinked a few times, trying to gauge if I'd heard correctly. "What does that have to do with anything?"

"Everything."

We stared at each other in silence until I finally caved. What could it hurt to tell him about a bunch of dead relatives?

"Mom was an elementary school teacher. She died in a car crash years ago. Her mom was from New York, and her dad was born in Ireland but came to America when he was a kid."

"That's it?"

"What did you expect?" I snapped. "And what does my mother's family have to do with Aiden?"

He looked up and down the alley as though checking for eavesdroppers. "It really would be best to discuss this elsewhere."

I crossed my arms. "Not gonna happen."

He pursed his lips. "Very well. You are descended of a fae line. A halfer, as humans so quaintly call them."

This time, the laugh that bubbled out wasn't funny at all.

"You're wrong," I said, shaking my head. "I'm one-hundred-percent human."

"It's not surprising you didn't know. You are many generations removed from your fae progenitor, but a single drop of magic in your blood is all it takes."

As tendrils of doubt began to take hold, I desperately grasped at the one fact I knew protected me from this man's lies. "I work with metal. I touch steel and iron every day. I can't be a faerie."

"A unique gift to be sure. One that, as far as I know, exists only in your bloodline. Even then it's rare." He held my gaze while he spoke, his voice never wavered. He believed what he was saying. "In fact, it's that gift that brought me to you. Your unique ability will help us find the killer."

"No." My head swung frantically from side-to-side as I twisted the key in the driver's side door of my Jeep. "There's no way. You're insane, and this conversation is over."

He frowned, a furrow creasing his brow. "I've upset you."

"Stay away from me!" I slammed the door, turned the ignition, and roared out of the alley in a squeal of rubber.

No way. I shook my head. *It isn't possible.* I repeated that chant all the way to David's house as *what ifs* flitted though my mind.

Parked in front of David's building, I rested my head against the steering wheel. Aiden's name hadn't been released yet. Crazy or not, that guy knew something about the murder. For all I knew, he might be the killer. I had to tell Garcia.

But if he told her what he'd told me, true or not. . . . I imagined being dragged away for "voluntary" testing. Surely the results would prove I was human, but I didn't like to think what those tests entailed. And what if I somehow failed the test? What if the PTF thought I'd known? If the PTF caught a halfer hiding their identity, that person was added to the registry and sent to the nearest reservation, unable to set foot on human soil for a minimum of one year. I swallowed the cold, hard lump in my throat. Exile, even temporarily, was not a consequence I was willing to risk.

DAVID STOOD IN the kitchen of his two-bedroom apartment, staring at a menu on the gray marble counter. Dark curls touched his shoulder where he pinched the phone to his ear, and a day's worth of black stubble stood out against olive skin that stayed tan even through the winter months. He wore a t-shirt that couldn't hide how much time he spent at the gym, and bare feet peeked from the bottoms of navy blue sweats.

Kicking my boots off so as not to track mud across the plush, cream carpets, I hung my faded hoodie next to a name-brand coat worth more than my entire wardrobe and flopped onto the brown leather couch with one arm draped over my eyes.

David shoved my legs aside to make room. The leather creaked, and a cloud of cologne wafted over me.

I peeked out from under my arm. "No Steven tonight?"

He shook his head. "He's at a photo shoot."

Like me, David had never celebrated a one-year anniversary. Unlike me, that didn't translate to long stretches of being alone. His current boyfriend was a male model who specialized in commercial advertisement. If you flipped through a popular men's magazine, he'd probably be in there somewhere.

"Did you tell him about Aiden?"

His lips pulled down at the corners. "We're not supposed to talk to people about the case, remember?"

"Yeah, but he's your boyfriend."

"It's not like we're married. Besides, he never really liked Aiden. I don't want empty sympathy." His head flopped back against the cushions, eyes focused on the popcorn ceiling. "How're you doing?"

"Surviving." I crossed my arms, hugging myself tight like I could smother the ache in my chest.

David rolled his head toward me, lips pressed tight. Then he grabbed my wrist and yanked me into his open arms. I stayed stiff against him for a moment, until the familiar sent of his cologne saturated me. The tension in my muscles started to melt. I breathed deep, enjoying the warmth, then pushed back.

He squeezed my shoulder, but let me go.

A stray strand of hair tickled my cheek, and I tucked it behind my ear. "What did the police tell you?"

"That Aiden was murdered." There was a hard edge in David's voice. "They said it was a home invasion, but I can't imagine what Aiden had that was worth stealing. You know how he lived."

Aiden had eschewed most modern luxuries. He didn't own a TV or computer. The one real piece of technology he had was his phone, and even that had been pitifully outdated.

"When did you last see him?" I asked.

"We went out for drinks two weeks ago. He wasn't acting any weirder than usual, but it was kinda hard to tell with him, you know? How 'bout you?"

"He called me," I swallowed past the lump in my throat, "the night he died."

"What?" David sputtered, mouth gaping like a water-starved fish. "What did he say?"

"It was the night of the opening." I cringed at the inadequacy of the excuse even as I uttered it. "I only listened to the message when the police told me he was dead." My fingers clenched to fists on my knees. I couldn't meet David's eyes. "What if I could have saved him? If I'd just answered my phone that night, I might have . . ."

I buried my face in my hands, struggling to breathe around the pain in my chest.

David rubbed smooth, even circles over my back until the trembling in my limbs subsided. "There's nothing you could have done."

"I hate feeling this helpless."

"Me too. It's my business to keep people safe, yet one of my best friends just got murdered." David ran a private security firm in Denver with clients all over the metro area, including Souled Art Gallery and Magpie Books.

"I don't suppose there's any secret security tricks you could do to find Aiden's killer?"

"Nothing the police aren't doing already." He scrubbed his face, looking as miserable as I felt. "What'd Aiden say in the message?"

"That he was being watched. He said I needed to pick up a present for my grandfather, and he hoped he'd talk to me tomorrow." My voice cracked on the last word. Aiden's tomorrow had never come.

David's fingers drummed against his knee. "You haven't got a grandfather."

I rolled my eyes. "Yeah, I know."

"What do the police think?"

"That it's some kind of secret message, but I've got no clue what it could mean."

David opened his mouth, but the doorbell rang. While he paid for our General Tso's Chicken and Mongolian Beef, I turned on the TV and flipped through movies, happy for the distraction.

"How about *Legend of the Drunken Master*?" I asked when he came back with the food.

"Perfect."

We settled in with our takeout boxes and chopsticks, and I tried to forget everything else and immerse myself in a normal movie night.

The food disappeared to a soundtrack of amplified punches and bad dubbing until only a single savory nugget of breaded chicken remained at the bottom of the carton. David's chopsticks moved in for the kill, but I swooped in and speared it at the last moment. My lips sealed over the spicy meat with a wide smile.

Moving his mouth to give the impression his voice was out of sync, David shook his fist in exaggerated outrage. "You dare to steal the last morsel?"

Following suit, I said, "Victory is mine!"

"You shall pay dearly for this transgression." Setting his chopsticks aside, David brought his fist around in a wide, slow-motion swing toward my face.

My own chopsticks clattered to the floor as I brought my arm up to counter the punch, then laid in with some of my own. Our mock battle raged on the couch in tandem with Jackie Chan's fight on the screen, complete with over-the-top sound effects and cheesy dialogue. Then David's fist came in for an upper-cut, but shifted at the last second from a slow-moving punch to a lightning-fast flash of fingers.

Giddy as I already was, the tickle sent me over the edge. My defense fell apart as David mercilessly targeted my armpits, and I threw myself halfway over the armrest in search of escape. Tears streamed from my eyes and my chest constricted around the silent laughter that wouldn't let me breathe.

Finally, as the credits started to roll, I managed to suck in a shuddering breath and shout, "Stop! For the love of god, I'm gonna pee my pants!"

Mockingly, David flopped back and announced, "Victory is mine."

It took twenty minutes and a trip to the bathroom to settle down after that, but when I left David's apartment I felt a million times better. I still missed Aiden, but the empty pit in my chest was, if not gone, at least lessened. I drove home on autopilot, eager to put the weekend behind me. My only thoughts when I stepped onto the gravel in front of my house were of bed and the prospect of a good night's sleep.

A branch snapped.

I turned away from the house, tracking the noise. Probably Cat looking for handouts again.

A thick hand wrapped around my neck, closing like a vise to cut off my scream.

My attacker pressed me against the cold metal of the Jeep, pinning my legs with his hip. Unable to pry the fingers from my neck, I clawed at his arm until my limbs grew heavy and numb. The world contracted to the glint of moonlight off a Cheshire Cat grin.

"Hello, Ms. Blackwood." Warm breath wafted across my face, bringing with it the sharp smell of decay. "Do you know who I am?"

I tried to focus through the pounding in my head. Had I seen this man before? At five-eight I'm hardly short, but my toes barely scraped the ground as he dangled me even with his face. He was wide as well, built like a linebacker. How had he approached without my noticing? His black hair was neatly trimmed above a waxy complexion, which managed to be both dark and pallid, and his ebony eyes swallowed the light around us, flat and black as a shark's. Not a face I knew, nor one I was likely to forget.

My lips formed words, but only a meaningless gurgle escaped my throat. Abandoning my voice, I jerked my head from side to side and prayed he'd let go before consciousness abandoned me completely.

"Well, I know you, Ms. Blackwood. I've been watching you for a while now. We have a mutual friend, you and I." He loosened his grip enough that the darkness closing around the edges of my vision stopped its advance but didn't recede. Then he leaned close and inhaled deeply, burying his face in my hair. "James Abernathy has been a very naughty boy, and you're going to deliver a message for me. You can do that, can't you?"

I nodded. If he wanted me to deliver a message I had to be alive, right?

"Good, girl," he sneered. "Tell Mr. Abernathy you've had a visit from Bryce. He'll recognize the name. His presence is required at the home of my master. He has two weeks to comply. And in case he thinks of refusing, remind him that he couldn't protect even one little girl he seems to care for. Should he cross us, we'll bring his world down around him."

My stomach twisted as his tongue slid over my skin, starting at my collarbone and slithering up my throat in a long slimy trail over skin prickled with goosebumps in the cool night air.

He chuckled at my involuntary shudder. "Mmmmm, you smell divine."

A growl diverted his attention, and he spun so fast I feared my neck would snap from being swung like a rag doll. His grip tightened. My field of vision was shrinking fast. I could barely see Cat on the porch, back arched and teeth bared.

"Well, well," his voice sounded distant. "Looks like there's more than one claim on your pretty little neck."

The collar of fingers disappeared. Gravel bit deeply into my knees and palms as I collapsed, gasping and coughing, to the ground. My lungs were on fire.

When my vision cleared except for a few lingering spots, I carefully

29

lifted my head. My assailant was nowhere in sight. I hadn't heard a car, nor passed one on the road to my house. The nearest crossroad was a mile away. He must have walked, or run. Unless he was still there, hiding somewhere. The thought sent shivers down my spine.

Cat butted his head against my side, then yowled in protest when I snatched him up and surged to my feet. Stumbling as fast as my leaden legs would carry me, I ran for the door.

Between my trembling hands and Cat writhing to be let down, it took three tries for me to open the lock. In the relative safety of my living room I slammed the door, threw the bolt, and collapsed to the floor. Cat bolted out of my arms but stopped just out of reach, luminous eyes pinned on me.

Light-headed from adrenaline and oxygen-deprivation, I pointed a shaky finger at him and said between gasps, "You can stay inside tonight."

After several deep breaths, the fear knotting my stomach started to loosen. Then it transformed into a more comfortable emotion—anger. How dare someone come to my home, a place that was supposed to feel safe, and threaten me and my friends. I clenched my fists. First Aiden, now James? What the hell was going on?

I pulled out my cell phone. I was damn well gonna get some answers.

A HOT SHOWER did wonders to calm my nerves while I waited for James to arrive. I'd always felt pretty secure in my ability to take care of myself, but being caught off-guard twice in as many days had really shaken my confidence. Not to mention making me rethink living so far from town. Clearly, my half-assed approach to Aikido training wasn't cutting it. I needed to up my game.

I was still under the scalding stream when the doorbell rang.

I shut off the water, but paused with my hand on a towel. James lived in Golden. Even if he'd been at the gallery in Boulder when I called, I hadn't been in the shower all that long.

I wrapped the towel around my torso, dark snakes of wet hair sticking to my neck and shoulders, and crept into the hall. The living room lights blazed, blinding me to the world beyond the windows, and I cursed my own short-sightedness.

A set of staccato beats hammered the door while I crouched in indecision.

"Alex, let me in." James's deep, commanding voice catalyzed me to action.

Crossing the living room, I paused with my hand on the knob.

"How did you get here so fast?" I called through the solid comfort of the door.

"I was already out and drove at a ridiculous speed. Now let me in."

Flipping the lock, I swung the door open, relieved to find a friendly face. Not that the expression on James's face was in any way friendly. He looked ready to rip someone's head off.

"Thanks for coming."

He stepped through the doorway, pushing me farther into the room. "Are you all right?"

I glanced at his long-fingered hand where it rested on my damp, bare shoulder, and was suddenly painfully aware of how exposed I was.

Tightening my grip on the paltry cover of my towel, I took a step back, breaking the contact. "I'll live."

James's gaze dropped to my throat, and the line of his jaw tightened. A flash of molten silver swirled through his icy blue eyes like metal in a crucible.

My breath caught, and I took another step back.

He turned to close the door, sealing us away from the night.

My heart beat loud in my ears while I waited for him to face me again, waited to see the familiar blue of my friend, but he was a statue in crimson silk and tailored slacks.

"Make yourself comfortable while I get changed."

The long, dark fall of his ponytail bobbed between the peaks of his shoulder blades. "Take your time."

I kept my eyes on him until my bedroom door blocked him from view. He never moved. It didn't look like he was even breathing.

Tilting my chin in front of the mirror, I found what had caught James's attention. A ring of purple bruises circled my neck in the shape of a handprint. Good thing I wasn't due at work the next day, I didn't own enough makeup to cover all that.

Turning, I caught a flash of silver in the mirror and froze.

Just light reflecting off the curtain rod behind me, nothing special. That must've been what caused James's eyes to flash, some trick of the light and my over-active imagination.

Dragging a comb through my damp tangles, I rummaged for a baggy t-shirt and a pair of loose pajama pants in the pile of laundry on my floor.

When I returned, James was perched on the couch, looking out of place on the worn and faded fabric of my hand-me-down furniture.

It was odd, seeing James in my house. For all that we'd become friends and colleagues in the two years since we'd met, our time together was spent in public places like the gallery. Even our Tuesday night tradition of meeting to discuss art, the world, and life in general always took place at a restaurant. Other than the day he'd come with an offer to show my work, James had never set foot in my house. And while I'd spent plenty of time in the impersonal apartment he kept above the gallery, I'd never seen his home.

Looking at the gaudy knick-knacks collected from all the places Mom and I had lived, and the eclectic pictures I'd purchased in support of fellow artists, I cringed at what he must think of the mish-mashed colors and styles. Then I gave myself a mental shake. James was a friend, I didn't need to impress him.

Not that I could.

Compared to James, I had all the sophistication of something you'd find on the bottom of a shoe. James wasn't like ordinary people; wasn't like me. Even without his titles or prosperity, his fancy suits and shiny cars, he'd never be average. And I'd never been anything but.

After a moment of wistful regret, I came back to reality and headed for the kitchen. "I'm gonna make some hot chocolate, you want anything?"

"No, thank you." James was regarding Cat, who glared from a nearby chair with his ears back.

"That's Cat," I said by way of introduction.

"Where did you get him?"

I shrugged. "He started coming around a few months back. Doesn't seem inclined to leave."

"Interesting." He settled back with a contemplative look.

Tonight's attack deserving of genuine comfort food, I added a big dollop of whipped cream and a drizzle of chocolate syrup to my cocoa. Carefully carrying my steaming mug to the living room, I settled on the unoccupied side of the couch. The cocoa was too hot to drink, so I cradled it in my lap, curling around its warmth as I faced James.

"You said your attacker had a message for me. What was it?"

Down to business then. "His name was Bryce. He said you'd know him. You have two weeks to visit his master."

"That was it?"

"He was annoyed with you, said you'd been naughty." I swallowed hard before adding, "He also pointed out that you couldn't protect a single girl, and if you crossed them they'd bring your world down."

I thought I'd gotten my fear under control, but as I relayed the message I remembered Bryce's tongue on my skin and my hands started to shake.

I didn't see James move, but he was suddenly there, setting my mug with its cocoa dripping down the sides on the coffee table and cradling my shaking hands in his larger, steady ones.

"I am so sorry." He looked into my eyes, and I looked down at my lap, unable to meet the intensity of his gaze.

I started to say, "It's not your fault," but stopped abruptly when I realized it was. Bryce only attacked me to get to James.

"Don't worry, Alex, I'll take care of this. It has nothing to do with you."

His condescension grated. How could he say it had nothing to do with me? I was trying not to dwell on the "girl he seems to care for" part of Bryce's message, which I'd purposely omitted. I was obviously a target because of my relationship to James, platonic or otherwise, and I wasn't some child to be kept in the dark.

Pulling my hands carefully from his, I asked, "Who's this guy you're supposed to see? Bryce's 'master.' What's that mean?"

He settled back, stony-faced. "You're better off not knowing, Alex. I don't want you involved."

"News flash, I'm already involved." I balled my hands into firsts and pressed them to my lap. I'd be damned if I was going to risk losing another friend through my ignorance or inaction. "If you won't tell me, I'll have David look into this Bryce guy and find out for myself."

We sat in silent confrontation for a moment, then the hard lines around James's eyes relaxed. "All right, but promise you won't go looking for trouble."

"I promise."

"Bryce's master is a businessman whose headquarters are in Denver. You can think of him as a mafia boss. He has many underlings to do his bidding, including Bryce. He makes a point of absorbing or running out any competing business in the area, so the fact that I have steadfastly refused to join his little group and acknowledge him as my superior is of great annoyance to him. He and I have very different business practices, and it bothers him that I remain successful."

I quirked an eyebrow. "Why would a mob boss want a local art gallery? I mean, I love your gallery, don't get me wrong, but it hardly seems worth it."

"It's not the gallery he wants. It's me."

I pursed my lips. I'd never worried much about James's secretive nature. We all had a right to privacy. But Bryce had been fast, strong, and silent. More than any human had a right to be. More than the fae who'd come to my studio. If James was mixed up with people like that . . .

"James," I bit my lip, took a deep breath, and made myself ask, "are you a faerie?"

Silence rang in my ears for an endless moment, then his laugh melted the tension.

"No, Alex. I am no fae."

My shoulders dropped as the breath I'd been holding escaped. "Then why is he after you? Are you the mob boss for a rival gang or something?"

"I'm just a man who doesn't like to be pushed around."

"So it's extortion?"

He hesitated. "I guess you could say that."

"What's this guy's name?" Had I met a real mob boss without knowing it?

"I can't tell you." His expression said he wasn't going to budge on that one, so I moved on.

"What are you going to do?"

"First, I'm going to make sure you're safe."

I thought I saw another flash of silver, but it was gone in an instant.

"Then, after many long, boring hours of discussion, Bryce's master and I will once again come to a compromise that leaves us both unhappy, but able to coexist."

"If you've compromised with him before, why is he coming after you like this?"

"I'm a thorn in his side, but he hasn't the means to bring me to heel. So we exist in an uneasy truce."

I ran a hand over the bruises around my neck. "I'd say your truce is broken."

"Indeed." His hand fluttered toward me, then settled back with the other in his lap. "I promise you, I will make certain no more harm comes to you because of this."

I almost laughed at his earnestness, but that would have belittled the honesty in his eyes. Instead, I simply said, "Thank you."

"Having said that, I must request you not report this incident to the authorities."

I blinked twice, sifting through the words. "But he attacked me."

"I know, but it will only complicate matters if the police are involved."

I thought of the fae who'd visited my studio, the stalker at the book-store, and Aiden's murder. If there was any chance this was connected, I'd go to the authorities no matter James's wishes.

"I've had some other strange encounters lately. Are you absolutely sure that Bryce coming after me tonight was just about getting you to talk to his boss?"

"What encounters?"

"Two fae stopped by yesterday. Does Bryce's boss employ any faeries?"

James sat up a little straighter and narrowed his eyes. "No. No fae would work for him."

"Not even Bryce?"

"He's not fae."

"You seem pretty sure."

"I am. There's no way the two incidents are related."

I tapped one finger on my knee. James seemed confident Bryce was no faerie . . . but he hadn't seemed human. Then again, my perception had been skewed by fear and adrenaline. Maybe Bryce only *seemed* super-humanly fast and strong. Or maybe James didn't know Bryce as well as he thought.

"What about the local murders? Could Bryce be behind those? He seems violent enough. Maybe there are other people his boss isn't happy with."

"I promise, Alex, this was an isolated incident. There's no reason to tell anyone about it. Please, trust me."

I glared, but grumbled a terse, "Fine."

"Thank you. Now, it's late, and you've had a taxing evening." He stood up, pulling me with him. "It's time for you to go to bed."

I'd been wide awake during our conversation, certain that thoughts of Bryce would keep sleep at bay, but as James spoke, my eyelids started to droop. The tension drained from my body, muscles relaxing in a wave, and I swayed on wobbly legs. I'd experienced adrenaline crashes before, but this was like popping a Valium.

With one arm tight around my waist, and the other holding my arm, James led me down the hall and over to my bed. A jolt of energy shot through me when I realized James was in my bedroom, but it was quickly drowned out by exhaustion. I barely registered when he pulled the covers up to my chin and pressed his lips to my forehead.

I mumbled something that was supposed to be "good night," but came out as gibberish.

"Pleasant dreams, Alyssandra," he said from the doorway.

My last coherent thought before sleep took me was regret that I hadn't gotten to drink any of my hot chocolate.

Chapter 4

I WOKE TO MY *American Idiot* ringtone blaring from the nightstand, and groping blindly, knocked my phone to the floor. With a groan, I rolled onto my stomach to retrieve the noisome device.

"'Lo," was all I could manage in my post-sleep stupor.

"Alex? Did I wake you?" It was David.

"Um, yeah. Gimme a sec." I sat up, rubbed the sleep from my eyes, and took a long stretch before putting the phone back to my ear. "What's up?"

"James called this morning. He asked me to install a security system at your place. When I asked why, all I could get out of him was that he doesn't like you up there all alone. But he's never had a problem with it before, and he wants this done ASAP. Did you tell him about Aiden, or did something else happen?"

So he hadn't told David about Bryce. Not too surprising since James defaulted to secretive. Still, if he was going to involve David, he could at least have come up with a convincing story. Now it was up to me. If David knew I'd been attacked, especially so soon after losing Aiden, he'd go straight to the police no matter what I'd promised James.

"The day we found out about Aiden, two guys came here looking for an antique box they thought I had. They didn't believe me when I said I didn't know what they were talking about. I ended up smacking one with my tongs, and it turned out he was a faerie. They took off after that, and I haven't seen them since."

"You were attacked?" David's voice came out an octave too high, and I was glad of the distance that prevented him from shaking me as I knew he wanted to. "Why didn't you tell me? Did you report it?"

"Of course I did, and I didn't tell you because we had enough going on with finding out about Aiden."

"But you told James?"

I looked to the ceiling, searching for inspiration. "We were talking, and he could tell I was upset. Since we're not supposed to tell anyone about Aiden yet, I told him about that."

"When? He called me like two hours after you left. Did you go straight to his place? No, don't answer that. It's none of my business. Anyway, whatever you said freaked him out. He's footing the bill for a top-of-the-line system."

"Really?"

"Yeah. Honestly, I'm kinda relieved. I never liked the idea of you up there all alone, and after what happened to Aiden . . ."

"Aiden lived in the city."

"I'll still feel better knowing you've got backup if you need it. It wouldn't hurt you to own a gun either."

"You know I hate guns."

"I know. I'll need to find out when Oz is free for the install."

The great and powerful Oz, short for Oscar, was the technical wizard of David's security firm. There wasn't a piece of hardware or software he couldn't make sing and dance given half a chance. While he spent most of his time on larger projects like installing security systems for business tycoons or crashing the economies of small nations, he'd been known to help me out from time to time with updating my website in exchange for a home-cooked meal.

"Tell him I'll bake cookies, that should bump me to the top of his priority list."

"You always did know the way to a man's heart."

"I'm not sure about hearts, but I've got the stomach covered."

"I gotta get going, Alex, but I'll call tomorrow to schedule the installation. Be safe, okay?"

"You too."

Glancing at the clock, I reached my arms above my head with a yawn. I was awake, I might as well get up.

On my way through the living room, I noticed the still full mug of cocoa on the coffee table. The whipped cream had long since melted, leaving a film of sticky, white residue around the top, and there were trails of cocoa dried to the sides where it had sloshed over the edge.

The physical reminder of my encounter with James left me

momentarily off-balance. Had he really tucked me in, or had I dreamed that? It was all a little hazy, like someone had pulled a gauzy curtain over my memory.

Dream or no, my stomach fizzed like a shaken soda at the thought of James kissing me goodnight.

Shaking my head, I scooped the mug up and dumped it unceremoniously in the sink. Since I hadn't gotten any last night, I made a fresh cup of cocoa for breakfast in place of my usual tea or coffee, but thought better of the whipped cream since I was no longer in such dire need of comfort. Sipping my chocolaty goodness, I settled in my favorite seat by the window.

I usually worked in the studio on my days off, but what if those fae goons came back? Then again, I'd given them more than they'd bargained for. Maybe they'd leave me alone. Either way, the studio was the safest place if they did show up. And while it seemed my house had become a truck stop for psychos, I wasn't about to let fear dictate my life.

I labored most of the morning over the project I'd started Saturday, using chasing and repoussé to create patterns in the copper elements. But after several hours, my scrap heap was piled high with discards, and I had yet to make a single suitable piece. Frustrated, I looked over the rejects. The sculpture I was creating was supposed to depict growth, but everything I made seemed to scream loss and confusion.

Giving up, I switched tracks. Maybe I just needed to get it out of my system. Art could be cathartic after all. I started a sculpture that would represent all the grief and guilt I felt at Aiden's loss, my frustration with recent events, and my disgust with the state of the world in general. I worked through lunch, sawing, hammering, riveting, without any real plan. I made adjustments as the mood struck me. The organic, free-form approach wasn't my usual way of working, but these were unusual circumstances.

With the sun starting its descent behind the mountain, I sat back from my work. The sculpture was perfect, and I hated it.

Loneliness, blame, and anger poured off the metal. I thought I'd feel better when the piece was done, but seeing it made me even more miserable, like the work had amplified those terrible emotions. Annoyed with my success, I threw a cloth over the sculpture and stashed it in a corner where I wouldn't have to see it. Then I cleaned up the studio, defeated.

The clock on the wall read a quarter past five when I got back to the house. Sophie wasn't due until eight. Plenty of time for a nice dinner to make up for skipping lunch. Going to the laundry room at the end of the hall, I pulled a lasagna out of the chest freezer that shared the space. I'd been saving it for company, but it had been a rough couple days and I was craving a heaping helping of melty cheese.

To distract my stomach until the food was done, I took a trek down to the mailbox. Living in the mountains had definite advantages, but convenience wasn't one of them. I couldn't get pizza delivered, ice cream melted before I got it home in the summer, my driveway became a glacier in winter, and the mailman refused to make the two-mile detour to bring mail to my door. I'd had to put a mailbox at the end of my "driveway," where it connected to the main road.

I took my time strolling down the pitted, gravel path. Many trees still wore the lingering colors of autumn, patches of red and gold jumping out between the evergreens, while bare branches reached up to scratch the darkening backdrop of the sunset sky. The air was crisp, promising that winter was just around the corner.

When I opened my mailbox, the first thing that greeted me was a sparkling, white grin. Gary Anderson's face had been showing up everywhere lately, plastered on billboards, pamphlets, posters. Now his likeness had followed me home in the form of an informational flier outlining his platform for the upcoming election. Flipping the card, I found a Purity stamp of approval on the back.

Taking an openly anti-fae stance was ballsy for a politician. Purity's radical hatred of paranaturals was offset by One Earth—a secular group advocating universal tolerance—so Anderson's Purity platform was sure to alienate more than a few voters.

I still wasn't sure what camp I fit into. While my father had been the very definition of a Purist, even before the term came into use, my mother had always been open to sharing the world. They fought about it the night Dad left. I didn't hate the fae like my father, but I'd never accepted them as my mother had. The election was less than a month away. I'd need to find an answer soon.

Under Anderson's smiling face was a newspaper's worth of local coupons on colorful, glossy pages; a postcard from my dentist reminding me I was due for a cleaning; three bills; and an envelope with no distinguishing features and no return address. Intrigued, I tucked the other junk under my arm and held the mystery envelope up for closer inspection.

There was no name, just my address printed on a label attached to the front and the usual postage marks. I slid a finger along the seam and pulled out a folded piece of paper. A little slip tucked inside fell to the ground. Retrieving the scrap, I turned it over to find a claim ticket from Smitty's Pawn Shop.

I'd seen Smitty's, it wasn't too far from the gallery in Boulder, but I'd never been inside. I certainly hadn't pawned anything there.

Pulling out my cell phone, I dialed the number on the back of the card. After three rings a recording told me to call back between the hours of eight and five, Monday through Friday, so I tucked the claim ticket into my wallet and started back toward my house and the waiting lasagna. I'd try again tomorrow.

THE DOORBELL RANG at eight-sixteen and I opened the door to find Sophie in designer hiking boots, Gore-Tex pants, and a multi-layered, all-weather coat. I met her in my faded jeans and flannel with a pack slung over one shoulder, gave her a wide smile, and stepped into the night.

"You were right about the moon." She gestured at the luminous orb. "It's nearly bright as day out here."

I nodded. "And we should have plenty of time to get up, sketch, and get back before it sets on us. But you brought a flashlight just in case, right?"

"Of course."

Hefting my pack so it sat evenly on both shoulders, I snapped the waist clip. "After you."

A small path wove through the underbrush from my house to the main trail leading to the boulder field. The path had started as a game trail, but it was mostly me who used it these days. Over the years I'd trampled quite a few paths from my property to hook up with various trails in the area.

I was a little nervous going out at night after my recent visitors, but Bryce had no reason to come back, at least until James's two weeks were up. The fae were more worrisome, but even if they came looking, they weren't likely to find me in the wilderness. I took a deep breath, straightened my shoulders, and let the cool night air carry my concerns away.

Once my eyes adjusted to the eerie effects of the moonlight, the trail was easy to follow. I walked as though we were strolling under an afternoon sun. After a few trip-ups and an occasional tug on my pack to steady herself, Sophie found her stride as well.

The trail opened up into a large clearing at the base of the boulder field, an excellent place to set up. The unobstructed light would give us enough illumination to work. Each choosing a patch of grass, we started pulling out the tools of our trade. I started with a simple sketchbook and charcoal. Sophie jumped right in with her watercolors.

The moonlit land was magical, a contrast of sharp silver highlights and deep shadows that swirled with color like a million tiny replicas of the layers of the night sky. The meadow around us was an island of silver grass dancing in the breeze. The forest, a sea of darkness breaking on its shore. Every shadow seemed to come alive, making the trees look like they moved just at the corner of my vision. Above the clearing, the remains of an ancient rock-slide snaked down the mountain like a silver river, ending in the moonlit boulder field. Even though I was just a few miles from home, I was sitting on an alien planet.

Sophie and I sat in companionable silence, each absorbed with our work. I did a series of studies, trying to capture the play of moonlight on the surface of a little stream that trickled nearby, passing in and out of shadows at the edge of the meadow like a child chasing waves. When I had enough perspectives to capture the feelings of playfulness and danger the scene evoked, I set out to find a new subject.

The corpse of a large tree perched at the upper edge of the meadow. Its bark had mostly fallen away, exposing white wood that shone in the night. The chalky branches created an inverted silhouette against the sky. I walked around the trunk, dragging my fingers along the surface until I came to the lightning scar that told me how the tree had died.

I smiled. This would be the subject for my next project.

I wandered back to where I'd left my supplies. Sophie was still focused on her painting.

"There's an awesome tree up there," I pointed it out, "but I need more elevation. I'm going to climb the boulders to find a better angle."

"Okay." She didn't look up. "Be careful, the boulders in that field shift when you walk on them."

"I'll keep that in mind," I said dryly. The thought of Sophie giving me survival tips was like a fish telling a bird how to fly. She'd never even been hiking before she met me. Still, the warning proved she'd been listening.

Tossing my sketch book into my pack, I started up the slope. It was slow going. Most of the boulders were large and well-settled, but every now and then one would rock precariously when I shifted my weight. The deceptive light also complicated matters, making distances difficult to judge and hiding angles that might turn an ankle if I hit them wrong. I climbed halfway up the slope before I was satisfied with the vantage I'd found for my first composition. Settling on a large, relatively flat boulder, I pulled out my sketch book, colored pencils, and watercolor kit.

A prickly feeling nagged at my subconscious.

At first, I thought my mind was playing tricks with my senses. After all, the world at night was full of motion caught out of the corner of my eye and noises in the dark.

I tried to ignore it, but the sensation grew until I felt like an army of ants was crawling just beneath the surface of my skin. When I couldn't take it anymore, I stood up and turned in a slow circle, surveying the area.

A flock of birds took wing from the forest to the south, and I squinted in that direction, trying to make out what had startled them into flying when they should have been asleep.

A moment later there was another disturbance, this one a good deal closer.

Without taking my eyes off the dark sea of trees, I called, "Hey, Soph! There's something moving in the woods. I think you'd better come up here."

Animal attacks on full-grown adults were rare, but both bears and mountain lions were known to frequent the area. If we had to chase off a predator, we'd stand a better chance together, and we had more options on the rocks than in the clearing.

As Sophie reached for her art supplies, the meadow fell silent. I hadn't even registered the background sounds of birds and insects until they were gone. The unnatural quiet made my hair stand on end, and goosebumps prickled across my skin. The whatever-it-was in the woods had reached us. Nothing I knew of moved that fast.

"Leave the damned supplies," I shouted. "Just get your ass up here!"

Even as I spoke, an enormous, wolf-like creature burst into the moonlight at the edge of the clearing with fangs that glinted in a long, narrow muzzle and fur as black as the shadows from which it sprang. Twigs and leaves shed from the beast's matted, muddy pelt as it charged toward Sophie, long legs devouring the distance between them.

My mind reeled. First faeries and now this nightmare monster bearing down on Sophie like death itself?

Fear swirled through my abdomen, but I pushed it aside. If I let myself feel it, I'd be paralyzed. I wouldn't lose another friend. I couldn't. Not after Aiden.

With no idea what I intended, I launched down the rocks, skipping from stone to stone as fast as my feet would take me, screaming for Sophie to move faster. She was barely halfway across the meadow.

Swerving to the side, Sophie angled toward the closer cover of the trees, but she was too slow.

The creature launched itself at Sophie's back before I made it to the bottom of the boulder field. One terrified shriek escaped as she fell, cut short when she hit the ground.

I reached the meadow, slowing only to grab a fallen limb that lay in my path. Tall grass whipped my legs, snagging my jeans, slowing me down. My lungs burned as I tried to suck in more air and push my feet even faster.

Ten feet away.

Sophie was on the ground, struggling to keep the creature off her, stumbling and sliding as she tried to regain her feet.

Five feet away.

The creature lunged. Its teeth, dripping with saliva and a darker liquid, caught Sophie's leg and turned her fancy hiking gear into so many tattered rags.

Two feet away.

Sophie screamed. Blood splattered across my face as the beast's clawed forearm finished its arc, tearing through the front of Sophie's designer jacket.

I slammed into the monster's side as hard as I could, with all my weight, all my momentum, and all my rage. The impact was barely enough to force a stumbling step from the creature, but enough to draw its attention away from Sophie, motionless on the ground.

When I bounced off its body, I rolled to the side, so the monster's teeth snapped closed on empty space when its head whipped around. I wouldn't have thought it possible for a creature so big to move so fast. I couldn't stay ahead of those fangs for long. My muscles screamed from the forced sprint across the clearing, and my breath came in gasping sobs that didn't fill my lungs.

As the beast lunged again, I jabbed its face with the broken end of my branch, using its own force to power the blow. The beast jerked its head, knocking the branch toward the ground. Coarse wood bit deep into my hands as the stick tangled in the creature's legs, and I was pulled off my feet.

A giant paw pinned my shoulder, and I shrieked as the bone of my upper arm cracked. Another paw batted away the flimsy protection of my stick, flinging it out of reach.

My chest reverberated with the creature's growl. Blood trickled from a long gash on the snarling muzzle, mingling with the mud already caked there, but the wound slid well beneath the bright golden orb that watched me with a mixture of hatred and hunger.

With nothing left between me and a painful death, I stubbornly threw my free arm up in a pathetic attempt to block the teeth coming toward me. As they closed around my forearm, muscle pulled away from bone in shreds. All I could do as reality ebbed away on a tide of blood was glare into the face of the monster that had killed me and wonder what in seven hells had happened to my life.

The creature's weight suddenly lifted, and pain burst through me as blood tried to pump back into my ruined limbs. I writhed for a moment, trying to wrap my mind around the thought that I wasn't dead yet.

What had happened?

There was a yelp, then snarls. Furred bodies tumbled past my head.

I tried to shift, to see what was going on, but every motion sent waves of pain and nausea rolling through my broken body.

Another yelp, and a shower of dirt clods pelted me like rain.

Tipping my head, I could just make out two monstrous shapes as they clashed and sprang apart in a series of moves precise enough to have been choreographed. The newcomer was larger and faster than the first. Not that it mattered. I was as good as dead, and Sophie hadn't moved since the beast sent her sprawling.

The sounds of combat grew distant, like someone had turned the volume down on the world, and my focus drifted up to the night sky. The moon was two days from full, but it was glorious; a silver beacon burning in the heavens. Its lower edge brushed the tops of skeletal trees. If the evening had gone according to plan, Sophie and I would have worked for another hour before packing up. Time enough to find our way home without stumbling in darkness.

I wished I could tell Sophie I was sorry. Even as the thought formed it spun away into the growing haze of my mind. Some distant part of me realized I was in shock, and when I gave in to the sleep pulling at my consciousness I would never wake up.

At least my last sight would be beautiful.

Then the stars disappeared.

A dark shadow in the shape of a wolf's head crept into my vision, imposing itself on the peace of my last moment. I tried to work up a curse for the beast, but didn't have the strength. From the silhouette, two bright eyes stared into my own. They were hazel eyes, green around the edges with golden flecks and a starburst of brown in the center.

My brow crinkled with a distant spark of recognition. Where had I seen those eyes before?

Chapter 5

DAD'S YELLING. HE always had a quick temper, but he usually hid it better. Mom is yelling, too. She doesn't usually yell back. I'm hiding under the covers in my canopy princess bed. When the yelling stops, the front door opens and closes, then a car engine catches, and I know he is gone.

I run down the stairs in my nightgown, nearly tripping in my haste. The front door is locked and I lose precious seconds wrenching it open. The taxi pulls away as I run outside. My bare feet slap the pavement as I race down the middle of the road, trying to catch up, but the cab pulls farther away. Just before I lose sight of it, I think the figure in the window looks back at me, but I can't be sure.

I walk back to the house of my childhood, and there is my mother, crying in the living room. I want to run to her, but I'm angry. Why did she have to say those things? Now Daddy is gone and he's not coming back. It's all her fault.

But that isn't right. Dad would have left no matter what she said. He left us both.

Mother won't stop crying, and now I see that her face is bloody. A long gash runs across her temple from where the side window buckled in on our old Corolla. A crimson curtain covers her cheek and neck, just as it did in the hospital the last time I saw her.

I try to get to her, but waves of blood and tears swirl around my ankles. The nightgown sticks to my legs as I wade forward, pulling me down even as the waters rise. I'm not even halfway across the room when I lose sight of her, drowning in sadness and loss.

Aiden's voice echoes out of the abyss, "They're coming . . . "

I floated in darkness, but sound carried through the void. Voices, pitched strangely, as though trying to yell and whisper at the same time. I couldn't make out the words.

Slowly, I lifted one eyelid to verify that the darkness was only in my head. Bright light stabbed my eye and it snapped closed. Sucking in a breath, I gritted my teeth and tried again, even more slowly. Through a curtain of lashes I could just make out the light above me, hanging naked from an unremarkable ceiling. Turning my head, I opened my eyes a little wider and found I was looking through bars.

What was going on? Was I in prison?

Beyond my cell was another cage. The occupant was laid out on a metal table, much as I imagined myself to be. There was blood everywhere, on the body, the table, the floor. Whoever they were, they couldn't be alive. What had happened to them? Would I suffer the same fate? Had I already? Maybe I was a ghost.

"She's awake."

"Keep her calm. I need to put her under again."

"Alex, can you hear me?" A face floated into my vision. It was a handsome face. Full lips that looked like they'd be soft to kiss. A strong jaw covered in coppery stubble. Shaggy, chestnut hair that turned reddish-gold in the light and curled around his ears and the nape of his neck.

"Marc," I croaked. My throat was raw, as though I'd swallowed a rasp.

"Don't talk." He pressed a finger to my lips. "Luke is fixing you up."

Fixing me up? What was wrong with me?

Then I looked into his hazel eyes, green around the edges with a starburst in the middle, and the world turned upside down.

I tensed all over, trying to push away from the man in front of me, from the memory of those eyes, and from the sudden knowledge of who was in the room across from me.

"Almost there, just hold her steady." I recognized the second voice as Luke's. He was a practitioner, a rare human who could wield magic. He was also a regular at the bookstore, often requesting obscure titles for his magical studies. Why was he there? Did he know about Marc? I had to warn him.

But even as I opened my mouth, my mind slipped back into darkness. Marc's hands fell away as I relaxed. From a great distance I heard him say, "We need to decide before she wakes up again."

THE NEXT TIME I woke up, my senses came back faster. I didn't hear anyone, so I opened my eyes and looked around. To my left was the barred wall I'd seen before, to my right was a small table laid out with a collection of surgical equipment, containers of dried herbs, and some vials of liquid. Off to one side, looking like a rumpled pile of dirty laundry, was Luke, fast asleep and snoring softly. He was wedged in a corner between the table and wall, head bobbing on his chest as it rose and fell in deep, even breaths. His dark skin blended into the shadows, obscuring his features, but the glasses drooping to the end of his nose glinted in the overhead lights. Close-cropped black hair clung to his scalp, and at least a day's worth of stubble covered his jaw.

There was no sign of Marc.

Assured that Luke was out for the count, I took stock of my own condition. Starting slow, I wiggled my fingers and toes. All my digits seemed to be in working order, so I moved up to my arms. I had a visceral memory of my left arm in tatters, and had to take several deep breaths before working up the courage to raise it where I could see the damage. White bandages wrapped from the palm of my hand to the middle of my upper arm. At least the arm was still there, and if the bandages were white the wounds couldn't be bleeding much.

My right palm was also bandaged where the wood of my make-shift weapon bit in. A black brace wrapped my upper arm like a pressure cuff, soft and solid at the same time.

I pulled my knees up until the soles of my feet were flat on the table and looked down at my thighs. They were covered by a white sheet, the kind people draped over corpses in cop shows. My garb hadn't even registered on my previous foray into consciousness. I'd had other, more pressing, concerns. Now I was wondering what had happened to my blood-soaked clothes from the attack, who had undressed me, and just how many people had seen me naked?

I glanced at Luke, still sleeping against the wall. He was a healer; that was sort of like a doctor. Surely he'd seen lots of naked people. He would have been very professional, more interested in my wounds than my body.

The thought of Marc being there while I was naked made my cheeks burn, so I pushed the thought aside and tried to focus on the present.

I was able to roll onto my side and swing my legs over the edge of the table. From there, I levered myself into a sitting position. Trying to straighten made me gasp, so I settled for huddling over my knees, gripping my sides to ease the pain in my ribs. They were at least bruised if not broken. Blinking away tears, I wrapped the sheet around myself and gripped it to my chest. Then I faced the bars and wondered again what kind of place this was.

The room across from me was empty. What had they done with the body? It had to have been Sophie lying there when I'd first woken up.

A sob escaped and tears spilled down my cheeks. I'd lost another friend, another person I'd foolishly let myself get attached to. Guilt and loss twisted through me, but I slammed a mental lid on the rush of emotions. I'd broken the rules, let people in, started to care. Now I was paying the price.

Luke's hand settled on my back, and I stiffened at the unexpected contact. He didn't speak, just stood with me while I forced my emotions back to a manageable distance and settled my breathing.

My gaze fell again on the empty table in the far cell, and my stomach twisted. I had to know. I owed her that much. Swallowing the bitter taste in my mouth, I asked, "What happened to Sophie?"

His smile was sad and a little too tight, but he said, "She's recovering."

For a moment, I didn't react. I couldn't. I just sat, dumbfounded, and stared as though I could see the words he'd spoken hovering between us. Then, after a few stammers, I managed to choke out, "She's alive?"

He nodded.

I flung my arms around him in a joyful hug despite the pain that flared through my ribs. Luke staggered as he took my weight. Nerves screamed all over my body, but I didn't care. My friend was alive.

"Take it easy, Alex." Luke scolded. "It's going to be a while before you're fully recovered. Not dead and healthy are not the same thing." With a grunt of exertion, he settled me back on the table.

The sheet had fallen loose during my exuberant display, and my cheeks burned again as he picked it up, shook it out, and wrapped it around my shoulders. His eyes stayed politely averted the whole time.

Once the sheet was back in place, he patted me on the shoulder and mumbled, "You're gonna be fine." He said it so quietly it seemed more for his benefit than mine, but I smiled in gratitude.

If Sophie and I were alive, it was because of Luke. Like many practitioners hamstrung by the PTF's dictate that they not learn the darker arts reserved for the Church's Sorcerer Troops, Luke focused his magical studies solely on healing, lending his skills when modern medicine failed.

I wiped my treacherous tears and looked at him through blurry eyes. "Thank you."

He patted me on the shoulder. "Just don't go throwing yourself around anymore and undo all my hard work."

I gave a sheepish grin and nodded.

"I'm not kidding, Alex. You're lucky to be alive."

My smile slipped as still-frame memories of the attack flashed through my mind like an epileptic flip-book with half the pages missing.

I gripped Luke's arm. "It was Marc."

Frowning, Luke shook his head. "He was there, but he's not the one who attacked you. In fact, he saved your life. Another few minutes and you'd have been too far gone to bring back."

I tried to think back, to remember more clearly what had happened, but my head was full of cobwebs.

The black one. It attacked us. Marc must've been the other.

I opened my mouth, but Luke held up a hand to cut me off.

"I know you've got questions about what happened, and we'll get to that, but first, how do you feel?"

"Sore, overwhelmed, tired, hungry, thirsty, a little dizzy, and a bit ridiculous that I'm sitting here in nothing but a sheet."

The corner of his mouth twitched up. "I think I can take care of some of that. But let's make sure you know your limitations first."

He gestured to my sheet-covered body. "You lost a lot of blood, so you'll be woozy for a while. Your legs are okay other than some scratches and bruising. You had three cracked ribs. I did what I could to speed the healing, but they were a pretty low priority, so they're gonna hurt for a while. Both palms were lacerated. From the edges of the wound it looks like you were holding something jagged but not sharp that tore rather than cut you. Your right arm was broken in two places, snapped like a pencil. I set the bones and started them mending, but you'll need to keep that brace on for a few days. No heavy lifting, and yes, that includes your hammer, so stay out of the studio at least until Saturday. When you do go back, start slow. I don't want you re-injuring it."

He paused for a breath, letting it out slowly, and I braced for bad news. He'd saved the worst injury for last.

Indicating the bandages he said, "Your left arm was pretty severely lacerated. We're talking multiple tears that went all the way to the bone. That's where you lost most of your blood. Luckily, Marcus had enough sense to tourniquet before moving you. I was able to re-knit most of the tissue, so you should regain full use of your arm."

The air I'd been holding came out in a loud *whoosh*.

"But," he said, "the muscles, tendons, and ligaments were all torn loose. That's not an injury that can heal overnight, even with magic. It's going to take a while, and probably a decent amount of physical therapy, before you get your strength back in that arm."

"Time and work I can handle, I'm just glad I'll still be able to use it. Honestly, what you did is amazing. I can't even begin to thank you enough."

"Before you get all mushy on me I should warn you—I was able to repair most of the core structure, but even magic can't make a wound like that disappear entirely. You're going to have scars."

My stomach twisted at the news, but I managed to smile. "Do you really think I'm shallow enough to worry about scars when not long ago I was lying in a field, sure I was dead?"

He held up his hands in a placating manner. "I never presume to know what a woman thinks about her looks."

"I'm grateful for what you did, Luke, and no amount of scarring will lessen that."

"Right," he said, rubbing his hands together. "There's no reason for you to stay down here anymore. Let's go find you some food and clothes."

"And answers?"

"After." He wrapped one wiry arm around my waist and helped me slide off the table and onto my feet. I had to rearrange the sheet, wrapping it under my armpits and holding it closed with my left hand so my right was free to grip Luke's as I struggled for balance.

"Take your time," he said. "There's no rush."

I toddled slowly at first, trying not to trip on my unsteady feet. Then, as my dizziness began to recede, I focused more on my surroundings.

The cell I'd woken up in was one of several that lined a stone hallway. I couldn't tell if any others were occupied. "This place looks like a dungeon."

"You're not far off." The tight line of Luke's lips dissuaded further questions, so I shoved my curiosity aside and focused on not falling over as I shuffled my feet over the floor.

My room was the closest to the exit, so it was only a few steps to the reinforced door at the end of the hall. That led to a storage room, which looked more like what I'd expect to find in a person's basement, with shelves of canned goods and various storage boxes lining the walls. There were also a couple steamer trunks, a large chest freezer, and several cases with padlocks on them.

To the left was another door. This one opened to the bottom of a staircase that doubled back over the dungeon rooms. I had to pause twice during my trek up the steps, but Luke was patient, waiting quietly until I was able to continue.

"Don't worry, you'll be back to your old self in no time."

"Right," I wheezed.

The top of the stairs dead-ended at another heavy, metal door. Some-one was obsessed with security. Then again, anyone with a dungeon in their basement would be.

We entered the house proper through the laundry room, which was larger than my own and boasted a top-of-the-line washer and dryer. Several baskets of rank-smelling clothes were stacked between a sink and another huge freezer. A set of French doors looked out over a rough wooden deck, and I blinked in the afternoon sun. A forest scene much like the one out my own windows spread beneath a pale, uninterrupted blue sky.

Luke turned to take us farther into the house.

The living room was large, but it had a comfortable, lived-in feel, as though many people spent time there. The couches and chairs were good quality but worn, the rugs were thick but frayed around the edges, and literature ranging from *Game Informer* magazine to the latest Danielle Steel novel were strewn about the various tables. A picture on the mantel showed Marc brandishing a three-foot fish at the camera with a smile that practically split his face in two. I shuddered at all those exposed teeth.

"You all right?"

I gestured to the picture. "This is Marc's house?"

"Mm hm."

We passed a set of stairs and entered a long hallway. Closed doors echoed the cells below. Halfway down, Luke opened one and directed me inside. "You can get cleaned up in here while I make some food."

The bathroom had a large porcelain tub with a shower fixture that looked like heaven itself.

Luke slid the brace off my upper arm. "Don't use this arm while the brace is off. The bones have started to re-knit, but they won't hold up if you strain them. Don't worry about keeping the bandages on your hands dry, I'll change them when you're done regardless."

He started the faucets, but hesitated before leaving. "Do you need help getting in the tub?"

"I'll be fine."

"All right. Don't drown."

Once the door clicked shut behind him I dropped the sheet and turned to face the refugee in the mirror. Sunken eyes looked out from bruised sockets set in pale, sallow skin. My hair was a nest of dreads, with leaves and twigs snarled in the tangles. I'd be lucky if I didn't have to cut the knots out.

The ring of bruises Bryce had left still circled my neck, but they were barely a footnote to the kaleidoscope covering the rest of my body. No wonder I was sore. My right arm, where Luke had removed the brace, was dark purple and swollen to half again its normal size. My ribs were camouflaged in purple, blue, and black. Even my legs, which had escaped serious injury, were covered in scrapes and bruises from my many tumbles. One of the toes on my right foot was jammed, the nail broken and jagged.

At least most of it was temporary. The swelling would go down, the bruises would fade, and I'd look like myself again. I didn't want to consider what was hiding under the bandages still covering my left arm. Despite what I'd told Luke, part of me was worried about the scarring. Pushing that thought aside for a stronger moment, I carefully climbed over the rim of the tub and eased into the bath.

LUKE KNOCKED AGAIN, "Are you done yet, Alex? I don't want to stand here all day."

"I'm getting out now." With a sigh, I turned off the faucet and tried to wring the water from my hair with one pathetically weak, bandaged hand. Standing, I braced against the tub while a dizzy spell passed, then grabbed one of the fluffy towels from the rack and wrapped it around my torso. Walking to the mirror, I wiped the fog away. I felt a million times better now that I was clean, and I looked a little less like death warmed over.

Luke was lounging beside the door when I came out. "Feel better?"

"Much."

He pushed away from the wall and indicated another room, the door standing open. "I found some clothes. Let's see if any fit."

The bedroom we walked into was obviously designed for guest use, with a bed, dresser, and nightstand, but no personal effects. The room reminded me so much of a hotel I half suspected there would be a Bible in the nightstand.

On the end of the bed was a pile of mismatched clothing. I rummaged until I came up with a loose broomstick skirt and a button-up shirt two sizes too big.

"I'm not gonna win any fashion awards," I noted, holding my selection up for Luke to see. "But I should be able to get into these without much trouble."

"All right. Let me re-wrap your bandages."

I sat obediently on the bed while Luke peeled the bandages away. At first I was reluctant to watch, but my curiosity got the better of me, and I peeked at the damage.

There were about twenty puffy, red lines marking the edges where my skin had been jigsawed back together. They ran along my forearm, starting slightly above my elbow and tapering off on the back of my hand. I'd expected to see stitches holding the patchwork together, but there weren't any. "What's holding them closed?"

"Magic, of course," he said without looking up from his work.

"Wow. You must be a really strong practitioner to do all that in a night."

His hands stopped. He looked up. "Alex, it took more than a night to put you back together."

Thoughts raced through my head of being in a coma for weeks or months. Did my friends think I was dead?

"Don't panic," he chided, correctly interpreting the look on my face. "You've been out about a day and a half. It's Wednesday afternoon."

I pulled my hand loose from his ministrations to smack him lightly on the arm. "Don't scare me like that."

"Sorry." He snatched back my hand and finished wiping it clean with a sterile pad. "This is going to sting."

"Oh, good, I could use some more pain." I gritted my teeth in preparation.

Luke produced some greenish slime from a jar that smelled like a moldy herb garden.

"What's that?"

"You don't want to know." He proceeded to smear it over the puckered seams on my hands and arm. It stung like the cold pain of ice held against your skin too long, but quickly faded into a more tolerable tingling sensation.

"I hope you enjoyed your shower, because you need to leave this on for at least twenty-four hours."

"What does it do?"

"It'll make the injuries heal faster and prevent infection."

"Cool."

I sat as patiently as I could while Luke rewound my arm and hands with fresh bandages. Once he finished, I jumped in with the questions he'd promised to answer before he could defer them again.

"So what's going on here? Is Marc a shape-changing fae?" I'd heard rumors of fae who could transform into animals, but they were rare, and the creature I'd faced in the woods had been wild, unreasoning, more like. . . . I shuddered. After the fae came out, people claimed to have proof of all sorts of things—ghosts, aliens . . . werewolves—but the PTF had never found any evidence to substantiate the claims.

With a sigh, Luke picked up a sandwich from a tray sitting on the nightstand. "Here, I ate while you bathed."

I took a bite of the sandwich, but gave him a look that said I still expected an answer.

He swiped a hand over his head, flattening his hair like a carpet that sprang back into place once the pressure was gone. "You've heard of werewolves?"

The sandwich turned to ash in my mouth at the echo of my earlier thoughts, but I choked it down. "Men who turn into monsters at the full moon. The PTF dismissed them as fiction."

"Which is exactly how people throughout history responded to stories of the fae before they came forward themselves," he pointed out. "And I wouldn't say the PTF has dismissed them, more like put them on a back burner."

The sandwich churned in my stomach and a cold sweat prickled on my forehead. As if the fae weren't enough to deal with, now there were other storybook monsters running loose? But I couldn't deny what I'd seen.

"There are a lot more things that go bump in the night than just the fae, despite the PTF's lack of evidence."

"So Marc is a werewolf." It made sense, but my brain was having trouble grappling with the idea. What was next? Loch Ness? E.T.?

My mind jumped to Bryce and the way he'd seemed more than human. James had been sure he wasn't a fae . . . but what about a werewolf? Then my eyes and thoughts settled back on Luke. "What about you? Are you a werewolf?"

He shook his head. "Werewolves have amazing healing abilities, but they have to survive long enough for them to kick in. Even a werewolf can't come back from the dead. Since they can't be taken to a hospital without revealing their secret and putting them all at risk, they call me, or someone like me, when they need to be patched up. Though given how tough they are, it doesn't happen often. I mostly reset bones that have healed wrong."

"Why did they call you for me? I'm human. Why not take me to a hospital?" Then I remember that, in tales about werewolves, the people who survived attacks turned into monsters themselves. In a quavering voice I asked, "I am still human, aren't I?"

The question hung in the air for one terrifying moment before Luke placed his hand on my shoulder and said, "You're not going to turn into a werewolf."

A relieved sob escaped, and I jerked my hand up to quash it.

"In all honesty, Alex, we're not sure what's going on with you. Your fear was well justified. Normally, anyone who survives a werewolf attack becomes one. We don't know why you didn't."

"Is that what happened to Sophie? Is that why she isn't here?"

"Yes. Don't worry, Marc will take care of Sophie."

"Is he keeping her in one of those cages downstairs?"

Avoiding my gaze, he said, "There's no one else in the house today." Which wasn't exactly an answer.

"So where are they? Shouldn't Marc be the one explaining all this?"

"He's busy."

"With what?"

"Convincing the pack to let you live."

My eyebrows shot toward my hairline. Then the corners of my lips lifted. Surely he was joking? But Luke's forehead was furrowed, and the line of his mouth was drawn tight.

The muscles pulling my face into an uncertain smile went slack. "Excuse me?"

Luke clenched his hands, eyes drifting to the faded carpet under his shoes. "The more conservative members of Marc's pack were all for letting you bleed out once they realized you weren't going to change, and they're not happy you're still breathing. As far as they're concerned, it's a pass/fail test—turn into a werewolf or die."

My jaw dropped, and I crossed my arms over the knot in my stomach.

"Werewolves are very protective of their secret," he said.

"So protective they'd let me die?"

"More than that. They'd kill to keep it."

My mouth went dry as I searched for words.

"Marc is speaking on your behalf, making the case that you can be trusted."

"What can I do to convince them?"

He shook his head. "Just trust Marc to talk some sense into them."

"But—"

He raised a hand. "There's nothing you can do. Marc will come see you when they've decided."

"To tell me, or kill me?"

Luke's smile was weak and didn't reach his eyes. "That depends on what they decide."

Chapter 6

RED AND GOLD streaked past the window as I chewed at the ragged edges of my nails. The awkward silence in the cab of Luke's truck as he drove me home made my skin itch. I still had so many questions, but after twenty minutes of interrogating him between bites of sandwich, it was clear he was done answering. I'd have to get my information from another source, namely Marc. Not that I was looking forward to that visit.

To distract myself from the thoughts running circles through my head, and keep my hands away from my mouth, I rummaged in the bag Luke had returned to me from the night of the attack. I wished I could believe someone had retrieved it for me, but more likely, they'd just been cleaning up the evidence. Luke hadn't mentioned what became of my clothes, and I didn't ask. It's not like I'd ever want to wear them again.

The bag looked like it had been chewed on, with several large holes torn through the fabric. My art supplies had been hastily shoved inside, my sketches were crumpled, and most of my charcoal sticks were broken. The case for my watercolors was cracked, but the paints were all right.

In one of the side pockets I found my cell phone, or what was left of it. The screen was a web of cracks, and the back cover had fallen off. The battery was missing.

"Shit."

"What's the matter?"

I held my phone up for Luke to see.

"Yep, it's a goner. Wanna borrow mine?"

I shook my head. "There's a landline at my house." I bit my lip.

"Assuming I can find the phone."

He arched an eyebrow, and I shrugged. "I never used that line, and the only calls I got were from telemarketers and political ads, so I unplugged it and put it in storage."

"But you kept the line active?"

"Sol asked me to." I smiled out the window. Sol hadn't asked so much as demanded as a condition of helping me buy the house. "Said he didn't trust the reception on my cellphone. Wanted me to have the land-line for emergencies."

Marc's house was closer to mine than I expected. In all my wanderings I'd never come across it because a barbed wire fence with signs advertising "private property," "keep out," and threats of violence surrounded the sprawling perimeter. As a crow flies, we lived about a mile apart. However, that mile translated to four by car along the winding mountain roads. All my bruises were shouting in protest by the time we pulled up behind my Jeep.

"What happened to Sophie's car?" I asked as Luke helped me from the cab.

"Marc's people took care of it."

Nothing ominous about that at all.

Cat was pacing by the door when I hobbled up. "Miss me?"

With Cat weaving around my ankles and Luke hovering near my arm, I unlocked the door and pushed into the comfort of my home. I didn't even try to stop Cat from following me in.

Luke helped me get settled on the couch, then pulled a plastic bag of herbs from his pocket. "Mix one tablespoon of this in hot water every six hours until it's gone. It tastes like shit, but make sure you drink it all."

"Gee, thanks."

"I'm sure Marc will stop by as soon as he can," he continued. "Remember, their secret is very important to them. More important than the life of a single person. Don't give them a reason to doubt you."

"What if he can't convince them?" The tightness in my chest made it difficult to breathe, let alone speak, so the question came out as a strangled croak.

Luke's jaw clenched. He stared at the floor. "Get some rest. You should be fine in a couple days so long as you follow my instructions and don't overdo it."

He stopped with his hand on the door. "Stay away from them if you can, Alex. Once you get dragged into their world, you can't climb free. When Marcus comes, keep your mouth shut. Then get on with your life like none of this ever happened."

Before I could respond, the door closed, and I was left with only my spiraling thoughts and some stinky herbs.

I stared at my shaking hands. Was this what a death sentence felt like? But my fate wasn't certain. Marc would come through for me. He had to. In the meantime, there was nothing to do but move forward as though I'd still be alive tomorrow.

Putting water on to boil, I headed to the bedroom at the back of my house that I used for storage. It only took a minute to find the cordless receiver for my old phone. It took another five to find the charging base. Blowing off the dust, I carried the ancient device back to the kitchen and plugged it into the wall.

Since I hadn't shown up to relieve Maggie at ten like I was supposed to, it was a safe bet she was still at the bookstore. Luckily, that was one of the few numbers I had memorized, so the loss of my phone's contact list hadn't crippled my ability to call.

"Magpie Books, how can I help you?"

"Maggie, it's Alex."

"OhmygodAlex!" She practically shrieked into the receiver. "Where the bloody 'ell have you been? When you didn't show up for your shift I tried to ring, but kept gettin' your voice mail. I left like a dozen messages. I even asked David to check on ya, but he came up bugger all!"

I loved Maggie's accent, but the more worked up she got, the more pronounced it became. Sometimes she was downright unintelligible, and her rapid-fire speech made it even worse. When she finally paused for breath, I jumped in. "I know, Mags. I'm sorry I worried you. Something came up and this is the first chance I've had to call."

"What came up?"

I didn't want to lie to Maggie, but I couldn't tell her the truth either. Not without putting her in danger. I'd already lost Aiden and had Sophie to worry about. I wouldn't let anything happen to Maggie because of me. "I'm sorry, Mags, but I can't tell you. Just trust me on this, okay?"

Static crackled through the silence. When she spoke again, her accent was back to a manageable level and her words no longer slurred together. "You need to ring David. He's off his trolley with this."

"I will."

"And you owe me for skiving off yesterday. I had to pull twelve hours before Jake came in. If anyone else did that, I'd sack 'em."

"I know, and you'd have every right."

The line stayed quiet so long I feared the call had dropped until

Maggie asked, "Is this about what happened to Aiden?"

That floored me. As far as I knew, the cops had a lid on Aiden's identity as the latest victim. "How do you know about that?"

"I read it in the paper this morning. I'm sorry, Alex. Aiden and I didn't agree on much, but I know he was a good friend to you."

"Yeah." My voice hitched. "Thanks, Maggie."

The silence stretched for a long moment, then Maggie surprised me with, "A guy came looking for you yesterday."

My mouth went dry as images of Bryce and Mr. Smith raced through my head. "What guy?"

"He said his name was Malakai. He wanted to apologize for upsetting you. Did something happen?"

The stalker from the bookstore. The haze of my exhaustion lifted as my heart sped up and my palms grew sweaty. "Maggie, if you see that guy again, call the cops."

"What? Why?"

"Just trust me, okay?"

"Are you in some kind of trouble?"

Good question. "I'm fine."

"I know you're big on independence, but remember, you don't have to face everything alone. You've got people who care about you."

Like Aiden. Like Sophie.

Don't get attached. Mom's warning echoed through my memory, her words muffled against my hair as tears splashed my scalp. *The only people we can depend on in this world are you and me.*

Then the accident happened, and it was just me.

"Thanks, Mags, but this isn't something you can help with."

She sighed again, a signal that she wouldn't press the issue. "I assume you won't be in today?"

"Sorry. I promise I'll be there Saturday." As long as I wasn't executed by werewolves.

"You'd better. I can't run this place by my lonesome."

"You wouldn't have to if you'd hire more help."

"For your information, I've got someone lined up to start training today. If all goes well, she'll be full-time by the end of the month."

"Really?" I'd been wrapped up in my own affairs lately, but I hadn't realized I was that out of the loop. "Who is she?"

"Name's Kayla. She's a part-pixie halfer. Seems nice enough. Getting her degree in microbiology of all things."

"Impressive."

"Yeah, hopefully it means she's not dim. What're you doing Friday?"

The question was so out of the blue I answered without thinking. "Nothing."

"Good. I'm coming to your house for dinner."

"Wait, what?"

"Charlie has a client meeting, so he'll be busy schmoozing, and you and I haven't seen each other outside of work in ages. We're due for a girls' night."

I shifted my grip on the phone. "It's not really a great time, Maggie."

"Why? You just said you were free."

"Yeah, but—"

"I'll even bring dessert."

My mouth started watering at the thought of one of Maggie's masterpieces. Surely with enough clothes and makeup I could cover the evidence of the attack, and she wasn't wrong about it being a while since we hung out socially . . .

"See you at six." Maggie's voice carried a ring of triumph, and I pictured her grinning as she ended the call.

Sighing, I stared at the phone. David deserved a call, too. He was probably imagining I'd met a similar fate to Aiden, just as I would be if our positions were reversed, but I wasn't ready for him yet. Maggie wouldn't force me to talk. David was another story. If I didn't give him answers he could swallow, he'd show up at my door and wring them out of me. I needed to buy time for him to cool off, and for me to think up a convincing story.

Abandoning the phone, I went to the computer and sent an email to let David know I was alive, then made a mug of foul-smelling tea from the herbs Luke had left. The odor alone was enough to make me gag, but I pinched my nose and took an experimental sip. My stomach churned as the tea hit my tongue, and I clamped my lips closed to avoid spraying it into the sink. Luke hadn't been kidding about the taste.

Wrapping a blanket around my shoulders, I curled up on the couch. Cat startled me by jumping up next to me, but as he made himself comfortable on my feet and his purr filled the silence hanging over the room, I began to relax. I brushed my fingers over his head, and he tipped his chin up, rubbing his cheek against my hand. Maybe a pet wouldn't be so bad. Resting my head against the back cushion, I let myself be lulled by Cat's warm vibrations as I absently stroked his fur and watched the world outside my window.

In the short time I'd been gone, the aspens had lost many of their leaves to the winds that tore across the ridge lines and shook the evergreen sentries that stood guard over the valley. The birds that migrated had left for the season, but those that remained chirped their songs in defiance of the coming cold. Sunlight shone through the treetops, and the land passed in and out of shadow as clouds floated by to block the light.

A POUNDING ON my door brought me upright with a jerk, and my heart hammered against my chest in echo to the persistent knock. I groped for bearing in the gloom until my eyes settled on the pale circle of a wall clock. I'd slept through most of the day.

Had Marc come to deliver his pack's verdict? The thought froze me in place.

Then again, wasn't there a full moon?

The pounding came again.

I rubbed at the beginning of a headache and shouted, "Who is it?"

"James Abernathy. Open the door."

I sat up a little straighter, but ignored the command. Deflecting Maggie on the phone was one thing, by the time I saw her I'd be in much better shape. But here, now, James would want real answers. Answers I couldn't give. "I'm feeling a little under the weather. Can I call you tomorrow?"

"I am not leaving until you open this door."

Shit. I really wasn't up for company, but what if it was about Bryce or some other impending peril? I pulled the door open a crack, trusting the backlight from the living room to obscure my injuries.

"What is it, James?"

His hands lifted, reaching halfway to me before falling back to his sides. Voice tight, he asked, "Where have you been?"

"What?" I'd been missing less than two days. Maggie knowing was inevitable, and of course she'd tell David, but James?

"When you missed dinner last night, I tried to call."

Damn. I scrunched my eyes and pinched the bridge of my nose. The day I'd lost was Tuesday—the one day he was guaranteed to notice thanks to our standing dinner arrangements.

"When you didn't answer, I came to check, but couldn't find you." His hands bunched into fists. "Given recent events, your absence was . . . unsettling."

I owed him an explanation. Too bad I couldn't tell him the truth.

"Sorry, James. Come on in." Keeping my face down, I stood back from the door and gestured for him to enter. The blouse I'd chosen had long baggy sleeves and the skirt came to my ankles, so I could hide at least some of my injuries. But the bandages on my hands were visible, and the bruises and scrapes on my face would be obvious in the harsh light of the living room.

Lips pressed to a tight line, he stepped inside but didn't pass me. Instead, he carefully lifted one of my bandaged hands.

"I know it looks bad, but I'm all right." I pulled my hand away.

He let it go, but his eyes held mine, unblinking. Ice, and heat, and some emotion I couldn't identify swirled beneath the silver-blue surface.

"Your face—"

"I know." I swallowed, trying to ease the dryness in my throat. He was too close.

"Alex, who did this to you?"

I shook my head, cringing when the muscles in my chest protested the movement.

"Alex—"

"Have you eaten?"

"What?" His brow scrunched, turning his eyes to pools of shadow.

"How about I whip up some dinner to make up for skipping out on you last night?"

He pursed his lips, deep lines etching his face. "I don't care about the missed dinner, Alex. I just want an explanation."

"And you'll get it, I promise. But I'm hungry." I gestured toward the dining table.

James paced to the middle of the room, arms folded across his chest, radiating displeasure.

Skin crawling beneath his inspection, I closed the door and carefully walked to the kitchen, trying not to let my soreness show. "What are you in the mood for? I wasn't planning on company, so we'll have to make do with basics."

James let out a sigh, relaxed his stance, and joined me in the kitchen. "Anything is fine."

"Pasta it is then." I pointed to a large pasta pot, sitting above the cabinets. "Grab that pot, will you?"

Normally, I wouldn't let a guest help me cook, but in my current state it couldn't hurt to let him do the heavy lifting. Besides, it would help keep him occupied with something other than pulling apart the explanation of my recent whereabouts.

Even James, tall as he was, couldn't quite reach the shelf where I stored my pots without the step stool tucked off to one side. The picture of composed, sophisticated James, with his expensive clothes and perfect hair, balancing on tiptoes to get a pot for pasta was enough to make me burst out laughing.

While laughter would normally have been a welcome way to break the tension, it quickly became a coughing fit. I collapsed into a chair and wrapped my arms around my sides as the jostling inflamed my battered ribs.

James appeared at my side, one hand hovering just above my shoulder as if afraid to touch me. "Are you all right?"

"Fine," I wheezed. "Like I said, I'm a little under the weather."

"And I'm still waiting for an explanation."

Nodding, I took the pot to the stove and set some water to boil. "I don't remember everything."

James leaned back against the counter and crossed his arms over his midnight blue shirt. "Just tell me what you can."

I nodded. Werewolves aside, I needed to hide the fact that Sophie had been there. I didn't want anyone wondering what had become of her. "After all that's happened lately, I needed to clear my head. So Monday after dinner, I hiked to a meadow not far from here."

"You went for a walk, alone, at night, after being attacked . . . twice." He held two fingers up for emphasis. "What were you thinking?"

I bristled at his tone. "You said Bryce would leave me alone, and I figured if anyone came looking I'd be harder to find in the woods than sitting here at home. As for hiking alone, it's not like I was stumbling through the dark in an unknown area. The moon was nearly full, so there was plenty of light, and I've hiked that path hundreds of times. Now do you want to hear the rest of the story or not?"

"Please, continue," he said in a more subdued tone.

I pulled a box of noodles out of a cabinet and dumped them in the water.

"So I was in the meadow making charcoal sketches when a bear came out of the forest. He was probably foraging, looking to put on some weight for hibernation. We get a lot of that around here. Anyway, we startled each other, and he took a swipe at me."

A muscle jumped in James's neck. The strain around his eyes and mouth made my heart ache, but a warm flutter danced through my stomach. Part of me was pleased by his reaction.

I shoved that warmth and all its complications aside, pushing it back to the corner of my mind where the part of me that still believed in happy endings crouched like a feral beast.

Grabbing a glass with shaky hands, I took a drink of water and tried to refocus my thoughts.

"The bear outweighed me by a ton and was strong as hell, but most animals prefer food that doesn't fight back. So I grabbed a fallen tree limb and did what I could. When I got a good jab at its face, it decided I was more work than I was worth and scampered away, but it landed a couple hits that left me pretty bruised and tore up my arm."

Since I hadn't gone to a hospital, it would be hard to keep Luke's involvement secret. Besides, it wasn't like he'd done anything wrong. He was a publicly registered practitioner who used his magic to help people all the time.

"Since I was losing blood, I called a practitioner I know and asked him to meet me at my place rather than drive myself to the hospital. Unfortunately, I stumbled on the way home and broke my phone. That's why I didn't answer. I don't remember much beyond that. Luke said he took me back to his place because I was in worse shape than he'd thought and he needed some special herbs to patch me up. He kept me under while he worked. I just came home today."

I tipped the noodles into a colander and got a face full of steam.

It was a pretty lame ending for the story, but I didn't want to embellish more than necessary to make it believable. Keeping the story close to true would make it harder for him to catch me in a lie.

James's steady gaze made me squirm. He seemed almost disappointed, like he'd expected a more fantastic tale. One with giant monster wolves perhaps?

"I'm glad you're all right," he said at last. "May I see your arm?"

"It's all bandaged up right now. Luke told me to leave the goo on for at least a day."

"Ah, well, I suppose that's that then." His mouth twitched up for a moment like he was suppressing the urge to smile. "It's fortunate I'm paying for your security system. I imagine the personal attentions of a practitioner would be quite expensive. As I understand it, they are generally called only when a person is beyond help by normal medical means."

The water glass froze halfway to my mouth. I hadn't considered what Luke's services might cost. I'd been so wrapped up in what had happened and finding out about the werewolves, I hadn't stopped to think that Luke wouldn't be working for free. I was grateful for what he'd done, but it's not like I was the one who called him. Maybe I could get the werewolves to foot the bill? Sure, I'd bring that up with Marc right after I found out if he was there to kill me.

"Alex? Alex?" James finally caught my attention.

"Sorry, what was that?"

"Are you all right? You went very pale."

"I'm fine," I gave a half-hearted smile. "Just tired. Luke said I'd be pretty weak for a few days."

"I shall take that as my cue to leave then." James pushed away from the counter.

I gestured to the pasta draining in the sink. "What about dinner?"

The corners of his mouth curved up, but the tension didn't leave his eyes. "Another time."

I followed him to the door. A gust of frigid night pushed through when I opened it, snapping my hair and making me shiver. The setting sun had taken the day's warmth with it. "Sorry again for worrying you."

He paused on the threshold and set one hand on my shoulder. "You are not immortal, Alex. Neither are you replaceable. Please be careful."

The butterflies were back, and my sudden lightheadedness had nothing to do with blood loss. The musky scent of his cologne flooded my senses, and for one terrifying moment I let myself imagine he might kiss me. Then I slammed the thought away. It wouldn't happen. It couldn't happen. I didn't want it to happen. Did I?

The worn edge of the door frame dug between my shoulder blades as I drew back from his touch. "Good night, James."

His grip tightened briefly, then fell away.

SUNLIGHT STREAMED through my bedroom window. I laid there for a long moment. Then, careful of my ribs, rolled onto my side. A warm lump of gray fur greeted me.

I blinked twice, then reached out to poke the intruder. Fur twitched under my hand, and a pair of slitted green eyes lifted to peer at me. Cat yawned, dousing me with a cloud of warm cat breath, then closed his eyes and tucked his nose back under his tail.

"What're you doing here?" I glanced at my open bedroom door, trying to remember if I'd let him in last night. More and more, I was getting used to having Cat underfoot.

I scratched behind his ears, making them twitch. "If you're sticking around, I should invest in some kitty litter." Cat's purr rolled through the mattress for a moment, then tapered off as he fell into a deeper sleep.

I worked my way off the bed by increments, pleasantly surprised by the ease with which I could move and breathe compared to the night before. I was still sore, but the intensity of the pain had faded to a distant, throbbing, ache.

My dinner dishes were still on the table when I shuffled to the kitchen in search of breakfast, and the dirty pasta pot and colander sat beside the sink. I wrinkled my nose at this scene of domestic neglect, but headed straight for the kettle. While the water heated, I scooped more of Luke's foul-smelling herbs into a mug. He'd given me enough to last two days. If I felt as much better tomorrow as I did today, that would be plenty of time to get me back to a decent condition. I really did owe him huge.

Suppressing a sigh at the thought of repaying that debt, I carried my stinky tea over to the computer. David's reply waited in my inbox. After several lines chastising me for making him worry, he wrote that Oz would be over to install my new security system early Friday morning.

I regretted making Maggie and James worry, but felt worse about David. After what happened to Aiden, he must have been a mess. My recent disappearing act had proven pretty conclusively that—despite being an introvert living at the back end of nowhere—there were people who would miss me if I were gone.

I licked my lips. Marc would convince his friends I wasn't a threat. He had to.

My thoughts circled back to Aiden, as they always seemed to lately. A quick Internet search brought up the article that identified him as the latest victim. The article didn't include much. A few lines about his work as a park ranger and a generic lament about a life cut short. The rest was more anti-fae propaganda.

Recalling the man in the alley, and his seemingly genuine belief that I could somehow solve this crime, I pulled up every article I could on Aiden's murder and those that preceded it. There were dozens. Some were opinion pieces or political posturing. Others read like speculative fiction, the details turning my stomach.

While all the victims died in their homes, that's where the similarities ended. Some houses were ransacked, others didn't seem to have anything out of place. Some doors were broken, others were still locked. Some people died from simple bullet wounds or severed arteries while others had been tortured. Page after page of grizzly descriptions, quoted laments from grieving relatives, and calls to action scrolled past.

Photos of the victims punctuated my search. A young woman with piercing green eyes smiled on the arm of her fiancé, full of hope and promise. An old man with wild, wispy hair walked hand-in-hand through a farmers' market with his equally ancient wife, leaning together for support. A middle-aged woman strained the seams of her business suit as she sat feeding pigeons on a sun-dappled park bench. My heart grew heavier as I clicked past each life-filled face until Aiden stared back from my computer screen.

If a pattern lay buried somewhere in that mess, I couldn't see it. Pushing back from the computer, I massaged my temples. How stupid to think I could provide any useful insight when Garcia's task force had failed to make a connection. What did I know about murder investigations?

I cursed my own uselessness, and might have wallowed longer but for a knock at the door.

Chapter 7

MY STOMACH CLENCHED. It was probably Marc. But was he there to talk, or to finish what the other wolf had started? What if it was Bryce, or Smith and Neil, or some new insane threat? My lungs pumped faster as my brain raced with possibilities. Was this how Aiden had felt?

Shrugging into a baggy beige cardigan to hide my arms, I crept around the room and peeled back a corner of curtain to peer through the front window.

Standing on the porch was a man in his mid- to late-thirties. He was an inch or two shorter than I was, but twice as wide, giving the impression he'd been compacted. His mouth was a little too large, turning down at the corners in a perpetual frown. His hair was close-cropped dirty-blond, thinning on top. Dark glasses covered his eyes, so I couldn't tell where he was looking, but I didn't think he'd noticed me yet.

I hesitated long enough that he knocked again, adding, "Ms. Blackwood? I'm with the PTF."

I chided myself for letting my paranoia get the better of me and opened the door a crack. "Can I see some ID?"

He flipped open a little leather wallet with an official-looking bronze badge. "My name is Paul Johnson. I work in the Denver office."

I opened the door the rest of the way. "Are you here about the fae I reported?"

"Not exactly." He tucked his sunglasses into a pocket, and settled his pale blue eyes on me. "Mind if I come inside?"

Stepping back, I indicated the couch, then took up position on one of the chairs. Sweat broke out on my palms as my mind skipped between the stranger behind Magpie and his crazy claim that I was part fae, and the werewolves and Luke's assertion that the PTF hadn't discounted them entirely. I swallowed, and willed my voice not to shake. "What's this about?"

"I'm investigating a case that may be connected to the report you made. I take it you haven't received my messages? I've been trying to contact you since Tuesday. When I got no response, I thought it best to come in person."

"My phone broke Monday night."

His lips pursed, like he was trying to decide if he believed me, and I resisted the urge to shift under his scrutiny.

"You were friends with a man named Aiden Daye, correct?"

"Yes." A thrill of hope raced through me. Maybe they'd found Aiden's killer. If the PTF was involved, that meant faeries. Maybe those Purity activists were right.

"You're aware of what happened to him?"

I nodded. "I spoke with the police. Is the PTF investigating his death as well?"

Side-stepping the question, he asked, "How well did you know Mr. Daye?"

"We've been friends since college. We never dated, if that's what you mean, but David and I were the closest friends he had."

"I see." He fell silent and pursed his lips, as if trying to decide what to say. "What I'm about to tell you is sensitive information about an on-going investigation. You cannot tell another living soul. Do you understand?"

I nodded.

He leaned forward, propping his arms on his knees, and I found myself mimicking his pose. The intensity of his stare made my skin itch. "Mr. Daye was under investigation for trafficking faerie artifacts."

"What!" I jerked back as though I'd been burned. "Aiden would never be involved in that."

"Are you sure?" His eyes never strayed from my face.

"Yes. We were very close. I know he wouldn't do that."

"He was also suspected of being an unregistered halfer."

My mouth gaped like a fish out of water until I pulled myself together enough to stammer, "There must be some mistake. I'm sure I would have known if Aiden was a faerie."

"Do you know many fae, Ms. Blackwood?"

"Well, no," I admitted.

"Then how can you be sure? Most fae can easily pass for human, and many halfers don't even realize themselves what they are. That's why what we do at the PTF is so important. Otherwise, normal humans have no way of telling who is who." It sounded like a speech he'd practiced often.

I thought back to the stranger in the alley and his assertion that I could be a halfer without even knowing. How certain was I, really, about anything these days?

"Aiden was just an ordinary guy . . ." Even as I said it, I remembered all his idiosyncrasies—sweeping for bugs, worried people were watching him. Maybe he really had had a reason to be paranoid. I tried to remember Aiden in my studio. Had he ever touched the metal there, the iron or steel?

I'd been his friend for years, surely he would have trusted me enough to tell me? But as I considered it, I wondered if that was true. Aiden knew I didn't care much for the fae. I didn't hate them as much as the Purists, but I still blamed them for their part in the war and what it had cost my family.

I shook my head. If he'd been a faerie, why not just register like he was supposed to? He might have lost his job with the city, but surely that was a small risk compared to deportation?

As my brain wrestled with the implications, I couldn't help feeling Aiden had become a stranger. It was like losing him a second time.

"Are you sure?" I demanded. "Do you have proof Aiden was a halfer?"

"There's evidence, but since he was still under investigation, it's inconclusive."

"So you're not sure."

"Not one hundred percent, but near enough. If we'd already proven him fae, his death would have fallen under PTF jurisdiction. But regardless of his fae status, the circumstances of his murder overlap my current investigation."

"The illegal artifacts."

"Yes. We were tracking a certain object in Mr. Daye's possession, but it went missing when he died. The fae who visited you were probably after the same item, thinking Mr. Daye passed it to you before his untimely demise. As I understand, it was a small silver box. Can you recall Mr. Daye having any such object?"

I imagined Aiden's house. He'd kept it neat and tidy, almost sparse. Most people collected trinkets from their life—photos, souvenirs, mementos. Not Aiden. His walls had been empty except for one picture of his grandmother and a picture of him, me, and David from a trip we took in college. I had a copy of the same photo on my mantel, with "The Three Musketeers do Mexico" scrawled across the bottom in David's sloppy handwriting. Aiden had two cases of books, all non-fiction. No trinkets used as bookends or shelves of knickknacks.

"If he had a box like that, I never saw it."

"I see." His frown deepened. "It's very important we retrieve that box, Ms. Blackwood. Faerie artifacts are dangerous, and trafficking in them is a serious crime."

"I told you, Aiden wouldn't have been involved with that." Halfer or not, Aiden had been a good man.

"Not knowingly perhaps. If you remember anything, or find any information pertinent to my investigation, you'll let me know?" He smiled in a way that was supposed to be congenial, but felt fake.

I took the card he offered. "If those fae were looking for the box you think Aiden had, do you think they killed him?"

"It's a good possibility. The PTF is cooperating fully with the task force investigating the possible serial killings, though no fae connection has been established yet. But your friend's death may not be related to the others. More likely, he was killed for the faerie artifact, and his murderer either has the box or is looking for it. Either way, tracking down that artifact is our best chance to find his killer."

Catching Aiden's killer obviously wasn't this man's top priority, but he was right about the box providing a strong lead.

"I'll let you know if I think of anything."

"Thank you, Ms. Blackwood."

I stood to show Mr. Johnson out, but a knock at the door interrupted us. With a PTF agent present, I didn't feel the need to spy before answering.

Marc had finally come for the visit Luke promised. The afternoon sun caught red highlights in his chestnut curls, creating a soft, coppery halo that would have been inviting if not for the intense hazel eyes that accompanied it. Swallowing hard, and praying that look didn't mean he'd come to kill me, I kept my eyes trained on his broad chest as he pushed past me without being invited.

"Not interrupting anything, I hope." His voice carried a low rumble, the hint of a growl. Finding a PTF officer in my living room probably wasn't the best way to assure a werewolf his secret was safe with me. Then again, how would he know? It's not like agent Johnson had a neon sign above his head that said PTF.

"I was just leaving." Agent Johnson stepped up to the door, and Marc shifted to create a space for him to pass.

My fingers twitched to stop Johnson, but that would only delay the inevitable. If Marc's pack had decided to kill me— No. Marc had to have convinced them. I swallowed and tried to keep my voice even as I said, "Goodbye, Mr. Johnson."

"Please call if anything comes up, Ms. Blackwood." He nodded to Marc. "Good day."

Marc opened his mouth as soon as the door closed, but I held up a hand to forestall him. "Shh."

He bristled, but pressed his lips closed and waited until Mr. Johnson got in his car and started down the drive before asking, "What was a PTF agent doing at your house?"

"You know him?"

A muscle in Marc's jaw twitched. "I've seen him before."

I lifted my chin, forcing myself to meet his glare. "He had some questions for me."

"What did you tell him?"

"Nothing that concerns you."

"Alex," the rumble of his voice reverberated in my chest, "if the pack has been compromised I need to know. Now."

Facing off against an angry werewolf might not have been the brightest idea, even if he hadn't come to kill me, but I was tired of being interrogated. Fists balled at my sides, I forced my voice to remain even. "Yours isn't the only secret in the world. It's got nothing to do with you."

We stood like statues locked in a staring contest for a moment. Then he let his arms fall to his sides and gave a curt nod. "Sorry, but when you've got a secret like ours you tend to get a little paranoid."

"There's a lot of that going around."

"Are you in some kind of trouble?" Now that suspicion had taken a back seat, concern laced his voice.

"You tell me." I took a step away from him. "Luke said you'd come with a verdict."

He nodded. "I've convinced the others to let you live."

I stumbled over to the couch as my muscles went slack with relief. "Thank goodness." It was barely a whisper.

Marc smiled, but it wasn't a friendly smile. "You're my problem now, Alex. If you do anything to compromise my pack, or the secret of our existence, I'll deal with you myself."

I swallowed at the threat and tried to keep my voice from shaking as I said, "I won't betray you."

"I believe you. That's why you're still alive."

"Thank you." Twisting my hands together in my lap, I added, "Thank you, also, for the other night."

His smile fell, and his gaze shifted to the window. "You're welcome. And I'm sorry."

"Sorry? For what?"

"For the fact that it happened at all. It shouldn't have."

"What do you mean?"

"I knew there was a rogue in the area," he admitted. "If I'd found him sooner, this all could have been avoided."

That "if" held the weight of responsibility. He'd been beating himself up for what happened. I knew how he felt.

I couldn't ease my own guilt over dragging Sophie into the woods that night any more than I could forgive myself for ignoring Aiden's last phone call, but maybe I could ease Marc's conscience. "If you hadn't been there that night, Sophie and I would have died, no question."

He gave a non-committal grunt.

"Speaking of Sophie . . ." I wasn't sure what to ask. Sophie only survived because she'd become a werewolf herself. I couldn't even imagine what she was going through. "Um, how's she doing?"

Marc's look sent a chill down my spine. "She's alive."

"Where is she now? Can I see her?"

"No, Alex." Steel edged his voice, but pity too. "You won't be able to see Sophie for quite a while."

"Why not?"

"Sophie's a new wolf, brand new. She's got no control. Emotions run high in young wolves, tempering with time and training. The wolf who attacked you was also young, changed about four months ago. If Sophie saw you right now, she'd rip your throat out."

I gulped at the memory of gnashing teeth sinking into my flesh, and shuddering, rubbed the scars hidden beneath the flimsy cloth of my sweater. "Sophie will be like that for months?"

"She's better off than Tim. She has an established pack to support her, and an alpha to control her until she can control herself."

"Who's Tim?" I made the mental leap. "The rogue? How do you know his name?"

"We got the whole story out of him after the attack."

"Wait, you didn't kill him? Sorry, that came out more bloodthirsty than I meant. It's just, I thought he died in the fight."

"Werewolves are exceptionally hard to kill. I could have killed him if necessary, but he submitted once it was clear he couldn't win the fight. The damage he sustained has already healed."

"So what, he gets to go on with his life all la-dee-da after what he did? He could have killed us! He very nearly did. And what about poor Sophie? She's gonna flip when she finds out the monster that attacked her is still on the loose."

Marc gave me a second to calm down, then said, "He's not on the loose, and she already knows."

I jerked back. "Really?"

"Yeah."

"So where is he?"

"Contained."

"He should be put down."

"He's not a dog, Alex. He's a victim."

I snorted and crossed my arms.

"He's also a useful example for Sophie. Knowing his story will help make clear the choice she'll have to make."

I sat forward, uncrossing my arms. "What choice?"

"The same one Tim is making right now. To join a pack, mine or any willing to take him. We'll teach him control and try to give him back some semblance of the life he lost. In his case, there's also a trail of bodies and people looking for answers, but we can help with that, too. What we can't allow is for him to go free. Rogues like Tim and the wolf who made him are a threat to us all."

"So what's the choice? I didn't really hear one in there."

"The choice," he replied solemnly, "is that he can either live by our rules, or die by them."

I raised an eyebrow. "I thought he wasn't a dog."

"Hence the choice."

"That's not much of a choice. No one's gonna choose to die."

"You'd be surprised," he said quietly. "We're monsters, Alex. You've seen it yourself. We can't ever be fully human again. Some people would rather die with as much of their humanity intact as they can than live like that."

My thoughts circled back to Sophie and what that night had cost her.

"Sophie will have to make that choice?"

"Yes."

"What do you think she'll choose?"

He looked at me for a while before answering. "It isn't my place to say, but I have hope she'll choose to stay with us. She doesn't have the guilt Tim has to deal with, and she has the pack to support her. We'll do what we can. Hopefully it will be enough."

"I need to see her."

"You can't."

My hands balled into fists. "She's my friend."

Marc sighed and ran a hand through his curls. "That trail of bodies Tim left behind, you think it was all hikers he came across in the woods?"

That damped my anger like a bucket of ice water.

"Tim was a ranch hand in Texas. One night, about four months ago, the cattle got spooked, and everyone ran to calm them down before they trampled each other. Tim was the first one out. What he found was a werewolf having a buffet."

A memory of matted fur and glistening teeth flashed through my mind, and I hugged myself tight to suppress a shudder.

"He'd grabbed a shotgun when he ran out. Not sure if that makes him more or less lucky than you with your stick. A normal shotgun won't slow a werewolf down much, but it sure will piss him off. When Tim pulled that trigger, rather than running off like a coyote or fox, that werewolf just got angry. Tim survived the attack, but come the next full moon . . ." Marc shrugged, his jaw tight.

"He woke up a week later, blood-soaked and alone more than fifty miles from the ranch. He read in a paper that everyone on the ranch had been torn apart and eaten by some kind of wild animal. See, Alex, when a new werewolf wakes up, it wakes up hungry, and it doesn't think of humans as anything but food. Tim worked on that ranch for years, he knew every person who lived there; workers, families. And he killed every last one of them."

My stomach churned. I was no longer upset that Marc wouldn't let me see Sophie.

"If that all happened in Texas, why didn't the pack there take care of him? What's he doing here?"

"The nearest pack started searching as soon as they discovered what had happened, but Tim was already headed north, trying to outrun what he'd done. He passed into my territory two days before you were attacked. He was still human at the time, which made him harder to track. It wasn't until he shifted that I was able to pinpoint his location.

Unfortunately, you and Sophie were closer to him than I was."

I hugged myself tighter, nails digging into my upper arms. "I never should have brought her out there."

"There's no way you could have known."

I shook my head. "I just wish I could help her. I hate the thought of her having to rely on strangers to convince her life is still worth living."

"Right now, the best thing you can do for your friend is to stay away from her."

Marc and I sat in silence, each lost in our own thoughts for a time. No matter how I looked at it, he was right. The best place for Sophie was with the other werewolves. They could help her understand what her life had become. My presence would only muddle the issue and remind her what she'd lost.

"How many werewolves live here?"

Marc shifted in his seat. "It's best you don't know too many specifics about the local pack. Many of them are still uncomfortable with you knowing about them even in a broad sense."

Thinking of Aiden, I asked, "Why don't you just register with the PTF? Then you wouldn't have to hide."

Marc's face clouded up, and for a moment I thought he would leave without answering. But after a few calming breaths, he said, "We're not fae, Alex. Fae are beings that come from, and generally live in, another realm. Werewolves are, or at least were, people. Regular human beings until something terrible happened to them. We don't have anywhere else to go. This is our home.

"Then there are the rules dictating where the fae can live and what kinds of jobs they can hold. The logic is that people don't want the fae in sensitive positions because they wouldn't have humanity's interests at heart. But werewolves were all human to start with, and many still think of themselves that way. Some people become werewolves after spending years as teachers or doctors. Should they have to give that up? It's hard enough trying to fit back into a life when you don't feel like yourself anymore. Aside from all that, the PTF monitors for dangerous and violent behavior. Never mind that most of us can get through our daily lives without incident, they'd lock us up and throw away the key as soon as they saw what we become."

I nodded along with his explanation. It was true, the PTF would never let them go back to their lives after transforming into dangerous beasts. I thought of Sophie being carted off to a PTF facility for the rest of her life and balled my fists at the injustice of it.

"You're right. You wouldn't be free if people knew about you." I looked him in the eye and promised again, "Don't worry, Marc, I'll keep your secret."

"Enough about werewolves," he said. "How are you doing? Luke said he expects a full recovery, with the exception of a few scars."

"They're not even as bad as I thought they'd be." I pushed up my sleeve to show him. "They already look like they happened months ago."

"Luke knows his stuff. In all honesty, I didn't expect you to make it once we knew you weren't going to change."

"Yeah, Luke mentioned it was rare for a person to survive without changing."

"Rare," he snorted. "Try unheard of. I'm not sure what to make of you, Alex."

"This hasn't happened before?"

"Well," he hedged, "not exactly. I have a theory, but I need to do a little research before I voice it."

I braced my hands on my hips and glared. "Why can't you tell me now? Even a theory is better than nothing."

He shook his head. "Not in this case. When I know, you'll know. I promise."

I pressed my lips into a thin line, but he didn't budge.

"Other than the scars, you're back to your usual self?"

"Not quite," I admitted. "But I will be. Actually, the most annoying thing is my phone."

"Your phone?"

"Yeah. It got broken." I pulled the mangled carcass out of the drawer where I'd stashed it.

"May I?" I dropped the mess into his outstretched hand and he started fiddling with bits. "The sim card seems intact, you just need a new phone."

"Yeah, just," I snorted. "Like that's not the expensive part."

"I've got a spare you can have," he offered. "If you let me take this I can make sure it works."

"I didn't mean to imply you had to fix it. I was just complaining."

"Still, I feel responsible."

I opened my mouth to argue, but stopped when I saw the strain in his face. He was looking for something, anything, to make amends, to ease his guilt of failing to stop Tim before he got to me and Sophie.

I patted his arm. "Thanks."

He stared at where my hand rested on his sleeve for a moment, then cleared his throat and stood up. "I have other matters to attend to. Take care of yourself, Alex."

"And you take care of Sophie." After a moment's hesitation, I added, "Tell her I'm sorry."

Marc smiled. "I will."

I opened the door for Marc and found Cat sitting just outside.

Marc lunged so fast that the breeze of his passing blew my hair into my face. Fast as he was though, Cat was halfway across the porch before Marc made it outside.

"Geez, Marc, it's just a cat."

"What?" he demanded. "You know that cat?"

"He's been hanging around for a while now." I smiled at Cat. "I might even keep him."

"But—" Marc turned as Cat started hissing.

"Not you too," I scolded the ball of raised fur. "I guess it's natural that cats and wolves wouldn't like each other."

"Something like that." Marc glared at Cat, who glared right back. "You shouldn't take in strays, Alex."

I snorted, "You're one to talk."

"Ha!" His bark of laughter seemed to break the stalemate between them, and Cat sauntered off around the corner of the house as though that's where he'd intended to go all along.

Marc watched him go. "Don't get too attached. Strays are fickle."

I waited in the doorway until Marc drove out of sight. Then Cat came strolling back.

"You planning to leave me?" I asked.

He rubbed against my ankle and swaggered into the house.

Smiling, I closed the door, praying I was done with visitors for the day.

Chapter 8

FRIDAY MORNING brought gray skies and a crisp breeze. Most of the deciduous trees had been stripped bare by a front moving in over the divide, leaving just a few denizens of the branches too stubborn to let go. The first winter storms would pull them down. Until then, they were little bursts of color waving like flags in the wind.

I'd healed enough to wriggle into a pullover sweater to fight the chill that had settled in during the night. If not for the scars that decorated my arm and a lingering fatigue, I might have imagined the whole attack. Oz was scheduled to come over early to install the security system, so I'd set my alarm for the first time in days. I was in the kitchen, pouring coffee, when he arrived.

"Hey, Oz. Long time no see." It had been nearly five months since I'd last bribed him to update the inventory on my website. I'd seen him in the bookstore a few times, but we hadn't talked much. Oz and I were casual friends, but we didn't get together without a reason. He was easygoing, had a great sense of humor, and was just sarcastic enough to suit my tastes.

"Yeah, been a while."

He hadn't come in, though I'd stepped aside to let him. Instead, he stared at me like I'd grown a second head. For a mortifying moment I worried I'd done something ridiculous, like forgetting to put pants on when I came out of the bedroom. I looked down. Nope, the sweats were still there, it hadn't been a dream.

"What's up?" I asked.

Obviously preoccupied, his big brown eyes blinked a few times before he came back with, "Hmm, what?"

"You're looking at me funny. What's the matter?"

"What? Oh, no, it's nothing." He ran a hand through his short brown hair, making it stick out crazily around ears that were slightly too large for his face, and finally stepped inside. "Sorry, I'm not quite awake yet."

That was a cop-out answer, but I let it slide. I didn't want people prying into the weirdness my life had become just because I was acting a little strange. I couldn't hold it against him for doing likewise.

Instead, I offered a conspiratorial grin and said, "I know the feeling. Want some coffee?"

"That'd be great, thanks."

I walked into the kitchen to get the coffee, and he kept talking, raising his voice as I moved away rather than following me.

"David said to give you the works. He'll stop by later, probably around lunch."

"Typical. He always shows up for food." I handed him a steaming mug. "If I got the cream and sugar wrong, feel free to doctor it yourself."

"This is fine. Do you want me to start in the studio or the house?"

"Does it matter?"

"Not to me, but it can get noisy and I'll have stuff laying all over while I'm working, so you may want to be wherever I'm not."

"A little noise and clutter doesn't bother me. Just do whatever works best for you and I'll try not to get in the way."

"Okay." He set his coffee on an end table and went back outside.

I peeked out the window. Oz was unloading equipment from his truck. It was perfectly reasonable, but his departure felt abrupt, like he couldn't wait to get away. Something was definitely bothering him, and I couldn't help but feel his discomfort was directed at me.

I marched to the full-length mirror in my bedroom and stared at myself. The scars on my arm were covered, and the baggy sweater hid the brace. There was some discoloration on my face and neck from the bruises, but I'd put a layer of concealer over them so they wouldn't be noticeable at a glance. My hair was brushed. I was fully dressed. I'd had a shower.

With a sigh, I gave up trying to solve the mystery and went to watch the production unfolding in my living room. To hell with Oz. If I made him uncomfortable for some reason he didn't care to share, that was his own damn problem.

Watching Oz install the security system wasn't nearly as interesting as I'd thought it would be. He wandered from room to room with a laptop and a little optic thingy. When I asked what he was doing, he said he was finding the best places to set up cameras and sensors for full coverage. Every now and then, when he thought I wasn't looking, I'd catch him staring at me.

Tired of feeling like a freak show, I excused myself. I felt stronger, and I was antsy to get back in the studio. No doubt Luke wouldn't approve, but I wanted to see how well I'd recovered, and the only way to test it was to get back to my normal routine. I tried not to be offended that Oz seemed relieved when I left.

It took less time than I would have liked to run out of energy. I wasn't even working with metal. I'd started slow, making wax models of the chess pieces I planned to cast for Sol's Christmas present. In less than two hours, my arms were lead weights. The upper part of my right arm ached beneath the brace. Speedy recovery or no, I had a ways to go.

When I returned to the house, Oz was nowhere in sight.

"Hello?" I ventured. After a moment, I raised my voice, "Hello?"

Oz's head popped out of the ceiling in the hallway.

"Ah!" I lurched back, heart pounding. The last week had ruined my appreciation for surprises. "You sacred the shit out of me."

"Sorry." He gave the first real smile I'd seen all day, albeit upside down. "I had to get in the attic to connect to the house's power supply. I'm almost done here. Then I'll get started on your studio."

"How did you get up there?"

He looked embarrassed, "I jumped to grab the ledge and used the wall to scramble up. Sorry if I left any scuff marks, I'll clean before I go."

I chuckled at the mental image. "Why didn't you just get a ladder? I saw one on the truck."

He cocked his head to the side. "Because I'm lazy." Then he was gone, back up the hole in the ceiling.

OZ FINISHED THE installation in three hours. Enough time for me to make a run to town for groceries and bake two batches of chocolate chip cookies. By the time David showed up, I had sandwich fixings, salad, and iced tea all ready to go. The boys came in together after Oz gave David a tour of the work he'd done.

"Hey, David, I—" My words were muffled by his chest as he pulled me into an embrace.

"Don't you ever do that to me again."

"I'm sorry. I didn't mean to worry you."

"After what happened with Aiden, I thought . . ."

"I know. I'm sorry." I'd been apologizing a lot lately.

Oz cleared his throat. "You need me for anything else, Boss?"

David took a step back, but kept his hand on my shoulder. "No. Everything looks great, as usual."

"Cool. Then I'll pack up and leave you to it." Oz started to back away, but I grabbed his arm.

"Oh, no, you don't. You've been working all morning. Leave the cleanup for a bit and come have some lunch."

Since I'd phrased it as more command than question, Oz couldn't refuse without being rude. He'd relaxed a lot since first showing up, but he still seemed wound a little too tight. He even cringed when I grabbed his arm. I didn't know him well enough to pry into his problems, but I didn't like seeing him so anxious either. The only way I could think to help was to make sure he at least got a decent meal.

I was glad of my decision when I saw the way he laid into the sandwich meat. I thought I'd bought enough to last the week, but watching Oz and David load their plates, I wasn't sure it would last through the meal. I stuck with salad, partly because the meat disappeared so fast, but mostly so I wouldn't feel guilty about the cookies later.

Once everyone had eaten their fill I got a Ziploc bag, filled it with cookies, and handed it to Oz. "For the road."

"Thanks," he said, eagerly taking the bag.

David helped Oz collect his gear and haul it to the truck. After waving Oz off from the driveway, he came back inside and snagged another cookie from the dwindling pile on the counter.

Shifting my weight, I chewed the inside of my lip and stared out the window at the place where Oz's truck had disappeared behind the trees. "Have you noticed . . ." I trailed off, shaking my head. I didn't know Oz very well. I had no right to pry. Besides, I had enough to worry about without involving myself in other people's problems.

"Noticed what?" The last cookie vanished into David's mouth.

"Nothing." I shook my head again and pushed back from the counter. "You ready to show me how this system works?"

We walked around the house, and David pointed out the security cameras that, together, would record anything that happened in the common rooms, and show who walked through which door in the hallway. There weren't cameras in the smaller rooms, which was fine by me since I didn't really want recordings of what I did in my bed or bathroom. He also pointed out sensors that would send an alarm if a window was opened or broken while the system was active. Around the perimeter, there were five motion-activated cameras to catch visiting cars and anyone trying to break in, and two to cover my studio.

Once I knew where the hardware was, David showed me a panel beside the front door that made it all work. The internal elements ran independently, meaning I could turn the window sensors off but leave the cameras running, or vice versa. The external cameras were on a separate loop. They would stay on, activated by their individual motion sensors. All the footage was fed into my computer for later review.

"Oz set it up already." David indicated an icon with the mouse. "This shortcut will let you access the footage from the cameras. We have it set to store about a week's worth of data, so if there's something you want to keep, make sure to save the file somewhere else. You know how to do that?"

I nodded.

"Good. There's one more thing. It's important, so pay attention."

Dragging me back to the console by the door, he indicated a large red button just under the key pad. Then he removed a small black box with a similar red button from his pocket. "These are panic switches. Most systems just have the one on the control panel, but I figured you'd need a portable one in case something happens in the studio. If you push this button it will trigger an alarm at my security company. Whoever is on duty will call your phone and ask for your password. You get one chance to answer. If you answer correctly they'll know it was a mistake and reset the alarm. If you answer wrong, or if you don't answer your phone, they'll assume you need help and call the police."

I bit my lip. "They'll need to call the land line." I indicated the old phone sitting in its cradle on the counter. "My cell broke."

He sighed. "That'll be a problem if you're in the studio."

"I'll get a new cell phone soon. Hopefully, I won't push the button before then."

"Hopefully you never push it." He dropped the little panic button onto my palm along with a slip of paper with my password written on it. "Tear that up as soon as you have it memorized."

I nodded.

"It only works if you actually press the button, Alex, so keep it on you. That said, this button only works here. If you're in town getting mugged and you press it, nothing will happen. Okay?"

"Okay."

"Now, let's talk about why you needed a security system in the first place."

DAVID SETTLED ON a stool at the counter, and I poured us each a glass of milk to go with the plate of remaining cookies he'd transferred to the space in front of him. Breaking off a piece to dunk in his milk, he asked, "What the hell, Alex? I know you don't back down from a fight, but you've never gone looking for trouble. First you don't tell me about getting attacked in your studio, then you disappear for days right after our friend gets murdered, and here you are looking like someone used you as a punching bag."

I guess the bruises were more noticeable than I'd thought. "First of all, let me just say that none of this was my fault."

He raised an eyebrow but didn't interrupt.

I sighed. I hated lying, but it couldn't be helped. I had to be careful, though. David was good at sniffing out lies.

"I went for a hike Monday night and was attacked by a bear. I managed to fend it off, but it tore up my arm. So I called a practitioner friend to patch me up. He kept me at his place a couple days to recover. I was unconscious while he was fixing me. I didn't know how much time had passed until I woke up."

He folded his arms, glaring suspiciously. "That's really what happened?"

"That's it." He didn't seem satisfied, so I added, "Look, I've got the scars to prove it," and lifted up my sleeve.

David let out a soft whistle as he turned my arm this way and that, tracing the network of white lines with his fingertip. "Okay, babe, you win. I'm glad you're all right."

"Me too." I pushed the sleeve back down.

"What about the visitors that spooked James enough to commission security? Have they been back?"

"Not that I know of. They could have come while I was gone, but I doubt it. Nothing looks out of place." I stared at my hands, fingers twined in my lap, trying to decide what to say next. Agent Johnson had ordered me to stay silent about his investigation, but David had known Aiden better than anyone. If there was any truth to Johnson's claims, surely David would know? "I need to talk to you about the box those guys were looking for."

"Oh?"

"A PTF agent came by yesterday. I thought it was about my report, but it wasn't."

"What did he want?"

"He asked about the box the two fae wanted. He's looking for it, too, and thought I might have it, or know where it is, because of Aiden . . ."

"Aiden? What does he have to do with it?"

I swallowed hard. Now that it came to it, I wasn't sure I should say anything. They were only suspicions after all, Johnson hadn't given me any proof.

"Just spit it out, Alex, you're killing me here."

"Aiden was, well, might have been . . . a halfer. It's not for sure. They're still investigating."

David sat in stunned silence for a moment. Finally, he asked, "What about the box?"

"It's a faerie artifact. Johnson seemed to think Aiden was involved in something illegal."

"Does he think that's why Aiden was killed?"

"Maybe, or it might just be a coincidence."

"I wonder why the police didn't bring it up in their questioning. Surely they'd be working with the PTF on such a high-profile case. Especially with all the anti-fae stirrings lately."

I couldn't believe he'd just ignored the whole "Aiden was a fae" thing. Finally, I burst out, "Did you know Aiden was a halfer?"

"Of course not."

"Then how can you be so calm? Doesn't it bother you? Shouldn't we have known if he was secretly a faerie?"

David sighed and ran a hand through his hair. "I know you don't have the warmest feelings toward the fae, but whatever else Aiden was, he was our friend. I'd like to think he trusted us as much as he was able. If he really was hiding a fae identity, it wouldn't have been worth the risk to tell anyone. Not even his closest friends. Besides, he might have been protecting us."

"What do you mean?"

"Knowing about an unregistered fae and not reporting it is like harboring a known fugitive. If the PTF found out about him, and we'd already known, you and I would have been in a heap of trouble, too."

"I hadn't thought of that," I admitted.

"At least that would explain his paranoia. Especially if he was hiding a magic item on top of masking his identity. Those things can go for a tidy profit on the black market, but they're pretty much a death sentence if you get caught with one."

"There's a black market for faerie magic?"

"Of course," he smiled. "There are always people willing to buy powerful items, no matter the cost or legality."

"How would you know?" I demanded.

"I work in security, Alex. It pays to be well-informed."

I looked at David, just sat and really looked. I always saw him as the carefree slacker I'd known in college, skipping classes and procrastinating his homework, skating by with a C-average. Somehow, he'd grown into an efficient, professional man, and I'd missed it. When had he gotten so serious?

"I'm starting to feel like I don't know my friends at all," I muttered.

"Don't be ridiculous," he grabbed me in a playful headlock and tousled my hair. "You know everything there is to know about me."

I pushed him off with a scowl. "I didn't know about this whole black market connection of yours."

"I never said I was connected. Knowing about something and being a part of it are entirely different. Besides, that stuff's just what I do for work. It's not who I am any more than a part-time clerk at a bookstore is who you are, or a fae in disguise is what Aiden was. Don't let the facts about a person's life distract you from what's really important."

He ruffled my hair again, and I slapped his hand away. "Okay, Mr. Dalai Lama."

Propping his elbows on the counter, he cracked the knuckles first on one fist, then the other. "So your visitors were looking for an artifact the PTF thinks Aiden had, and may have been killed for."

"Yeah, but don't tell anyone. Johnson made it clear his investigation was a secret. I could get in a lot of trouble just talking to you about it."

"I'll keep that in mind. And on that note, I'd better get going." He gave me one last hug and a kiss on the forehead. "Take care of yourself, and don't forget to use that panic button if you need it."

"Will do," I promised. "Thanks, David."

I stood at the window to wave goodbye, and was pleased to see the first big drops of rain splash down.

I loved rain. I loved everything about it. The way it smelled, sounded, everything. I settled in my favorite chair to watch the storm.

Cat jumped onto my lap. I almost pushed him off, but he started purring and the soothing rhythm made me smile. I scratched his head and watched the patterns as tiny rivers streamed down the windowpane. There were several flashes of lightning, followed by chest-rattling rolls of thunder that told me the heart of the storm was still a ways off.

The world dimmed then darkened, and I imagined the sun had dipped toward the horizon, its passage hidden by the storm clouds rolling across the sky.

I was brought out of my reverie by Cat's claws in my thigh.

"Ow! What the hell?"

Hissing, he darted into the bedroom.

Since he'd been fine through most of the storm, I didn't think it was the thunder that had Cat running for cover. I walked over to the dining table where I'd set down the panic button, and with a silent prayer that it wouldn't go off, slipped it into my pocket. Better safe than sorry.

I got back to the window just in time to see a set of headlights come up my driveway. I was getting really sick of company.

The man who got out was obscured by the rain, but I was fairly certain it was no one I knew. He paused on the porch after his dash from the car, brushing rain off his brown leather jacket. Once he'd gotten himself in order he knocked, but I let him wait another minute before calling out, "Who is it?"

"Ms. Blackwood? My name is Malakai," he answered. "We met briefly in the alley behind your place of work."

My mouth went dry. I hadn't been able to make out his features in the rain, but the voice was the same. I wasn't likely to forget it any time soon.

"Please, may I come in? It's quite damp out here."

My hand was in my pocket, but I hesitated with my finger on the button. "What are you doing here? And how do you know where I live?"

"I promise to answer your questions, but I'd really prefer not to do it through a closed door."

I had the panic button in my hand, and while I wasn't back to full health, thanks to Luke's ministrations I was hardly helpless. I was less inclined to dismiss him as crazy after all I'd seen and heard. If he really did have information, wasn't it was worth the risk?

Keeping the chain in place, I opened the door enough to get a good look at him. He was soaked through. "I don't suppose you're here to tell me you've solved Aiden's murder on your own."

He grimaced. "Unfortunately, no. Though I have made some progress. Will you hear me out?"

"You've got five minutes."

Chapter 9

HE GLANCED BETWEEN me and the still mostly closed door. "Are you going to let me in?"

"No."

His shoulders slumped. "You're not making this easy."

"Why should I? I don't know you from Adam, and there's a serial killer on the loose."

"I suppose that's fair. Though I do hope you'll change your mind quickly." He shivered for effect.

"That depends on what you have to say."

"I should warn you, some of it may be difficult to believe. But I assure you, it's all true."

After all I'd been through, I shuddered to think there were more hard truths coming my way.

"First of all, did you know Aiden was part fae?"

"Yeah, I did." I didn't mention that I'd only just found out and was still coming to terms with it. David's speech about Aiden being a friend and nothing else mattering made the whole thing seem less important than it had a day ago.

"That simplifies matters." He didn't ask how I knew, or seem surprised that I did.

"Would it shock you to learn that I'm a fae?"

I took an involuntary step back before my brain caught up with the conversation. If this Malakai person was related to Aiden, as he'd claimed, and Aiden was part fae. . . . "I guess that makes sense."

"Don't misunderstand. I'm not some half-breed with a smidgen of magic buried deep inside. I'm a full-blooded fae."

I looked him up and down. He seemed so ordinary. But that was the whole point of faerie glamour, right? To blend in. "Do you have a visa?"

He pursed his lips. "What will you do if I say no?"

Under the rules of the peace treaty, if the PTF caught a full-blooded fae without a visa, they were within their rights to execute it. To the best of my knowledge, that hadn't happened in years.

"I don't know. I guess it depends on how this conversation goes."

"I see. Well, rest assured, I do have a visa. I wasted a whole day getting it." He sounded disgusted, and looked like he wanted to spit. "Your precious PTF protectors certainly like to drag their feet."

I shrugged. "Yeah, well, that's bureaucracy. So why did you come to me? If you want to help catch Aiden's killer, you should take what you know to the police."

"Don't you care what happened to him?"

"Of course I care, but that doesn't make me qualified to do anything about it."

"On the contrary," he held up a finger, "it makes you uniquely qualified."

I stared in confusion. Maybe he was crazy after all.

"The fae look at crime and punishment differently than humans." He puffed a breath into his hands and rubbed them together. "In simplest terms, humans seem to believe in some universal truth and justice to which all beings can be held accountable. Fae society isn't like that. If a person is wronged, that person is responsible for seeking their own justice by whatever means they have at their disposal, provided they do not break any of their lords' laws in doing so."

"What about the weak or the poor? How do they get justice?"

He shrugged. "You'll not find many weak or poor among the fae, but those incapable of protecting themselves form groups or join the service of a stronger fae in exchange for protection. Lesser fae could bring a crime to the attention of their lord, but few are foolish enough to do so. In general, it is not in one's best interest to come to the attention of a lord."

"That sounds like a terrible system."

"Be that as it may, it is the system by which we live. Aiden was kin. As such, I claim the right of vengeance."

I crossed my arms. "How exactly were you related?"

"We were distant cousins."

"But you care enough to hunt down his killer?"

"It is my duty."

"So it's got nothing to do with a certain silver box?"

The flash of surprise in his eyes told me I'd hit the mark.

"I admit, recovering the stolen artifact is part of my job, but part only. As those nearest Aiden, it falls to us to avenge him."

"You, maybe," I scoffed, "but I'm no faerie. Humans have professionals for that. I don't subscribe to your vigilante system of justice."

"That is only half true."

"Right." I rolled my eyes. "You think I'm a halfer. I told you before, you're wrong." Despite my denial, my stomach twisted and I began to feel lightheaded. So much of what I thought I knew was in shambles.

A worried expression creased his forehead. "Perhaps you should sit while I explain the rest."

While his concern seemed genuine, I suspected he just wanted an excuse to come in out of the rain. "Your five minutes are up."

"But we still have so much to discuss."

I ground my teeth. I wanted to slam the door and pretend I'd never met him, but hearing him out might be the only way for the police to get his information since he seemed dead-set against talking to them himself.

I slid the chain off the door. "Okay. You can—"

Headlights flashed across the front of the house, momentarily blinding me.

When I could see again, Maggie was running up to the porch, a bundle cradled against her chest. Mud dripped from the hem of her pants to the dark cement of the porch as she stepped up beside Malakai.

"Maggie? What're—" I slapped a palm to my forehead. Dinner.

She shook the rain off her coat, shifting her load between arms, then grinned up at me. Her eyes slid over to my other guest, and the smile melted off her face. The box in her arms tipped, sliding trough her fingers, and I lurched through the door to grab it before it hit the ground.

"That's the man from before." Maggie's chocolaty skin had blanched. Her eyes were wide and staring. "You said—"

"It's okay, Maggie." I glanced at Malakai, who was, thankfully, holding very still. "Turns out it was just a misunderstanding."

"But—"

"Why don't you go on inside. I'll be right there."

Maggie looked between me, Malakai, and the open door. She bit her lip, took the box out of my hands, and sidled into the house, her eyes on Malakai the whole time. She left the door open.

Sighing, I ran a hand over my hair and pitched my voice so it wouldn't carry into the house. "You need to leave."

"We need to talk." He peeked through the open door. Maggie was standing at the kitchen counter next to her box, arms crossed. She frowned when she caught us looking. Malakai turned back to me. "Can't you get rid of her?"

I shook my head. If she thought I was in trouble, any attempt to chase her off would just result in more drama. "The fastest way to get Maggie to leave is to convince her nothing is wrong."

"But—"

I lifted one hand. "She should be out of here by ten at the latest. Come back then."

Grumbling, he nodded once and stalked back through the rain.

I waited until his taillights disappeared in the trees, then shut the door on one storm and walked into another.

Maggie stood, hands on hips by the entrance to the kitchen. The kinky black curls that gave her a feeling of vibrant energy even when she stood still seemed to writhe around her face, and her clear, mocha complexion was creased across her forehead and around her puckered mouth. The piercing green eyes I'd envied so much in college narrowed as I approached.

"What the bloody hell is going on, Alex? Who is that guy? You told me to ring the police if I saw him again. You were all freaked out. And now you're what, friends?"

Stepping up to the counter, I flipped open the top of Maggie's box. A glass dome greeted me, the cake inside only slightly squished where it had pressed against one side, smearing its chocolate icing.

"He's . . . an admirer." I lifted the cake out of the box and set it on the counter. Beneath it were some board games, a deck of cards, and a stack of movies. She'd come prepared.

Maggie's mouth screwed to one side. "I know you're not much for social interactions, but since when did a man showing interest warrant a call to the police?"

"I overreacted. When he first introduced himself he . . . came on a little strong."

She motioned to the front door. "What changed?"

I shrugged. Pulling the night's entertainment out of the box. "He's forward, but I don't think he's dangerous. Anyway, he's gone now. Girls' night, remember?"

She drummed her fingers on the counter, still frowning. "I just want to make sure you're not doing anything reckless. Losing Aiden like that was quite the bloody shock."

I clenched my fists. "I didn't *lose* him, Maggie. He was murdered."

Pressing her lips tight, she set one long, thin hand on my shoulder. Then her eyes shifted behind me, growing large, and her hand fell away. "Who is that?"

Fear spiked through me. I whipped around.

Cat blinked big green eyes. His tail swished like a streamer in a lazy summer breeze.

I collapsed against the counter and waved a hand at the furry intruder. "That's Cat."

"You got a cat?" Maggie pushed past me and knelt beside him. "You?"

I rubbed the back of my neck. "Not on purpose."

"But he's staying, right?" She glared at me, Cat half-pulled into her lap.

"Looks that way."

"Good." She gave him a scritch behind the ears. "It's about time you got some company up here."

I'd had more than enough company lately.

"How about some tea?" she asked, straightening. Tea was Maggie's answer for everything from flu to food poisoning, broken heart to boredom. Stepping into the kitchen, she looked around, sniffed the air, and frowned. "I take it you didn't make any dinner?"

My stomach twisted with guilt. "I—"

"Forgot I was coming." She sighed. "Honestly, Alex, if I didn't like you so much . . ."

I gave her a sheepish grin. "But you do."

She smiled back. "I'll make the tea. *You* find something for us to eat."

Cocking my head to one side, I pointed at the cake. "Found it."

MAGGIE WRAPPED her arms around me for a goodbye hug, and I stole a glance at the clock over her shoulder. 10:15. Malakai could show up any minute.

"Truthfully luv, you're sure you're all right?" The worry in Maggie's voice drove needles into my heart, but Maggie had a nice, normal life. I couldn't drag her into the madness mine had become. I wouldn't risk anyone else.

I nodded. "I'll be fine."

"Maybe you should come stay with me and Charlie for a while?"

I choked on a laugh. She and Charlie rented a small, two-story row house with barely enough space to keep from tripping over each other. I couldn't imagine how they'd managed not to strangle each other yet, and I wasn't about to join the mix. "Not gonna happen, Mags."

"Then hurry up and find someone to marry so I can stop worrying."

"Marriage isn't everyone's idea of happily ever after."

She raised her hands. "I know, and you've always been one to do things your own way. But I worry."

I gave her another hug. "I love you too."

Lifting her box, now with an empty cake holder, I stole another glance at the clock. 10:20. "Let's get you home before Charlie starts to worry."

The rain had petered off to a light mist, but my driveway was a river of mud. We slogged to her CRV and loaded the box in the back. A gust of wind tugged a strand of hair into my face and I pushed it back with a growl. "I love the rain, but it makes my hair so frizzy."

She tipped her head, pointing at her own wild mane. "Really? You're gonna complain to *me* about frizz?"

We both laughed as she climbed into her seat.

"See you 'round, Mags."

"I'd better. You pull another disappearing act on me and we're gonna have words."

I waved her off into the night.

Malakai didn't show up as I tromped back to the porch, or when I closed the door. He wasn't there when I looked out the window half an hour later after cleaning and putting away the dishes Maggie and I had used. Finally, I set my coffee maker so I'd have something to drink in the morning.

I pulled an afghan off the back of the couch and snuggled under it, tucking it under my legs. Damp still clung to my hair, and the chill of true night was setting in.

Cat jumped onto the cushion beside me, butting his head into my thigh.

Yawning, I scratched him behind the ears, and a long, low purr filled the silence.

I draped my hand over his vibrating side and let my head relax against the backrest.

Damn faerie better hurry up.

I BLINKED.

Watery light cast pale shadows across the living room curtains. The thick aroma of coffee drifted to me, and I blinked again. My tongue was stuck to the roof of my mouth. When I swallowed, the stale taste made me grimace. Every muscle in my body felt welded in place, and I groaned as I pushed away from the couch.

Cat yawned wide enough for me to see down his throat, stretched, and padded away down the hall.

The clock was blurry, and I rubbed my dried-out eyes. Morning had snuck up while I waited.

I rolled my shoulders, frowning when a sharp pain stabbed through my neck. Then I shuffled to the window and pulled back the curtain.

Malakai's little tan Toyota was back.

Why hadn't he woken me?

The rain was gone, replaced by a wispy fog that clung to the trees like cobwebs.

I poured myself a mug of steaming coffee and cradled it in my hands. I still wasn't sure what to make of Malakai's claim that I was a halfer, but what did he have to gain from such a ridiculous lie? And even if the screwy fae justice system had him looking for Aiden's killer, what made him think I could help? I took a sip of coffee and burnt my tongue on the scalding liquid.

Cursing, I set the mug aside. Time to find out if he was crazy or not.

Grabbing my robe, I pulled it tight to keep the damp chill off me as I tiptoed toward Malakai's car in my mud-caked boots. Mist beaded his windshield and clouded my view as I paced around to the passenger side. Malakai was sleeping, reclined in the seat, a faded blue blanket draped across his chest and lap. The back bench was a mountain of takeout bags, soda cans, and candy wrappers. He'd probably been living out of his car for days.

I chewed my lower lip and reminded myself that I had a nice new security system and a panic button that would bring the police if I pushed it.

Sighing, I slammed my palm against his window.

Chapter 10

MY LIPS QUIRKED with a twisted sense of pleasure when Malakai jumped. I'd had enough surprises lately, it was a welcome change to get the drop on someone else. I gave him a moment to orient himself, then knocked again. Once his eyes focused on me, I motioned him to roll down the window.

"Couldn't afford a hotel?" I asked.

He rubbed his eyes and grunted.

"Thought I told you to come back at ten."

"I got delayed. Didn't figure you'd appreciate a wakeup call at three a.m."

I nodded, leaning one hip against the cold metal of his car and crossing my arms. "You still wanna talk?"

He sat up a little straighter, looking at me with big, brown eyes. "Are you going to let me in this time?"

Stepping back, I tipped my head toward the house. "Let's hear what you've got to say."

He slid out of the car, then reached back and lifted a small, canvas backpack. Catching my look, he said, "Toiletries and such. I was hoping to use your bathroom to freshen up."

Keeping one hand in my pocket, thumb on the panic button, I let him proceed me to the front door. He looked to be in his mid-twenties, about my height but rail thin. His mousy brown hair stood up in tufts, and he walked stiffly, probably from being cramped in a car all night. I'd been on enough road trips to know how unpleasant that could be.

I pointed him to the bathroom and retrieved my now-cool-enough-to-drink coffee, then perched on the edge of a chair. When Malakai emerged, I motioned him to take a seat on the couch.

"So Mr. Malakai—"

"Kai, please."

I frowned. "Kai. What have you got to tell me?"

"First, I'd like to apologize for our initial encounter. I don't have much experience with humans. I didn't mean to upset you."

I snorted. It wasn't much of an apology, but the part about not having much experience with humans was easy to believe. I got the feeling he hadn't been off the reservation in a long time, if ever.

"I don't need an apology, I need answers."

"Shall we begin with you, or Aiden?"

"Tell me what you know about Aiden. Maybe, if I decide you're not full of shit, I'll listen to what else you have to say."

"Fair enough." He laid back on the couch and stared at the ceiling, like a psych patient about to unload their problems on a shrink. "I assume you're at least passingly familiar with the recent murders around here?"

I nodded.

"Your police haven't been able to find a connection between the victims because they are missing a crucial piece of information. All the victims were unregistered halfers."

"The PTF didn't find a fae connection. And wouldn't something like that have come out during the autopsies? Even if they were weak halfers, there should have been enough iron in the surgical tools to cause a reaction."

"Fae are animated by magic. It's our essence, similar to a human's soul. It's that magic that reacts to iron. When a halfer dies, their magic disperses. All that remains is their mortal flesh, so their corpses would seem human."

"Then how do you know what they were?"

He shrugged. "Humans can't tell the difference between someone with fae blood and someone without unless they perform tests, and those tests aren't infallible. Most fae can identify someone with magic in their blood at a mere glance. We also have the benefit of more accurate genealogical records. The fae registry of halfers is considerably longer and more detailed than what the offices of the PTF hold."

"The fae have a registry too?"

"Of sorts, but for different reasons."

"What reasons?"

"Let's just say we like to keep tabs on our relatives. All the people killed were low-level halfers, people whose fae ancestry was weak enough or far enough removed that they probably didn't know what they were. None of them had traits or abilities that would have brought them to the PTF's attention."

"But the PTF was looking at Aiden," I argued, "and I'm pretty sure he knew what he was. It would explain a lot of his behavior."

"True. Aiden's grandmother told him. Her grandfather was strong enough to do a few simple tricks. She got it into her head that people would be out to get her if they knew, and apparently passed that paranoia on to her grandson."

I'd met Aiden's grandmother a time or two before she passed. She'd raised Aiden after his parents died. That was something we'd had in common, our parents being gone, but I'd take a disappearing act and an accident over Aiden's story any day.

As he told it, his mother had a secret, but she'd loved his father so much that she refused to lie to him, trusting him to love her just the same. Aiden never said what that secret was, but now I could guess. She'd told him she was a halfer right around the time the war, and the faerie hunts were getting into full-swing.

Aiden heard shots. He'd run to the living room in time to see his father standing, gun in hand, over his dead mother. Then his dad turned the gun around and sprayed his brain across the wall.

I don't know how Aiden stayed sane after something like that, but he lived with his crazy grandma afterward and hardly ever talked about his parents. Thinking about that story, my heart twisted in shame at the way I'd let the shock of Aiden's secret change the way I felt about him, even if only for a moment.

"So the murderer is some sort of anti-fae extremist, like one of the Purity people."

He sighed, "Nothing so simple, I'm afraid. As I said, these were not people easily recognizable as halfers. It would have been difficult for a human to find them. However, they had something else in common."

He paused until I was forced to prompt, "What?"

"They were caretakers."

I let the silence stretch. When no more explanation was forthcom-\ing I arched an eyebrow and said, "Maybe you should pretend you're talking to someone who knows nothing about faeries."

He twisted his mouth like he'd eaten something sour and huffed, "A caretaker is someone entrusted with the keeping of a fae artifact.

Many artifacts have been created throughout the ages. Some simple, some powerful, but all highly sought after. Since the fae realms do not trust one another, they are always looking for an advantage. The easiest way to keep an artifact safe is to hide it here, in the mortal realm.

"Since no fae in his right mind would hand an artifact over to a full-blooded human, nor a fae outside their bloodline, artifacts not in use are given to their fae-human offspring and handed down through the generations as family heirlooms. Sometimes they obscure their connection to the family, or wait until the bloodline is diluted to the point of being virtually unrecognizable before entrusting an artifact."

"So Johnson was right. Aiden did have an artifact. That's why those fae were so intent on finding that box when they came to see me."

He sat up. "Other fae came here?"

"Right after Aiden died. They were looking for a little silver box."

"Many artifacts are masked as common trinkets. Tell me about these fae."

I pursed my lips. "First, finish telling me about Aiden's killer. Do you think a faerie did it to get their hands on the artifact?"

"That's one possibility, and probably the simplest of the theories we currently have."

"What's the other theory?"

"That there is a human moving against us who knows more than they should." He spoke quietly, as though voicing it might make it true.

"How is that worse?"

"If the killer is fae, this is a fae matter. We can seek justice on our own and the humans have no cause to interfere. They will not concern themselves over one fae killing another, and the murders will stop. If the perpetrator is human, it will be difficult to seek justice without involving the human legal system and revealing truths we would rather remain hidden. Such a path would likely cause more conflict between the humans and fae, potentially reigniting the war we so recently put to rest. Perhaps that is even the murderer's intention."

"You think someone is trying to restart the war?" The idea that anyone could think a return to war was a good thing was horrifying, but sick as it made me, I couldn't deny the possibility.

"It's something to consider. Even if that isn't the killer's primary goal, it may well be the result. We can't seek assistance from the human authorities without admitting the fae were aware of unregistered halfers living off the reservation, something that would constitute a breach in our peace agreement. However, if we seek our own justice and the criminal turns out to be human, the human government will see it as an unwarranted attack by the fae. In either case, the humans will react as they always do when frightened. They will lash out."

Maggie's black forest cake roiled in my stomach, threatening to come up. To think my friend's death could mean an end to the peace between faeries and humans was inconceivable, but I could feel the truth of his words settle over me like a cloak weighing on my shoulders. "Please tell me you're here to make sure that doesn't happen."

"That's one of my tasks, yes. I was sent to identify the killer, recover the stolen artifacts, and prevent a return to war."

"Yeah, sure." The giggle that escaped sounded a little hysterical to my ears. "Why not, right? 'Cause you're all of one guy. No problem."

He scowled, "You doubt my ability?"

"No offense, but that's a pretty tall order."

He puffed up with self-importance. "I'm not just one guy. I am a Knight of the Realm, and I am not alone."

That brought me up short. "Who else is working on this?"

He lifted an eyebrow. "You."

The bottom fell out of my stomach even as the giggles bubbled up again.

I needed to get a grip before I fell apart completely, so I took a couple deep, calming breaths before replying. "Look, I don't know who you thought I was when you came here, but you're wrong. Yes, I was Aiden's friend, but I'm just an artist. A human artist. There's nothing special about me. If I had any crazy skills or powerful connections to help catch Aiden's killer, I would have used them already. I can't help you."

He watched me carefully as he said, "I'm afraid you're quite wrong, on all counts. Are you ready to hear the rest of what I have to say?"

"I don't think I am," I admitted.

"I see." He stood as if to leave, but I stopped him with a gesture.

"Wait. Just give me a minute."

He sat back down, and I went to the kitchen for two glasses of water. I wasn't thirsty, but I needed time to strengthen my resolve before facing whatever Malakai had in store. Aiden had always been there for me. He'd gotten his ass kicked saving me. I'd already failed him once. If there was any way I could help find his killer, how could I refuse?

Handing over one of the glasses, I settled back in my seat. "Okay, go ahead."

Setting the water aside, he steepled his fingers and looked at me over the tops, pursing his lips. The steady throb in my chest provided a drumroll for my ears alone as I tried to counter the dryness in my mouth.

"My boss, to use a term that is familiar to you, is the Lord of Enchantment, one of the most powerful fae alive. He's the one who sent me to you."

My abdomen cramped, but I swallowed my denial along with the lump in my throat and croaked out, "Why?"

"Despite what you clearly believe, you are not human. Your fae blood, and your relationship to the deceased, make you uniquely qualified to solve this problem."

"I'm a metalsmith. I work with iron and steel all the time. Unless you're telling me not all fae are allergic to iron?"

He quirked an eyebrow, the sly smile on his lips answer enough.

Where my mouth had been dry before, it was now a desert wasteland.

Their allergy to iron was one of the universally accepted truths about the fae. It's how the PTF determined who was who, and how humans protected themselves. If it wasn't true . . .

Shimmering points of lights danced in my vision, and the sounds of the world muted momentarily around me.

Before my thoughts spiraled into total panic, Kai said, "Almost all fae are allergic to metals, iron being the strongest. Very few are allergic to silver or gold, but some breeds are. The traits and abilities of a specific fae play a factor in how strong the reaction will be to what. I'm sure you've heard that sea fae are more susceptible to iron than most? Well, there are two sides to every coin. Where there is a most, there must also be a least. In general, fae with an affinity for enchantment can handle any metal except pure iron."

"I handle iron just fine, so if that's the best you can do, I'm still no faerie."

"Be patient," he scolded. "I'm getting to that. There is one sub-classification with a higher immunity than the enchanters. To the best of my knowledge, only three imbuers currently exist. One is the Lord of Enchantment himself, his niece is the second, and the third is you."

I swallowed my denial, and instead asked, "What's an imbuer?"

"Exactly what it sounds like. They can imbue a substance with something else, something like a feeling, memory, or idea. With training, they can weave magic into items. That's how the most powerful artifacts are made."

"I don't understand. How can an idea be inside something, and what good would that do?"

"In your case, you do it through your art. When you work on a sculpture, you think about something in particular, right? Something you want to get across to anyone who looks at it."

"Yeah." I rolled my eyes. "That's sorta how art works. There's nothing magical about it."

"That may be true, but you've got a little something extra." He leaned forward to rest his elbows on his knees. "Let's say you want to make a sculpture that gives the viewer a sense of peace. While you're working on that sculpture you focus on that feeling. You remember every time you've felt safe and calm. As you work, those feelings and memories become part of your sculpture. When a person sees the finished work, they can't help but feel the same sense of peace you imagined while creating it."

"So you're saying people don't like my art for the art itself, but because I'm using magic to make them feel a certain way?"

"Not necessarily," he shrugged. "You're untrained, so you're not doing it consciously. Whatever leaks into your art is most likely just a byproduct of your mood. I doubt it's very focused."

I thought about how hard I concentrated on the idea I was trying to create when I worked on a piece and wasn't so sure about Kai's assessment. What if the only reason my art was successful was because of magic? An upheaval of my artistic identity wasn't something I was willing to take on faith. "Is there a way to test it?"

"It's not foolproof, but yes."

"How?"

"Do you have some clay?"

"Hang on." I went to my storeroom to look for an unopened box of the clay I used for small scale models of larger projects.

"Will this do?" I held the clay out to Kai.

"Yes, that's fine. Now, we're going to work with light because it's easy to see. If you were to imbue the clay with an emotion or memory it could be hard to tell if the magic worked. With this, you'll know right away."

"What do I do?"

"Just work the clay while you're thinking of light. You can make the clay into whatever shape you want, that's not important. What matters is your concentration. You need to set aside all your doubt and fear. Focus on the essence of light. Close your eyes and think about how light feels, its colors, everything that makes it what it is. Hold that firmly in your mind, mold the clay. When you've finished, open your eyes and look at what you've made."

I sat quietly for a good five minutes before I started working the clay. I had no idea what I was going to make, especially with my eyes closed, but I pushed and pulled as the mood struck me, following the contours with my fingers and making adjustments by feel. I imagined the heat of sunlight on my skin, the sound of fluorescents buzzing overhead, the warm glow from a fire, every type of light I could think of. Then I tried to find what tied them together. What was true of light in all its incarnations? Finally, when I'd captured the essence of light as best I could, I took a deep breath and looked down.

I'd molded the clay into an abstract form, but I barely noticed its shape. There in my hand, the clay was glowing.

Chapter 11

I JUMPED TO MY feet with a shriek, irrationally afraid the clay would somehow burn me. With a dull splat, the glowing form hit the floor, turning into a shapeless blob. It continued to emit a faint light.

I stared at it for I don't know how long. Eventually, hands guided me down to my seat.

"I'd call that a pass." Kai scraped the clay off the floor. "What do you think?"

"I think—"

The phone rang, and we both jumped, spinning to face it.

My heart was hammering so hard it sounded like a brass band had taken up residence in my ears, but I latched onto the phone as an excuse not to finish my hanging sentence because I had no idea how it should end.

I snatched the phone off the cradle mid-ring. "Hello?"

"Alex! Are you okay?"

"Mags? Yeah, why wouldn't I—" A cramp hit my stomach like a punch to the gut. I looked at the clock. I was supposed to be at work twenty minutes ago.

"Emma called. I'm on my way to open the store right now. What the bloody hell happened?"

"Sorry, Mags. Something came up. I can't make it in today."

"Something came up? Between when I left last night and this morning?" The blare of a car horn filtered through the line. "This has to do with that guy showing up at your place, doesn't it?"

I stiffened, gripping the receiver. "I'm just not feeling well."

"Bollox. You were fine last night. Hell, you ate half that damn cake."

"Seriously, Maggie, I'm just—"

"If the next words out of your mouth aren't 'on my way to work,' I'm calling the police."

Clenching my teeth, I growled, "Fine. I'll be there in an hour." I slammed the phone into its base, and considered unplugging the damn thing again. But that would just make the situation worse. If Maggie hadn't gotten hold of me, she'd have charged up the mountain, authorities in tow.

Kai was standing next to the couch, hands clasped in front of him.

"I need to go to work."

"Now?"

I shrugged. "Seems life doesn't stop just because some crazy fae shows up on your doorstep and turns your world inside out."

"I was really hoping to nip this investigation in the butt."

I cracked a smile. "Bud. Nip it in the bud."

He frowned. "Perhaps I could convince your friend to give you the day off."

"You go anywhere near Maggie, she'll call the cops."

"She doesn't have to see me."

I shivered. "Magic my friend, and I'll call the PTF myself."

He sighed. "Fine."

Rounding the counter, I dropped my empty coffee mug in the sink. "While I'm gone, you could make yourself useful by looking into the fae who paid me a visit. The PTF doesn't seem to be having much luck. None that they're telling me about, anyway."

He leaned against the counter, arms crossed. "What can you tell me about them?"

I gave him the briefest version I could of my mysterious visitors, the iron tongs, and the fish-faced fae.

"I'll see what I can dig up."

"I'll meet you back here around five."

"Before you leave." He trotted to the small backpack sitting by the couch and pulled out a thin black box the length of my forearm. "My lord bid me give this to you."

"What is it?"

"A gift, to assist and protect you."

I took the box, unhooked the small silver latch, and flipped open the lid. There, on a bed of velvet, was the most intricate chain I'd ever seen. It looked like one continuous piece of silver. I couldn't find any joints or links, but it coiled in a way that suggested fluid movement. The surface was etched with symbols so fine I couldn't pick them apart, creating one long interconnected image. It was beautiful. I reached out one tentative hand.

The moment my index finger made contact with the cool metal, the beautiful coil of silver came alive, spiraling up my arm like a boa constrictor seizing its prey. I gave a startled shriek and stumbled back, flailing in an effort to dislodge the thing. A blinding flash seared my vision and intense, burning pain flared through my arm as if it were on fire.

The box tumbled to the floor, and an instant later, I followed. One agonized scream ripped out of me as I fell. In the time it took to fill my lungs, it was over. The second scream died on my lips.

I lay on my side, cradling my arm to my chest, not sure what had happened. The box lay open on the floor in front of me, empty. The fabric lining dislodged and partially askew.

"Are you all right?"

I jerked back from Kai's hand and kicked out, forcing him to dance away. "Don't touch me!"

My breath came in ragged gasps, an after-effect of adrenaline that I was getting to know a little too well. My brain told me nothing hurt, but that couldn't be right. Pain like that didn't just disappear. I looked down at my arm. The fabric of the sweatshirt I'd fallen asleep in was burned through in a ragged spiral up the sleeve, the tattered edges charred black. I pulled the remains loose to look at the bare skin beneath.

Time froze as I stared, my mouth hanging open. Absent were the terrible burns I expected from the intense heat. No injuries, no scars. Instead, all the intricacies of that beautiful chain were imprinted in a perfect spiral up my right arm.

"Are you all right, Alex?" Kai kept his distance. His voice was higher than before, thin and strained.

I shook my head, too stunned to speak.

"Alex?"

"What . . . what was that?"

Looking away, he repeated tightly, "A gift from my lord."

Some gift. I fixed Kai with an accusing glare. "You could have warned me."

"My lord is not given to explanation, and the box was keyed to open for you alone. I didn't know what was inside, or what would happen when you opened it."

"Is it permanent?" I twisted my arm this way and that, trying to follow the pattern as it wound its way up my arm. "And why a tattoo? That's a pretty weird gift."

"It's not a tattoo, it's an enchantment, and yes, it's permanent."

"What does it do?"

He shrugged, eying the pattern. "If I had to guess, I'd say he's given you a charm to boost your natural fae abilities. I would need to spend some time deciphering it to be certain."

I closed my eyes and thumped my head into the wall a couple times before leaving it there. "Seriously. Just one normal day. Is that so much to ask?"

I WAS AN HOUR and a half late pulling into the lot. Maggie was behind the register when I made it up front. She narrowed her eyes as I approached.

"You don't look sick."

I focused on pinning my name tag in place.

"Are you gonna tell me what's really going on?"

I shrugged. "Nothing's going on."

"That right?" She crossed her arms. "So the fact that you've got some fae dude living with you is of no consequence?"

Choking on my own spit, I sputtered. "What? He's not living with me. And what makes you think he's a fae?"

"I called David after I hung up with you this morning. Had him run that guy's license plate."

"You . . ." My mouth moved like a suffocating fish, and my hands rose of their own volition as if seeking to strangle my friend. Maybe I should have let Kai magic her after all. "Why would you do that?"

She uncrossed her arms and let them fall to her sides. "You didn't leave me any choice. You're not talking, Alex. Not to me, not to David. We're worried about you."

I ran a hand through my hair. "So what exactly did this check pull up?"

"That car's registered to a fae off the reservation." She dropped her voice, setting one hand on my shoulder. "You've never been overly fond of the fae, Alex. Why are you letting that guy stay with you?"

I pulled back. "He's not staying with me."

She frowned. "The address listed on his PTF visa . . . it's *your* house."

I clenched my jaw so hard I feared my teeth might shatter. "Is it now?"

"You didn't know?" Maggie shook her head. "We have to tell the PTF he lied."

I lifted a hand. "No, Mags. I'll handle it."

"He—"

"He's got some information . . ." I glanced around and lowered my voice. "About what happened to Aiden."

Her brow furrowed. "All the more reason to call the PTF."

I shook my head. "It's complicated. Just . . . trust me, okay? I got this."

Maggie chewed her lower lip, fierce green eyes searching. "If you end up in a ditch somewhere . . ."

"You can say you told me so."

"This is bollox."

"Thank you." I gripped her shoulders. "Really."

She shook her head, worrying a silver pendant back and forth on its chain. I squinted at the pendant. Two sleek, abstract figures twined around a suspended crystal center. I'd made it for Maggie right before she and Charlie got married, something to remember me by in case she became one of those wives who forgot her girlfriends after finding a husband. I needn't have worried.

She followed my gaze. "It reminds me of you, of the times we spent together."

I licked my lips. Simple sentimentality, or had I imbued the piece without knowing? I shook my head and forced a smile. "Go salvage what you can of your day off."

Frowning until her pressed lips turned pale, she nodded, then headed for the back room.

I took a lap around the shop, pausing to wave hello to Emma as she bustled busily at the café.

Ancient Mr. Feltz—who made the journey from the retirement home up the road every morning—sat in his usual chair drinking coffee and reading the paper. A handful of other customers browsed for books. For one brief, shining moment, I was a normal person working a normal job in a normal store, and all was right with the world.

Then the front bell jingled.

I looked up, and nearly toppled the shelf behind me as I jerked back. The figure walking through the door was nearly eight feet tall, had jet black skin with iridescent gold veins, and shiny white hair that hung to his knees in a long, intricate braid. The fae's eyes were too big for his face and looked faceted; like close-ups I'd seen of spiders' eyes, all rainbow prisms and impossible to tell where they were looking.

Following close behind was a perfectly normal-looking man in a business suit. The two had been talking animatedly when they walked in, but paused at my forceful reaction.

"Are you all right, miss?" It was the businessman who spoke, but I couldn't tear my eyes from the fae standing in my store with no glamour. Neither could I form a response. Between Smith and Neil, and then Malakai, I'd had all the faeries I could take. I stood there, frozen, wondering what this newest fae had in store for me.

"Let's leave her be," said the fae, steering the businessman away by his elbow. He shot me a look over his companion's head, but I couldn't tell the meaning behind those prismatic eyes.

The pair ordered drinks from Emma, who served them with a smile. They took their cups to a table and continued their conversation in hushed voices. No one else was freaking out about the faerie in the room. The shoppers were still shopping. Mr. Feltz glanced up from his paper, but returned to it without comment.

After serving them, Emma walked over to me. "Are you okay, Alex? You've gone all white and sweaty. Are you feeling sick?"

"What? No. I mean yeah, I'm fine, Emma." I tore my eyes from the fae and tried to give my friend a smile, which felt more like a grimace. "Um, did anything strike you as odd about those last customers you served?"

Emma glanced at the couple in question and shrugged. "No. They got lattes and tipped well. Why?"

"No reason," I hedged. "Could you cover for a minute while I run to the bathroom?"

"Of course. You sure you're okay?"

"I'll be fine." I left Emma at the counter, darted back to the restroom, and locked the door. Bracing against the sink, I stared at my reflection. Was I going crazy? Was that person really a fae, or was I imagining it?

Maybe this had something to do with my "gift." I pulled up my sleeve and stared at the inked pattern, tracing the spiral with a fingertip. As far as I could tell, the tattoo looked the same as it had when it burned itself onto my skin.

I took a deep breath and splashed some cold water on my face. Assuming I wasn't going insane, the fae hadn't made any indication that he thought I could see what he really was, and no one else had reacted at all. Whatever was happening seemed localized to me.

Goody, because I wasn't feeling like enough of a freak lately. I just had to hold it together through my shift, then I'd see if Kai knew what the hell was going on. I really hoped he did.

After giving my reflection a pep talk, which did nothing to help me feel sane, I straightened my shoulders and went out to face the world. Once Emma was assured I was feeling all right, I made my way to the wall where we shelved our non-fiction titles and started scanning spines.

Pulling out a book on basic fae lore, I returned to the register and flipped open the cover. I ran my index finger down the table of contents until I came to the heading "Glamours." That seemed promising.

I skimmed the chapter, but didn't find anything about mortals seeing through glamours.

The businessman and the fae finished their drinks and stood to leave. I held my breath while they walked past, watching from the corner of my eye as I pretended to be absorbed in my reading. When the front chime sounded their departure, I breathed a sigh of relief and flipped to the section labeled "Charms."

It turned out charms could be anything; trinkets, jewelry, weapons, even people. One example claimed a gnome had been charmed so that anyone who shook his hand would have good luck for a week.

When I reached the end of the chapter, I flipped the page and stopped cold. The next chapter was titled "Curses," and the first line stated: *Charms and curses are two sides of the same coin.*

Kai had said my "gift" was a charm . . . but what if it wasn't?

Charms and curses worked the same way, usually the result of a powerful enchantment on an object or person. The only difference seemed to be whether the effects were helpful or harmful to the affected person.

I glanced at my arm, where the soft cream sweater I'd pulled on that morning covered the spiraling design of my new tattoo. Guess I'd just have to wait and see.

After reading the chapter on curses, I checked the table of contents again and flipped to a section titled "Lies and Lying."

While it is generally accepted that the fae are incapable of telling outright lies, you would be wise to take anything they say with a grain of salt. Lies by omission and inferred lies are not a problem for them, and most have had centuries to hone their skills at misdirection.

I tapped my finger on the passage and sighed. Kai couldn't lie. That didn't mean he was telling me the truth.

People came and went in a steady stream as I did my research, sometimes interrupting me to make a purchase or ask a question, but mostly just browsing. By the time Jake showed up at noon, I'd seen three more fae. None as startling as the first, but they definitely weren't human. One was a perfectly normal old man, except for being only two feet tall. My cheeks warmed, when I realized where his head overlapped his glamour, and where onlookers would think I'd been staring. Another had feathers instead of hair on her head. The last one I hadn't even noticed until he asked a question, and I found myself looking into eyes that were blue through and through. No whites, no pupils, just solid blue. I was starting to get used to it by the time Jake got there, so when he asked how the day was going I managed to keep a straight face when I said it was a pretty standard Saturday.

"You feeling better?" he asked. I stared blankly until he added, "Maggie was none too happy to work a double shift two days in a row. You must've been pretty bad to risk her wrath."

"Yeah, she can be scary," I said with a smile.

"Have you met our new hire yet? She started while you were out."

"Not yet, but Maggie told me about her. Kerry-something? She's a halfer, right?"

"Kayla, and yeah, she's part pixie. How cool is that?"

"Uh oh." I crossed my arms. "Found a new crush have you?"

"Shut up." He was blushing, so I knew I'd hit the mark.

"She goes to CU too, right?"

"Yeah. She's super smart. She's studying microbiology and bioinformatics."

"I don't even know what that means."

"I know, right?" He grinned. "Anyway, she's real nice, and she catches on fast. Maggie says she should be fully trained in another week, then we'll rework the schedules."

"Maybe we'll get to take regular breaks again."

Jake took up position behind the register while I moved off to put away a pile of books customers had changed their minds about, my own reading material tucked safely in the middle. I was facing out covers when there was a light tap on my shoulder.

"How are you doing?" Marc was standing close enough that the starburst patterns in his eyes were clear.

I shrugged. "All right, I guess."

"I don't have a lot of time, but I wanted to give you this." He held out a shiny new cell phone.

I looked it over. My last phone had been the cheapest I could get with my service plan. It could place calls, record contact info, and text, and the screen had displayed who was calling. However, the smartphone I was holding had a browser, GPS navigation, calendar, camera, even games. I got the feeling the device in my hand could replace the computer I had at home.

"This phone is way nicer than the one that got broken. Are you sure you don't need it?"

He waved his hand as though shooing a fly. "Don't worry about it. I put your sim card in already, so you should have all your contacts, and the number is the same."

"Wow, I can't thank you enough."

"Excuse me." The voice came from behind me, and I instinctively turned to see who was speaking. Then, with a yelp, I stumbled back into Marc, who caught me before I could fall.

The fae facing us was the height of a human, but that was where the similarities ended. Its skin was pale green, composed of millions of tiny scales, and its eyes were bright yellow. Out of its torso grew an extra set of arms, and both sets folded with an extra joint, like the claws of a praying mantis.

"Sorry," the word came from a set of serrated mandibles that spread to the sides. "I didn't mean to startle you. Only, I need to get a book off that shelf behind you."

"Oh, sorry," I said breathlessly. Pushing back against Marc, I scooted us both out of the way.

The fae had a set of claws at the second joint of its arm, so it was able to grasp the book without extending the extra segment. I couldn't pull my eyes away, fascinated by the strange anatomy.

"Good day," it said awkwardly, and retreated to purchase its prize from Jake.

"You want to tell me what that was about?" My cheeks grew red as I realized I was still pressed against Marc and quickly jumped away, spinning to face him.

How could I explain without sounding insane?

"Didn't you see the bug?"

"Bug?"

"Yeah, there was a big, freaky-looking bug there when I turned around."

"No, I just saw a guy that probably won't ever shop here again because the staff is crazy."

"Oh." Chagrined, I said, "Well, there was a bug there, too. Anyway, it just sort of caught me off guard."

"Sure, just like your friend accidentally fell while she was hanging that picture last week."

I blushed at the accusation. Then I remembered who that friend was. Pitching my voice low I asked, "How's she doing?"

"About the same."

I nodded and let it go. I couldn't do anything for Sophie right now. He shifted his feet. "I should get going."

"Right, of course. Thanks for the phone."

"No problem. Oh, and I added myself to your contact list, just in case." He walked out the door without a backward glance.

I scrolled through my contacts, looking for the new entry. Yep, there he was, Marcus Howard. I had his home, work, and cell numbers, as well as his address. I wasn't sure what to make of that, so I slid the phone into my pocket and went back to work.

I DROVE HOME on autopilot.

Kai's Toyota was there when I pulled up. I peeked in the window at the empty seats, then glanced at the surrounding trees. Where was he? I had more than a few questions for him after the day I'd had.

I took a slow breath and listened. The whisper of a voice came from behind my house.

Rounding the corner, I found Kai crouched on a rock, talking to my cat. Nothing weird about that, people talked to pets all the time, but Kai was waiting like he thought Cat might actually answer.

"He can't talk," I informed him. "Don't you have cats where you come from?"

"Ah, Alex." He looked up sheepishly. "I didn't hear you."

"Yeah, well, you seemed pretty focused on your conversation." I gestured to Cat, who stretched languidly and sauntered away.

"Just thinking out loud. And yes, I know cats don't speak."

"Right, well, come inside and I'll give you something new to think about." I led him around to the front and opened the door as I spoke. "Today at work I kept seeing faeries. At least, I think they were faeries. You look the same, so maybe not. Anyway, people walked in that were green or black or blue, with claws or wings or whatever, and no one else seemed to notice. Do you know what's going on?"

"Hmm . . ."

I flopped into a chair. "I may be going insane, and all you can say is hmm?"

"I don't think you're insane."

"Well, that's a relief." I lifted my marked arm. "Does it have to do with this tattoo thingy?"

"I imagine so." He settled on the couch across from me. "Again, I don't know exactly what the charm does, but it sounds like it's boosted your powers enough to grant you sight, meaning you can see through basic glamours."

"Then how come you look the same?"

"The simple glamours most fae wear are designed to work on mortals and mostly-mortals. They aren't intended to stop other fae from seeing them. With the charm's boost, you now have enough magic to see through them. Glamours like mine, however, are more complex. They can only be pierced by a fae stronger than the caster." He smirked. "You aren't strong enough to see through my magic."

"I shouldn't be able to see through any." I groaned. "It's really unsettling. Is there a way to turn it off?"

"It's a matter of control. Once you're accustomed to it, you'll be able to choose which image to see, the fae or the glamour."

I ground my teeth. "Does this thing have any other side effects I should know about?"

"Probably," he said with a shrug, "but none that I'm aware of."

"Right, since you don't actually know what it does. That's so reassuring." I sighed. "Did you learn anything today?"

"As a matter of fact, I did. I wasn't able to turn up anything about your visitors, but I did meet someone who's going to make our investigation easier."

"You know, you haven't actually told me what you want me to do yet. Even if I accept that I'm one of these people who can imbue things, that doesn't explain how I'm supposed to find a killer."

Taking a deep breath he said, "My lord sent me to you because he is eager to see this matter resolved. He believes we can learn more from the crime scenes together than I could alone. Imbuers can, by their very nature, perform something similar to readers. A true reader can tell the history of any object by touching it. An imbuer can read objects that have a highly concentrated thought or feeling trapped within, and more importantly, they can channel it."

He sat forward, resting elbows on knees. "You see, everyday objects can become imbued naturally in much the same way you create an imbued object with magic. It happens all the time. For example, if a person had a favorite seashell that they found at the beach and every time they picked it up they thought of that trip and how happy they'd been, the shell would become imbued with that memory. If a normal person picked that shell up, they might feel a brief, inexplicable happiness. If an imbuer, such as yourself, were to pick up that same shell and focus, you could see the memory stored there as though it were your own."

"You want me to go to Aiden's house and pick stuff up hoping to glean some of his memories?" I shuddered. There were no words for how creepy I found the idea of rifling through a dead man's memories.

"Not exactly. It's unlikely normal memories would be useful in our investigation, even if you were to find some. But repeated exposure over a long period of time isn't the only way objects become imbued. One burst of very intense emotion can also leave a residual imprint. For example—"

"The fear of being murdered," I finished for him. "This just gets better and better. You think that if Aiden was touching something when he died I might be able to see his memory of the murder."

"Yes. However, time is a factor. An item imbued by magic is permanent, unless you set limiters on it, while an item imbued naturally over time will fade. An object imbued by a sudden burst of emotion fades very quickly, so we need to visit the crime scenes as soon as possible."

"Scenes, plural? You want me to do this for more than just Aiden?"

"Of course. Aiden was not the only caretaker murdered. We should take every opportunity to discover the killer's identity and find the missing artifacts."

"What's so special about these things anyway? What do they do?"

"They could do almost anything. I don't know exactly, as my lord didn't tell me which artifacts were in danger."

"Your lord doesn't tell you much, does he?"

"Such is his right," he said tersely. "You will understand when you meet him."

"Meet him? Why would I meet him?"

"Now that he has acknowledged you, it's only a matter of time before he calls for an audience."

"Acknowledged me as what? A halfer?"

"Oh. I thought you understood." Kai looked distinctly uncomfortable. "As I said, imbuers are very rare. Such a gift is only known to exist in one bloodline, that of my lord. Having such an ability means you are a direct descendant of the fae Lord of Enchantment. For simplicity's sake, we can call him your grandfather."

"Wait," my head was spinning with the implications. "You're telling me I'm the granddaughter of a faerie king?"

"Many generations removed, but yes."

I rubbed my temples. "What did you mean when you said he acknowledged me?"

"Before I came, you were just a random by-blow. No offense," he added hastily. "Now you are recognized as a member of the ruling family and afforded the rights, privileges, and protection that that entails. In human terms, it would be the difference between a bastard and a prince, or in this case a princess."

"So I'm a goddamn faerie princess now?" I felt like laughing. My carefully maintained perception of reality had taken so many knocks that I wasn't even arguing any more. Just one more piece of impossible information to add to the stack.

"Something like that, but I wouldn't get too giddy if I were you. Anonymity has its advantages, and all fae gifts are double-edged blades. Being acknowledged also puts you in danger from anyone seeking to insult or harm the lord."

"Great, 'cause I don't have enough problems lately."

"One of which is this investigation. You have the ability to read the crime scenes, the right to investigate under fae law, and as a blood relative, my lord trusts you with the artifacts we will hopefully recover."

"Anything else?"

"What do you mean?"

I threw my arms up. "I don't know. Every time I think things can't get any weirder, something new springs up."

Kai's lip quirked. "I believe I'm all out of springs for the moment."

"All right," I sighed. "I'm going to take a shower, then we can discuss what our next move should be. We can't just walk into a crime scene."

I hadn't made a conscious decision to help, but Kai was clearly my best chance to find Aiden's killer. Besides, he seemed to know more about me than I did. Keeping him around until I got a few more answers wouldn't hurt.

"You can stay in the guest room until we sort this out." The way he beamed made me want to smack him, so I reiterated, "just until we find out what happened to Aiden. Then you're on your own."

"Whatever you say." His smile was still in place as he went to unload his car.

I hoped I wasn't making a mistake.

Chapter 12

BY THE TIME I came out of the bedroom, Kai had made himself at home. I peeked past the door to the guest room and saw that two suitcases had vomited their contents around the room. Kai sat on the bed tossing things as he dug into a third. I thought about objecting to the mess, but it wasn't worth the bother. He wouldn't be staying long.

Just long enough to upend everything I thought I knew about myself.

I couldn't get the thought out of my head that I was somehow a fraud as an artist, never mind as a human being. If I was using faerie tricks to make people feel a certain way about my art, what was the point? I'd always felt good when people picked up on what my pieces were meant to convey, but if I believed Kai, it was all a lie.

The reasonable course was to wait until things settled down and reassess my position, but I needed to regain some semblance of control over my life. I left Kai to his "unpacking" and called James.

"Good evening, Alex. I'm glad to see you've replaced your phone."

I drummed my fingers on the counter, focusing on the rhythm to keep from losing my nerve. "I need to talk to you about my work. Can I come by your place?"

"I'm not home at the moment. It would be simpler for me to come to you."

The redirect made me smile. Everything else in my life may have changed, but James's house was still off-limits.

"How soon can you get here?"

"Give me an hour."

I hung up before I could change my mind, or blurt out the whole messy truth on the phone. Sighing, I looked at my sweater-clad arm and drummed my fingers again. At least seeing him in person would put to rest any lingering suspicion about him being a faerie. Unless, of course, he had a special glamour like Kai's.

Kai joined me, digging through the fridge and coming up with the remains of a salad. "Who was that?"

"A friend."

"He's coming here?"

"In about an hour."

He sat at the table, speaking around bites of chard and kale. "As soon as we can, I'd like to visit the most recent crime scenes, see if you can pick anything up from them."

I shivered at the prospect of rifling through objects at murder scenes. "How am I supposed to get into the crime scenes? I doubt the police will let me in. Even, maybe especially, if I tell them I can pick up psychic vibes from dead people."

"With any luck, they'll never know we were there."

"And how do you propose we do that?"

"Magic, of course," he said with a smile.

"Care to elaborate?"

"As I said before, there are various classifications of magics. Different fae are better at different things. I've made the acquaintance of an illusionist who's agreed to help. He spends a lot of time at Crossroads, a local fae bar. We'll pick him up there on our way to the first crime scene."

"So he can sneak us in. Then what?"

"Then you try to find something that carries the memory of the victim's death."

I grimaced. "That is so creepy. If they were holding something when they died, won't the police have collected it as evidence?"

"Don't think so small. Perhaps the victim was pushed against a wall, or held with their face in a cushion. Since we don't know the details of the deaths, we can't count anything out."

"This is crazy. I can't believe I'm even considering this."

"Don't worry, Alex. Everything will be fine. With a little luck, we'll know who killed your friend after one day of work. I can get out of your hair, and you can get back to your boring, human life."

"My life is *not* boring."

We finished our meal in silence. Then Kai went back to his room, and I washed dishes. Not long after, the doorbell rang. I dried my hands and went to answer, but Kai got there first.

I barely registered James in the gap before he pushed through, lifting Kai by the collar. "What are you doing here?"

"Easy, big guy. I'm a guest."

James looked to me for confirmation and when I nodded, released his grip. Kai stepped back, smoothing the wrinkles from his shirt.

"What's going on?" James directed his question at me, but I was too surprised by his outburst to respond.

Kai said, "I'm here on business."

James narrowed his eyes, suspicion rolling off him in waves. "Aren't you a little young to be out on your own?"

I crossed my arms. "I take it you two know each other?"

"We're acquainted," James said tersely.

"Though it's been a while," added Kai.

"Good to know." I relaxed my stance, but my words were tight. "Kai, I need to talk to James. Alone."

"Say no more. I'll be in my room if you need me." James raised an eyebrow at that, but didn't comment as Kai retreated down the hall and shut himself in the guest room.

When James faced me, his expression was dark. "What's going on here, Alex?"

"It's a long story." I gestured to the dining area, the farthest we could get from Kai without leaving the house. I wasn't going to say anything Kai didn't already know, but I didn't like the idea of him eavesdropping.

James and I settled at the table with glasses and a pitcher of water, and faced each other in silence. I tapped my fingers against my cradled glass and pressed my lips together, searching for a place to start. "How do you know Kai?"

James thought for a moment. "I'm not sure what Malakai has told you. He is knighted to the fae Lord of Enchantment. It was in that capacity that I met him."

"So you know he's a faerie."

"One of the fae, yes. If you are interacting with them, you should not use the term faerie."

I frowned. "But everyone calls them that."

He shook his head. "Faerie is a human word that belittles the fae. It was used as a derogatory during the war, and there are those who might take offense at your use of it."

I took a sip of water and returned the glass to the table.

His eyes tracked the motion. "What's that?"

I followed his gaze to where the trailing end of my new tattoo peeked past my sleeve.

"Nothing." I tugged the fabric lower.

He narrowed his eyes.

I pressed my lips tight, then pulled my sleeve up with a sigh.

A shower of water and shattered glass pelted the table around James's clenched fist.

I stared for a moment, shocked by his reaction, then jumped up and grabbed the roll of paper towels off the kitchen counter.

James had barely moved. One clenched hand still rested on the table while he pinched the bridge of his nose with the other. Dropping a couple towels on the table and floor to sop up the water, I grabbed James's wrist to see how badly he'd been injured.

"I'm fine."

"Let me see." I pulled his hand open, but found no cut. The rhythm of his pulse was strong and steady under my touch.

He wiggled his fingers, rotating his hand for inspection.

"Hmph." I pushed his hand away and started collecting shards. I nodded at the tattoo. "I take it you know what this is?"

"A powerful charm. Though I couldn't guess its purpose."

Sharp pain stabbed through the arch of my foot.

"Shit!" I hopped to my chair.

James knelt, water soaking into the fabric of his designer slacks, and plucked the offending shard out of the carpet. He stared for a moment at the red-streaked edge, then tossed it on the table with the rest and lifted my foot.

I cringed. "How bad is it?"

He traced a finger over my sole, light enough to tickle, and I squirmed.

"Not bad." Despite his words, the color had drained from his face. James had never struck me as the type to get queasy at the sight of blood.

He pressed a paper towel over the wound. "Do you have band-ages?"

"In the bathroom."

The pain in my foot faded quickly to a dull ache, and even that was passing by the time he made it back with the first aid kit. He wiped the blood away and carefully placed a beige strip over the cut.

Straightening, he asked, "Do you have any wine?"

"What? Um, yeah." I guess water wasn't cutting it for this conversation. "There's some in the cabinet above the stove."

I cringed when he pulled out a cheap bottle I'd gotten for my last birthday and never got around to drinking. Not exactly the caliber he was used to. Might have been better to pretend I was out.

"Would you like some?"

"Sure. Glasses are next to the sink."

He opened the bottle, took down two glasses, and came back to the table. I carefully poured the burgundy liquid, and James cleared away the pile of broken glass, his movements stiff.

"I'm sorry, Alex. I shouldn't have lost my temper." He sighed heavily. "That seems to be happening a lot lately."

He dumped the handful of shards in the trash with a sound like wind chimes in a storm, drained half his glass, and refilled it before sitting back down.

For the first time, I noticed how worn out James looked. His neat appearance was rumpled around the edges. Little things, like a few strands of dark hair falling loose from his ponytail; his tie was slightly askew; his eyes, normally so bright and clear, seemed clouded.

I frowned, stomach twisting. Here I was, dumping my personal issues on James without even considering that he had his own problems to deal with. Problems like Bryce and his master.

"Is everything all right, James?"

"Well enough."

I crossed my arms and arched an eyebrow.

The corner of his lip perked up, but it didn't grow to a smile. "Perhaps not so well as I might have hoped, but nothing to trouble you over. You have concerns enough of your own."

He gestured to my tattooed arm with his wine glass. "Gifts from the fae come at a high price."

"So I've heard."

"And still you took it?"

"I didn't so much take it as it took me."

"I . . . see."

"Anyway, that's not why I called you tonight."

He poured himself another glass of wine.

I bit my lip, then blurted, "I'm taking my work out of the gallery."

He stared at me over the rim of his glass, the silence stretching until I thought I would snap.

"I know this is sudden, especially since the show just went up, and it violates my contract, but I need to withdraw my work."

"Why?" There was no anger in that word, no incredulity. In fact, his voice carried no emotion at all.

"It's a long story. I just—" My mouth worked while my brain struggled to find a reason that didn't require sharing a secret that could destroy my life.

James watched me mentally wrestle for the better part of a minute, then reached over and covered my hand with his. A warm tingle shot up my arm.

"It's all right, Alex. I know."

Those two simple words were like an ocean crashing over me.

He knew? How could he know? *What* did he know? My true nature, Aiden's murder by the serial killer, the PTF's suspicions, the artifacts, Kai's investigation, the existence of werewolves? This was why I hated keeping secrets. If I assumed I knew what he was referring to, I could easily spill something accidentally.

I swallowed hard and tried to keep my voice light. "You know what?"

"I've known about your family and your gift since the day we met."

The brittle edges of my forced smile collapsed. "What do you mean you knew? *I* didn't even know." Then I remembered that James knew Malakai, who worked for my great-whatever-grandfather, and it clicked into place. "You've met Malakai's boss."

He nodded. "I did a favor of sorts for the Lord of Enchantment, and he rewarded me with an imbued object. When I saw your work, I knew it was the same magic. Not as strong, of course, but the same. You had to be a relation of that lord. The gift of imbuing is not a common one."

"Why didn't you tell me?"

"Would you have listened? Besides, you were either hiding your identity or happy in your ignorance. Who was I to take that from you?"

"Yeah, Mr. Noble. Cashing in on magic art people can't help but like."

"Is that what you think is happening?" He rubbed a hand over his mouth and the shadow of stubble on his chin. "Your magic doesn't make your art irresistible, it only imbues a piece with the concept you're projecting when you make it. Can you honestly tell me, when you're working, the thought foremost in your mind is, 'Gee, I hope they buy it'?"

"No, I think about what the piece is supposed to represent—nature, or beauty, or rage, or whatever."

"Exactly. So when someone looks at your art they will see nature, or beauty, or rage. That doesn't mean they'll like your art any more or less. It means their reaction, whatever it may be, is stronger."

James knew more about art than anyone I'd ever known. Despite what I'd said, I couldn't see him putting pieces in his gallery that didn't have artistic merit just to make a quick buck. Especially since he wasn't exactly hurting for cash. My shoulders sagged as my anger receded, leaving me wrung out and exhausted.

"Sorry," I whispered, unable to meet his gaze. "I don't know what to think anymore. I feel like I've been turned inside out."

With a finger under my chin, he tipped my head until my eyes met and held his. "You, Alex Blackwood, are the same person you have always believed yourself to be. No one can take that away from you. Your relations don't matter. Your abilities don't matter. What matters is what you feel, and think, and how you live your life. Those are the things that define you as a person."

Warmth flooded my cheeks, and I pulled away from the electric spark of his touch. "Thanks."

He offered a smile that didn't reach his eyes. "Now, would you care to explain why a Knight of the Realm appears to be living with you?"

I cringed. "Not really."

We regarded each other, silently assessing.

James looked away first. "Be careful, Alex. Don't trust Malakai. The fae are wily, and ruthless, and they operate on a different system of values than you're used to. Whatever he's asking of you, I'd advise against it. He almost certainly has an ulterior motive."

"You don't seem to like him much."

"Like has nothing to do with it. The nature of the fae is fact, not a matter of opinion. Deception is in their nature." James opened his mouth again, closed it, and sighed. Then he pushed back his chair and stood. "I should go. It's late, and we both have busy days ahead."

I walked him to the door. "Thanks for coming, James. It means a lot to me."

"If there's anything you need, Alex, just ask." He brushed my cheek with the back of his hand, and a thread of heat flickered in my abdomen. "You are not so alone as you're always trying to convince yourself."

I blinked. That line had come often enough from Maggie and David, but James?

"When did you get to know me so well?"

"If you didn't spend so much time shielding yourself from others, you'd already know the answer to that."

He smiled and stepped out, and I pushed the door closed behind him.

I leaned my forehead against the cool wood. My cheek still tingled, and I pressed my fingertips over the sensation. Had closing that door been a mistake?

"You shouldn't trust him."

I turned to find Kai half in and half out of the hall. "Excuse me?"

"That man, he's lying to you."

"Funny, he said the same about you."

Kai gave a little shrug as if to say, "Don't say I didn't warn you," then smiled a crooked smile and disappeared into his room.

Chapter 13

FINGERS OF SUNLIGHT pierced the flat, white ceiling of the sky, burning off tendrils of fog that clung to the landscape. The night's chill was already receding, promising a return to warmer temperatures. I sat at the table with a warm bowl of oatmeal and watched a stiff breeze tear leaves from branches, scattering them across the ground and collecting them in ruts cut by yesterday's rain.

Kai poured a bowl of Captain Crunch and sat at the far side of the table. I glanced at the vacant chair James had used the night before. Part of me wanted to interrogate Kai about my enigmatic friend, but that somehow felt like a betrayal. James's secrets were his own.

Gritting my teeth, I stamped down the urge to pry and ate in silence.

When Kai finished, he wiped a sleeve across his mouth and retreated to his room. I glared at the dirty bowl and spoon still on the table. We'd need to have a chat about roommate etiquette if he stayed more than another day. For the time being, I bit my tongue and cleared both sets of dishes. Hopefully he would be out of my hair before it became an issue.

A few minutes later Kai returned, triumphantly waving two folded maps and a file folder. He opened the folder and skimmed through pages while I watched in mounting curiosity.

Finally, I couldn't take it anymore. "What are those?"

"Surely you didn't think I'd been idle since my arrival? This is the information I've been able to gain about the victims so far."

A paper filing system seemed entirely too mundane for a fae investigator, but I let it slide. "What does it say?"

He set the papers aside. "It's no wonder the police couldn't find a connection without knowing their true natures. These people had nothing in common. The good news is, we shouldn't have much to worry about when we do our investigating. Of the victims we're looking at, only one had a spouse, so we shouldn't be interrupted. The third to last victim, Antonio Dantes, left a widow. She's eighty-two years old, moved here from Italy, no other relatives. We'll knock first and hope she's not home."

"And if she is?"

He shrugged. "Then we lie and get her to tell us what she knows about her husband's death."

"I thought the fae couldn't lie."

"We can't, but halfers can. You can lie for the both of us."

He spread the first map out on the table. It showed the Denver-Metro area, marked with numerous red circles. The second map was of Boulder, and had similar marks. There were seventeen circles on the two maps.

My oatmeal sat like lead in my stomach. "Please tell me those circles aren't where people have died."

"As you like."

"Are they?"

"Are they what?"

"Don't be an ass," I snapped. "Are they murder sites?"

His lips quirked up at the corners. "Not all of them."

"Thank god," I breathed. "So what are they?"

"Some are murder sites matching the killer's MO. Others are known caretakers in the area. There's quite a bit of overlap."

"Known caretakers? Are there unknown ones?"

"Of course. I only know what my lord saw fit to reveal, and he only knows about caretakers from his own bloodline, at least officially. It's likely the murders that don't correspond to known caretakers were from other lines, but we can't be certain."

"How many caretakers are there?"

"As many as are needed to protect the artifacts not currently in use."

"How many is that?"

He shrugged. "No one knows."

Once he had the two maps laid out in more or less accurate alignment, he took a pen and wrote the number one inside one of the circles.

"This is where the most recent death occurred," he said. I recognized

Aiden's address. He wrote a two inside another circle, then three and four. "Number two is the second most recent, and so on. We'll go to these four sites and hope you pick up something useful. Anything older and the residual energy will likely have dissipated."

Leaning over the maps, I considered the locations. "They're pretty spread out. Do you want to visit them chronologically, or geographically?"

"A few hours either way shouldn't matter much at this point."

"Number four is in Boulder," I pointed to it on the map. "Let's hit that first. Then this one in Denver." I continued to trace roads until my finger came to the third circle. I swallowed hard.

Aiden.

OUR FIRST STOP was a bar on the outskirts of Boulder, where Kai had found the illusionist who'd agreed to help. The entrance was a rotting wood door in a dirty alley. I wrinkled my nose at the smell and asked, "How are they still in business? I can't imagine they get a lot of foot traffic."

"This isn't the kind of establishment that wants people walking in off the street. In fact, there are a number of spells in place to ensure that doesn't happen. If you come to this bar, it's deliberate."

That brought up a whole new list of concerns about what kind of establishment I was walking into, but rather than put my ignorance on display again, I kept my mouth shut, figuring I could work the answers out as I went.

Kai knocked. A second later we were confronted by a mountain with a face, and all other thoughts flew out of my head.

I stepped back, partly out of surprise and partly because I needed more distance to see up to his face. I'd met big guys before, but this one looked like if you hit him with a crowbar it would be the metal that bent. His features were chiseled. Not the chiseled-jaw look movie stars have, but like his whole face was carved from stone.

"Whatchu want?" His voice rumbled out a deep bass, vibrating my bones. I pictured this guy chanting 'fee fie foe fum' and barely managed to squelch the insane giggle that tried to bubble out.

Kai calmly said, "We're meeting someone." I guess he was used to talking to mountains.

The bouncer—what else could he be?—stepped into the dark space behind the door. I followed Kai across the threshold. Once we were through, the door slammed shut, casting us into darkness and cutting off our exit. My excitement at seeing a fae hangout evaporated. Maybe I should have stayed in the car.

I stood for a long, breathless moment, waiting for my eyes to adjust, or for something to jump out of the darkness. After blinking a few times, I was able to make out the hallway around me. Kai was outlined by a dim glow coming around a corner. I didn't see the giant anywhere. How could something so big disappear so quickly, and without making any noise? The thought sent shivers down my spine. This was not the world I knew.

I would be surrounded by the very people I'd spent most of my life trying to avoid or ignore. Not just halfers, but full-blooded faeries. What would my father think if he could see me now? Walking into a fae bar, letting a faerie live with me, helping avenge the death of a bunch of halfers? Then again, I was a halfer now, too. That would take some getting used to.

"Ready?" Kai's voice echoed eerily in the darkness, and I wondered if he was doing it on purpose.

That thought more than anything made me stand up straighter and put as much steel in my voice as I could. "Whenever you are."

With a chuckle, he led us through a labyrinth of hallways that stretched farther than the exterior of the building should have allowed. The light grew stronger with each turn. When we rounded the last corner, I found myself at the edge of a large open area leading to an even larger room.

There were booths and tables spread around the perimeter, a raised stage set against the far wall, and right in the center was a full-service bar. I'd expected the bar to be deserted at such an early hour, but a third of the stools were occupied. Apparently, the fae liked to start their drinking early, or maybe these were holdovers from the night before.

I forced a smile and gestured to our surroundings. "This is cool."

"Really?" Kai asked. "It feels a bit warm to me."

"I meant—"

"What's your pleasure?" A girl seemed to materialize beside us, all bright smiles and helpful solicitude. I'd worked at the bookstore long enough to know a customer service façade when I saw one. She had "hostess" written all over her.

"We're here to see Simon," Kai announced.

"Sure," she chirped, "follow me."

The girl's orangey-red ponytail swung rhythmically as she bobbed across the open space, Kai and I trailing after. From Kai's description of the bar, it sounded like only fae, and possibly halfers, were welcome. I couldn't imagine they'd employ a human, so either the girl was a human-looking halfer, like me, or wore a special glamour, like Kai.

A glance around the room confirmed that my tattoo was still letting me see through regular glamours, though few of the fae present were surrounded by the tell-tale shimmer. Guess being a fae bar meant glamours were optional. Many of the patrons appeared at least human-ish, but a few looked like they'd walked right out of a fantasy novel, or a nightmare.

Goosebumps sprang up all over my flesh.

The hostess led us to a booth along the wall where a man sat alone. He was short, maybe four-and-a-half feet tall, and he had huge, drooping ears that tapered to points. His skin was dark and waxy, sagging in wrinkles and folds to resemble the melted tallow of a candle. Tufts of white hair stood out from his head and ears, and he had the most impressive eyebrows I'd ever seen, like two snowy caterpillars resting on his forehead.

Our guide turned her too-bright smile back on us, and asked, "Will you be needing drinks?"

Kai shook his head. "We won't be here long."

She bobbed and darted off.

"Hello, Simon." Kai took a seat across from the man in the booth, and I followed suit.

"Malakai." When he spoke, his lips curled back, showing teeth so sharp they could have been filed.

"Ready to go?"

"Let me finish my drink," he grumbled, taking a slow swig. "Who's your friend?"

Kai had insisted I wear long sleeves and warned me not to show the tattoo to anyone unless he told me to. Apparently some fae would suspect my connection to the Lord of Enchantment if they saw it. Simon asking my relationship to the job was a good sign my anonymity was intact. I was still hoping to go back to some semblance of my normal life when this was over.

"She's tagging along," Kai replied. "That's all you need to know."

Simon shrugged and took another swig. "My payment?"

"All set. You can collect it when the job is done."

With a nod, Simon downed the last of his drink and belched. "Let's go."

The three of us marched out of the bar, Simon in the lead, then Kai, and I brought up the rear. As we approached the exit, the door opened. I could just make out the mountainous fae beside it. Where had he come from? The hallway looked barely big enough to hold, let alone hide him. I kept my gaze on him as I slid past.

Simon followed us to my Jeep, frowned, and climbed into the passenger seat. I guess he was riding shotgun. Pulling out of the lot, I headed north on Broadway, on the way to our first crime scene.

MELISSA ROW HAD lived in a small, two bed, one bath house. The yard was overgrown with knee-high weeds caged by a three-foot chain-link fence covered with clinging bindweed. Rather than stopping right in front, I parked three doors down on the far side of the street.

I was still in the dark about how Simon was going to hide us from onlookers, so I asked, "Are you going to make us invisible?"

Rather than answer, Simon swiveled in his seat to face Kai. "Is she serious?"

"Hey," I snapped. "I'm sitting right here."

"She's new." Kai gave an apologetic smile. "She's still learning."

"Whatever," Simon huffed. "Don't take too long. I've got a massive headache, and this job's not gonna help."

"Come on, Alex." Kai was out the door before I could do more than glare.

A gust of wind whipped my hair into my face when I stepped out, so I snagged a scrunchy and pulled the wild strands back into a messy bun.

Kai was two car lengths ahead when I circled around to the sidewalk. Refusing to trot after him like a trained puppy, I took half a dozen measured steps before I realized Simon was still in the Jeep. "Isn't he coming?"

"He'll work better if he can concentrate," Kai called over his shoulder.

I planted my feet on the pavement. "How exactly is he going to hide us?"

Hands on hips, Kai looked to the white-washed sky and sighed. Then he turned and walked back to me. "The easiest way to think about it is that he's making us inconspicuous. A strong illusionist can make someone invisible, as you suggested, but it requires an obscene amount of energy. A simple redirection or aversion spell would be enough to fool humans, but there may be fae watching, so Simon is disguising us. Anyone looking will see us as people who belong here, police or something. The details are filled in by the viewer's mind so it's more convincing."

When he set his feet to the pavement once more, I did trot to catch up. "Thank—"

He spun, one hand raised, and I jerked back, thinking he might slap me. But he stopped with his open palm hovering between us. "Don't."

"What did I do?"

"Humans toss thanks around like confetti, but gratitude means something different among the fae. Save it for a more meaningful debt."

"So I can't say thanks?"

"Not without admitting an obligation to repay it, and while I have no intention of taking advantage of you, there are plenty of fae who would."

"Right." I pressed a fist against the knot in my stomach. "Good to know."

He ran a hand through his hair, making it stand up crazily. "While I'm giving advice, here's some more—Don't ever ask a fae to explain their abilities. It's not safe. We don't like to discuss details about our magic. Especially not with outsiders."

"Doesn't having fae blood make me part of the gang?"

"Halfers, especially those raised by humans, are still considered outsiders for the most part. Besides, even a full-blooded fae wouldn't get a straight answer to a question like that. Of course, a fae would know better than to ask."

I rolled my eyes. "Maybe I should just not talk to any fae."

He smiled. "I think that ship has departed."

"Sailed," I corrected. "Let's just get this done."

Kai walked up the concrete path to the front door. Not surprisingly, it was locked and crisscrossed with police tape. Without hesitation, Kai touched his index finger to the lock and twisted the handle. The door swung open.

"Nice trick," I whispered.

Kai parted the police tape for me, and I ducked inside.

The inside of Melissa's house was as poorly maintained as her yard. Dim light filtered in around the edges of dingy curtains drawn across the windows to thwart curious onlookers. My shin smashed against a coffee table, and nearly toppled the stack of old magazines piled there. A plume of dust billowed into my face, and I sneezed three times.

"Careful," Kai hissed. "We don't want to disturb anything that might be noticed."

Turning to inspect the room, I said, "It'd take a lot to notice something out of place in here."

Almost all the available floor space was stacked with piles of junk. There were boxes of buttons, racks of scarves, binders whose labels claimed everything from DVDs to old trading cards, even a huge bin filled with stuffed penguins. Melissa had been a collector, and she hadn't been particular about what she collected.

Kai shrugged. "She was part-goblin after all."

"Really? A goblin?"

"Part-goblin. They tend to hoard anything they can get their hands on, and they're not big on cleaning."

"How are we supposed to find anything useful in this mess?"

"Start touching things. Things the victim might have touched as she died. We don't need to dig deep. It would be something near the surface, in easy reach."

"Won't I get my fingerprints on everything?"

"Don't worry, this happened weeks ago. The police would have examined the crime scene and pulled prints and DNA already. No one wants to leave a bloody mess around for months while they track down a killer. The police and forensic people come in right away, get all the evidence they can, then send in a cleanup crew to take care of the rest."

"If you live on the reservation, how do you know about police procedures?"

"The reservation is a recent development, and I'm not as young as I look."

"Right. So how do I do this?" I gestured to the clutter around us.

"You need to open yourself up to any residual feelings or memories. Clear your mind. Let your emotions take control."

I snorted. "Figures."

Reaching my hands to either side, I pushed farther into the mess, brushing things as I passed. The corridors winding through the clutter were narrow. In some cases, the passage grew so tight I had to turn sideways to get through without disrupting anything.

I chewed my lip as I worked, fighting to keep from slamming the door on my emotions as grief, anger, and disappointment snaked out of their cage and wormed into my thoughts. Gritting my teeth, I dropped my hands to my sides. "Isn't there another way to do this? Emotions aren't exactly my strong suit."

He shook his head. "You have to connect, empathize. That means opening yourself up."

"This is hopeless."

"You're thinking too hard. Just relax. Stop trying to control yourself."

I sighed, but put my hands back on the knickknacks around me.

We worked our way through the living room and kitchen, then up the hallway, through the bathroom and office, and into the bedroom.

I walked around, setting my hand on her dresser, nightstand, the old phone beside her bed. "This is the last room. I don't think we're going to find anything."

Which didn't mean there was nothing to find. A wave of disgust rolled through me. There might be a clue to Aiden's killer right under my nose, maybe even the identity of the killer, but I was too emotionally constipated to find it. I'd failed him again.

Tears pricked at the corners of my eyes, blurring the room.

My fingers trailed over the patchwork comforter on Melissa's bed. What would happen to all the stuff in her house? Did she have children? Parents? A boyfriend?

The world seemed to tip.

I sat down heavily on the edge of the bed. The light changed, like night had come in an instant. A surge of surprise rushed through me, disproportionate to the situation. Anger and fear danced around the edges of my shock. None of these emotions were my own, but they filled me like a balloon until I felt I would burst. The feelings were directed toward a hazy presence beside me, and I turned my head to find their target.

I wasn't alone on the bed.

Without thinking, I threw myself away from the shadowy form, tumbling off the bed and smacking my head against the wall.

"Alex!" Kai crouched beside me. "What happened?"

"I don't know. I was overwhelmed by . . . something. I was shocked. Betrayed maybe?" I rubbed small circles at my temples. "It was really weird."

"It seems she died in the bed. It must have been a strong emotion to linger so long." He helped me to my feet. "Can you try again? Remember, nothing in the memory can hurt you."

I wasn't eager to feel someone's dying moments, but I set my hand back on the bed.

"The feelings are weaker now. Surprise, anger, betrayal . . ." I shook my head. "I can't see the other person."

Kai frowned. "Describe what you experienced. Be as specific as you can."

I wracked my brain for details. "It was dark, night."

"Good, what else?"

"I was shocked. Angry and scared, too, but mostly I just couldn't believe what had happened." I frowned. I didn't even *know* what had happened. "Everything I felt was directed at the person next to me."

"Since only one victim was reported, we can assume that other person was the killer. Could you tell if it was a man or woman?"

"No, but I got the sense Melissa was in love with them."

Kai nodded. "If it was her lover who killed her, that would certainly be a powerful shock."

"So the killer was dating Melissa."

"Sleeping with her anyway," Kai amended. "Okay. Let's go before Simon gets impatient."

"I'm pretty sure he started that way."

"Touché." Kai pulled a slightly smushed candy bar from his pocket. "Don't mention what happened in here to Simon. I don't want him to know what you're capable of. It would be too easy for him to guess who you are."

"You don't trust him?"

"This is a job for him, and he's being well compensated. However, there's nothing to stop him from running to any interested party once we're done and selling what he's learned." He popped a piece of chocolate into his mouth, hesitated, then offered through chocolate-covered teeth, "Want one?"

I shook my head. "How do you stay so skinny eating junk like that all the time?"

He shrugged. "High metabolism. Besides, it's not all the time. We don't have stuff like this where I come from."

Magic and metabolism aside, if he kept on the way he was, he'd be in for a shock the next time he stepped on a scale.

We found Simon right where we'd left him, his head lolled forward and his eyes closed. It looked like he was sleeping, but when I opened my door, his head snapped up and he grumbled, "'Bout damn time."

Kai and I settled in without comment, and I motored off to the second stop on our morbid tour.

Chapter 14

ANGELA ESPINOSA had lived in a fancy new apartment building just off Alameda and I-25, the kind of place I could never afford. According to Kai, she'd been a successful young professional at an architecture firm in downtown Denver. The gated apartment complex had almost no street parking, which left me circling the block in search of a space. The wind picked up, chasing the clouds across the sky, and the sun turned my Jeep into a sauna. I would have liked to roll my sleeves up, but that was a big no-no with Simon in the seat next to me.

On my third time around the block, Simon pointed to an open space and said, "Park there."

"I can't park there, it's handicapped."

"Just park," he snapped.

"Fine." I pulled into the empty space. "But if I get a ticket, you're paying for it."

"Relax," he said, pointing to the handicapped sign I'd parked in front of. As I watched, the sign changed. It now read, "Permit required 6pm-6am."

"Okay, that's cool," I admitted grudgingly.

Kai rubbed his hands together. "I guess I'm up. Let's go, Alex."

As we approached the gate I asked, "Can you magic an electronic gate like you did the lock on Melissa's door?"

"No, electronics play havoc with magic."

"Then how do we get in without anyone knowing?"

"We'll ask to view an apartment as prospective tenants. Then I'll make whoever lets us in forget us."

My stomach cramped. "You can do that?"

"Magic may not work well on electronics, but people are easy." He grinned, and I shuddered at the show of teeth.

Kai rang the buzzer for the main office and the voice of a young-sounding woman crackled out of the box, "Hello? Can I help you?"

"Hello," said Kai. "We're looking for an apartment in the area. This place came highly recommended. Could we have a tour?"

"Yes, of course," came the voice. "I'll buzz you in. Just come to the administration office." The box emitted a beep, and the automatic gate rolled back.

We walked to the building marked office, where we were met by, I assumed, the owner of the voice from the box. She was a petite woman in a pinstripe pencil skirt and a white button-up blouse. Her dark hair was piled on top of her head in a tasteful bun. Her shoes were tall, expensive, and totally impractical for a walking tour.

"Hello, my name's Tina. Tell me, how did you hear about us?"

Kai reached out and shook the woman's hand. "It's a lovely place. Unfortunately, I think it's out of our price range."

"I understand," she said, without missing a beat. "If you change your mind, you know where to find us."

"Of course," said Kai smoothly. Then he flashed a bright smile, and gestured that it was time to go.

Once the office door swung shut behind us, I rounded on Kai. "I thought you said you'd make her forget us."

He started walking again, leading us toward Angela's apartment. "As far as she's concerned she took a nice, nondescript couple for a tour of one of their apartments. Unfortunately, we weren't interested."

"You made her remember things that didn't happen?" A heavy weight settled in my chest. If he could do that . . .

"It's easier to let the mind fabricate a plausible story to fool itself than it is to forcibly alter a person's reality."

"Like what Simon is doing to hide us."

He nodded. "If there's one thing that's always been true, it's that humans are masters of self-deception. How do you think the fae managed to stay hidden so long?" His voice dropped to a distracted mutter as he magicked the lock to let us into Angela's building. "People believe what they want to believe."

I frowned. "Then why not stay hidden?"

"Hmm?"

I cleared my throat. "If that's true, why didn't the fae just stay hidden?"

Kai pursed his lips. "Humans breed like it's a race to fill the world with bodies. Every time the population increased, they spread. They spread and spread until the whole world was full of them and there were no wild places left for us. Every gate to another realm requires certain criteria be met; a combination of trees, or a certain amount of salt in a body of water, or specific types of flowers. One by one, the places where those criteria were met were being overrun by highways, skyscrapers, shopping malls, condos. We had to change something, or all the portals we use to access this world would have been swallowed by human expansion."

We were in the elevator of Angela's building, heading to the fourth floor. I rode in silence, thinking about Kai's words. For once, the history books seemed to have gotten it right. Human expansion had forced the fae out of hiding like a rock thrown into a bush might flush out a flock of birds. But . . .

"Why don't you just stay in your own world? This isn't your home. If this place, overrun by humans as it is, is so terrible, why come here at all? Or fight a war where so many people died just to stay?"

Kai looked uncomfortable.

The elevator dinged, and the doors slid open to the fourth floor. We both stepped out and Kai turned to the right. Angela's apartment number was 408. Despite it being a more recent scene, no police tape adorned the door as it had at Melissa's house. But then, this was a high-end place. Maybe the reminder had upset the other tenants.

Kai stopped in front of her door, but instead of opening it, he stood with his head bowed. "Fae realms do not often link directly to one another. Without a crossroads, we would be cut off. And while the different races might not always get along, there are not so many of us that we can afford to become isolated."

Before I could frame a response, he swung the door open and marched inside. With his back to me, he said, "Let's not speak of this anymore."

Pressing my mouth closed, I stepped up beside him.

After the squalor of Melissa's house, Angela's home seemed almost empty. There were a few pieces of modern furniture placed tastefully throughout the apartment. The walls were painted in neutral colors with little adornment. The place barely looked lived in. Then again, the building itself was new. She couldn't have lived there long.

I turned toward Kai, but he stepped away, his frame rigid.

Had my questions really upset him so much?

I bit my lip. He'd said he was older than he looked. Was he old enough to have fought in the war? Had he killed people?

A wave of nausea rolled through me. People like my father . . .

I reached back to push the door closed, and my world disappeared.

MY FINGERS SLIPPED from the doorknob, slick with blood, and I crashed back to the floor. I didn't have the strength to try again, but if I didn't escape I was going to die.

I gazed back along the crimson trail that blazed through the otherwise white carpet. It led from my useless legs back to the kitchen. Where had the stranger gone?

A tremendous weight dropped on my back. I couldn't breathe, my ribs were on fire. Bones cracked under my assailant's knee while fingers twisted into my hair and jerked my head up. The scent of cigarettes filled the air. My vision was swimming so badly I had to close my eyes to keep from retching. Something slid around my throat.

"Last chance." The words were whispered in the gravelly voice of a pack-a-day smoker. "Tell me where it is, and I'll end this quickly."

How had he even known? How could he? But that didn't matter now. None of it mattered. I was going to die. There was only one thing left to consider—fast or slow.

"Box," I grated out. "Under the mattress."

The pressure around my neck tightened and my skin gave way to the sharp edge there. My cheek hit the floor, splashing in the puddle spreading beneath me. My face and chest were warm, but the rest of me was growing colder by the second. With my right hand, I reached out and pressed my palm to the door.

So close, so close.

My fingers left bloody trails as they slid down the painted wood.

"Alex!" The slap was hard enough to rattle my teeth. "Snap out of it!" Another slap swung my head in the opposite direction.

The sensation of having my head flop to the side made me start screaming. I flailed my arms, breaking Kai's hold, and fell back to the carpet. Clutching my throat, I twisted side to side, looking for the man who'd just killed me.

"Alex, calm down!" Kai was kneeling in front of me, trying to get hold of my shoulders. "You're fine! It wasn't you!"

It was the panic in Kai's voice that finally broke through my own.

My neck was intact, I could move, and the carpet was a pristine white. Whatever I'd just experienced, it hadn't happened to me.

I settled down enough for Kai to corral me to a love seat, where I took gasping breaths from between my knees. Kai disappeared, and a moment later a glass of water came into my field of vision.

"Here, drink this."

I reached out a shaking hand and slurped the water, spilling rivulets down my chin in the process. The feeling of liquid sliding along my skin caused me to drop the glass in my haste to wipe it away. At least the water had been cold, not the sticky warmth of blood.

"I'm okay," I said out loud, as much for my benefit as Kai's.

"What happened? What did you see?"

"It was a guy. He smokes, and he weighs a freakin' ton." I flexed my back to ease the pressure I imagined there. "She didn't know him, not like Melissa."

"Were you able to see him?"

"No, he was behind her. They'd been talking in the kitchen, but she dragged herself to the door after the first attack. She was already injured when the memory began. Then he came up behind her and knelt on my, I mean her, back." I shook my head. It was hard to remember that the things I'd felt hadn't actually happened. At least, not to me.

"That's it?"

"They spoke. He asked where it was, and she told him. A box under the mattress. Then he slit her throat, but not with a knife. It felt more like a circle around her neck with blades that faced in." I covered my mouth at the visceral memory and tried not to gag.

"Okay, wait here." Kai strode toward the back of the apartment. I was perfectly content to stay put, as I was feeling none too stable.

"It's gone."

Of course it was.

He sank into the seat beside me with a sigh. "A hole's been cut into the box-spring. Looks like that's where she hid the artifact she was guarding."

A stray thought that had been nagging at me clicked into place. "I think I've heard his voice before. I can't recall where, but it sounded familiar."

"Was it you who recognized it, or Angela?"

I bit my lip. "I'm not sure."

He sat in contemplative silence for a while. "Both sites smelled of magic. Did it sound like either of the fae who visited you?"

I tried to remember what the fae had sounded like, but it hadn't been important at the time. The memory of the killer's voice was fading as well, leaving only a vague impression of recognition.

"I'm not sure. Maybe." I shook my head. "What does magic smell like?"

"Lots of different things. It depends on the caster, and the spell. Unfortunately, I don't recognize any of the magic I've picked up so far. What I can say is that the same magic was used in both places." He leaned back into the cushions. "At Melissa's, I had no way of knowing if it was the killer or the victim that had used magic. But the magic here is the same, so our killer definitely has access to magic."

"That's good, right? Didn't you say it would be easier if the killer was fae? That would keep the humans out of it."

"Sensing magic would seem to favor the killer being fae, but there's also a possibility that whoever is killing these people is using the artifacts they've collected from previous victims. They could still be either fae or human, or anything between. So we haven't really learned anything."

"I wouldn't say that. We know Angela's killer was male. He was sleeping with Melissa Row, smokes, and may have spoken to me before. We also know he has access to magic." I lifted a finger for each point.

Kai stood and held his hand out to me. "Let's get moving before our luck runs out. We'll stop for something to eat before the next place."

I froze with my hand halfway to his, then let my arm drop. "I can't do it. I can't watch Aiden die through his own eyes. I didn't realize I'd feel what happened this deeply." I shook my head, hugging myself. "I don't want to feel Aiden's last moments."

Kai sat back down. We stayed that way for a while, side by side in silence. Then he said, "Aiden's death is the most recent. If he saw his attacker, this will be our best opportunity to identify him. I can't make you do this, but I am asking you. Please, Alex, if you want to know who killed your friend, this is the best way."

I had tears running down my cheeks by the time he finished. I loved Aiden, he'd been one of my best friends. Could I watch him die to find his killer? Was I strong enough?

"I can't promise anything, but I'll try." That last came out in a hoarse whisper, my voice cracking on the final word. I might be able to help catch a murderer, but at what cost? At the very least, I was going to have nightmares about this for the rest of my life.

WE ATE OUR hamburgers in silence. Simon dropped a snide comment about our taking so long, but I barely registered it through my somber mood. Kai was subdued too, all serious knight on a mission. I got the feeling he would do whatever it took to succeed. I didn't want to face Aiden's death, but I wasn't sure what Kai would do if I refused.

I didn't taste the fries as I pushed them into my mouth one by one, methodically chewing and swallowing. As uncomfortable as lunch was, dread made me drag it out as long as possible. But it couldn't last forever. When the burgers and fries were eaten, the drinks gone, we trudged to the Jeep, silently climbed aboard, and I drove us out of the lot and across town.

Aiden's house was just as I remembered, tidy beige bricks trimmed in white.

Standing on the path to the front door, my courage flagged. A trickle of sweat pricked on my scalp as I froze under the blazing sun. It seemed wrong that the day should be so bright and warm while ice was eating my insides. A gust of wind ripped the last few holdouts off a skeletal maple, tumbling them across the path and the neatly trimmed squares of lawn to either side.

"Come on, Alex. Let's get this over with." Kai pushed gently at the small of my back to get me moving.

This time Kai didn't have to use magic to get us in. I had the spare key Aiden gave me in case of emergencies. Once I had the door open, I froze. What if he'd died just inside, like Angela? I took a deep breath, and ducking the police tape, stepped in.

My first thought was that I hadn't visited Aiden's house in months, but my regret was quickly overwhelmed by the more pressing realization that whoever was in charge of cleaning up the crime scene hadn't come yet. Blood splatter decorated the wall to the right, and the carpet bore a rusty brown stain. Tiny plastic labels with numbers had been placed around the room, marking where evidence had been collected.

Bile rose in my throat and I covered my mouth with both hands, willing my lunch to stay down.

"Easy, Alex." Kai's palm was warm against my back. "Keep it together."

Once I was sure I wasn't going to throw up, I nodded and moved away from him. Standing in front of the place where my friend died, I thought I would lose my courage entirely, but it was quite the opposite. I wanted to be there with Aiden, to know anything that would help me find his killer.

Taking a deep breath, I set my palm flat against the largest blood stain.

Opening myself up wasn't a problem this time. With my hand

pressed to the tacky surface, there was no way I could hold back the torrent of emotions that tore through me. Love, loss, hope, rage, guilt, despair. They burst their chains and ate away my insides until I was an exposed nerve.

Darkness settled over the room. Pain danced at the edge of my awareness, but it was dim and a long way off. Aiden had been calm, resigned. He'd expected this.

Aiden spent his last moments on Earth thinking about the times he'd shared with David and me, missing us even as he died. Then David's face faded, and my own filled every corner of my perception. A tingling warmth spread through my limbs.

Then the tingles turned to pain, the heat to ice. Fear. Loss. Pride. I'd stayed strong. I'd carried the burden alone.

Cold shards dug into my heart, and tears welled in my eyes.

I'd made a mistake.

As the ghost of my own reflection faded away, I could feel my soul tearing free.

My palm stuck slightly as I staggered away from the wall, silent tears sliding down my cheeks.

Aiden had changed his mind, at the end, but it was too late. Whoever stole his chance for a future deserved to die. I balled my hands into fists. For the first time in my life, I wanted to make someone suffer.

"Alex?" Kai's voice was quiet, gentle, like he was addressing a stray dog whose temperament he was unsure of. "Are you all right?"

I nodded once, not trusting myself to speak.

"Did you get a look at the killer?"

I hated to dash the hope in Kai's voice, but there was nothing for it. "No," I croaked. "It wasn't a memory like the last one, just feelings. More like the first house. He was in pain, but he wasn't focused on what was happening to him when he died."

"Oh?" Kai's surprise was understandable. How many people could avoid thinking about their own murder as it was happening? "Only strong emotions leave imbued memories. If it wasn't shock from his murder you saw, what was it?"

"Regret." I said it as matter-of-factly as I could, but my voice cracked on the word.

Kai's lips pressed into a sharp frown, but he didn't press further.

I tried to blink away the pressure behind my eyes and clear the lump in my throat, but failed at both.

I'd never thought of Aiden as anything more than a friend. I'd assumed he felt the same. But seeing myself through the filter of Aiden's memory . . .

"Did you get *anything* useful from the reading?" The plea in Kai's voice was unmistakable. He was getting desperate for a concrete lead. Aiden's murder had been the most recent, and therefore our best shot at getting worthwhile information.

"He was sad he wouldn't see me or David again, and worried I'd end up in trouble because of him. Maybe he thought the killer would come after me next. Those fae did show up at my studio the next day."

Kai scratched his jaw. "If the killer didn't find what he was looking for with Aiden, but discovered he'd called you right before the murder, they might assume Aiden had given you the artifact or information as to its whereabouts."

"He was killed Friday. I told the police about Aiden's call the next day. I told David, too, but no one else. If someone knew about that call, they must have gotten it out of Aiden when they killed him or had access to his phone records." I ran my fingers down the wall beside the stains, not quite touching them. "Those fae came looking for the box right after Aiden died. Somehow, they knew I was connected to Aiden's missing artifact. As fae, they would have been able to tell Aiden and the others were halfers. Maybe they even have a list of caretakers like you. And they'd have plenty of magic." I glanced over my shoulder. "Was the same magic used here as at the other crime scenes?"

He nodded. "I don't know if your fae visitors are the murderers, but they obviously have some connection to the artifacts. We need to find them."

Aiden's dried blood coated my hand in fine brownish powder. I walked to the kitchen sink and scrubbed until my skin was raw, then used a nearby towel to dry off. The towel was blue with little white diamonds along one edge. He'd had it since college.

I stared at the threadbare towel as it shook in my hands. "Could you give me a minute? I'd like to say goodbye."

"I'll wait outside. Just don't take too long. I don't know how much more Simon's got in him."

"Yeah," I whispered. "Me, neither."

Once alone, I set the towel on its peg and walked back to the living room. There were few decorations on the walls, but there hung a match to the picture I kept on my mantel of the three of us—Aiden, David, and me. We were young and had that carefree liveliness that only the young possess. We were hanging off each other, making silly, drunken faces.

I ran my fingers over the image of Aiden's bright smile and said, "I'm so sorry, Aiden. Wherever you are, I hope you know I loved you very much. I miss you, and David misses you, and we'll remember you always. We know your secret. I'm sorry you had to carry that on your own, but it doesn't change how either of us feels about you. We love you, Aiden. Goodbye."

As if in a dream, I turned a slow circle, taking the place in for the last time; committing it to memory and locking it away. Aiden was gone. He'd been dead for a week, but this was the first time that fact felt real. Seeing his empty home, feeling his absence, I knew, really knew, that I would never see him again.

My body felt numb, as though every ounce of energy had been wrung from it, but my mind raced. Aiden was gone, but his killer was still out there. I *would* find him. I would see him brought to justice, whatever it took.

Chapter 15

THE LAST HOUSE on our tour d' death was a small brick building in the heart of Golden. The afternoon was wearing on, and I was wearing out. I was tempted to skip this place. Kai admitted it was an old enough scene we might not find anything, but we'd gotten lucky with Melissa, and we at least needed to verify the same magic had been used at all four locations. So tired though I was, I drove to Golden and parked three doors down from what used to be the home of Antonio Dantes.

According to Kai, Dantes had been an elderly Italian man with a smidgen of dryad in his blood. It was difficult to reconcile the image I had of dryads as sexy tree nymphs with an 82-year-old man, but when I saw the yard, I had to admit it looked like the home of a tree-spirit.

The house was small, almost lost in the center of the acre lot. Aside from the gravel paths winding through the urban forest, every inch of the property was covered in vegetation. Not a lawn or neatly arranged flower beds, but a wild and vibrant collection of trees, shrubs, vines, and flowers all growing together. Clumps of vegetables, berries, and herbs were interspersed with other flora rather than in a separate vegetable garden as most people would have.

I looked between the wild plants and the orderly bricks of the house. "If the guy was a dryad, why live in a house built of bricks rather than wood?"

"No dryad would live in a box of dead wood," Kai retorted. "That's like saying humans should live in tombs or cemeteries."

I wrinkled my nose. "I hadn't thought of it like that."

"Obviously." He rapped at the door. "There's a lot you don't understand about the fae. Maybe someday I'll take you to another realm. Give you a tour, a history lesson maybe." He winked, and pushed open the door to our last stop of the day after peeking in the windows to verify the widow wasn't home.

The inside felt like the kind of woodsman's cottage you read about in fairy tales. The rooms were small, but felt cozy rather than cramped. The walls were painted in warm, neutral colors, and everywhere I looked there were more plants. Some stood in large ceramic pots on the floor, others decorated the many shelves, and still others hung from the ceiling in beautifully tied macramé hangers.

I walked through the house, touching everything within reach. No alien emotions swept over me, but I had no way of knowing if there was really nothing to find or if I was simply failing to connect properly. I was tired and grumpy, and I'd had more than enough emotional turmoil for one day.

When I'd made a full circuit, I turned to Kai and shrugged. "I don't think there's anything imbued here."

"Not too surprising. The magic signature is pretty faded, and hard to make out over the energy coming from all these growing things. I'm pretty sure it's the same as at the other places though."

"So we're done?"

"Yep, let's go."

We were halfway to the door when it opened, framing an elderly woman with a shopping bag. She looked about ninety years old, with wispy white hair and a stooped back. Her parchment skin bore the remains of an olive complexion. Flinty eyes took us in over her beak-like nose, growing to the size of saucers as she absorbed our presence. She gave a startled shriek and the bag tumbled from her hands, groceries clattering across the floor.

I worried she was having a heart attack until she let loose with a string of Italian epithets. She cursed us seven ways to Sunday, then made a sign of the cross and spat at us.

I couldn't blame her. I'd feel the same if I'd come home to find two strangers in my living room, especially considering what happened to her husband. Still, we needed to calm her down before somebody called the cops.

Raising both hands in a placating manner, I tried to sound as calm and non-threatening as I could. "Please, ma'am, we're sorry to have startled you. The door was open when we knocked. We came in to make sure everything was okay."

She was still glaring at us and puffing like she'd run a marathon, but at least she wasn't shrieking in Italian anymore.

I picked up an apple that had rolled against my foot. "Let me help with this mess."

"Who are you? Why are you in my house?"

I looked to Kai. Wasn't Simon's spell supposed to make the observer fill in a plausible identity?

He gave an infinitesimal shake of his head. Something had gone amiss with Simon's spell. We were on our own.

Stepping forward, I said, "We're looking at houses in this neighborhood, and we heard there'd been some sort of crime here. We were hoping to find out what happened. You can't be too careful when you're deciding where to raise a family."

The woman's expression softened at the word family, as I'd hoped it would, so I continued to paint the story of an innocent couple stopping by to talk. "When we knocked on the door, it swung open. We called out, but no one answered, so we thought we'd better check to make sure everything was okay. We're sorry to have startled you."

By now the woman had composed herself. "All right then. Help me clean up this mess." She slowly bent down, looking like she might topple.

"We'll clean up. Why don't you sit down?"

"Don't sass me," she said with a stern look. "Still, I might as well put the tea on. Bring those to the kitchen when you're done." She huffed off, while Kai and I began collecting the spilled groceries.

"Did you magic her?" I inquired under my breath.

"Of course," he whispered. "You think she'd believe us so easily otherwise?"

"What happened to Simon's spell? Why isn't it working?"

"No idea, but I've got this under control. Let's see what she can tell us about Antonio's death. We'll deal with Simon when we're done."

"You think he's okay?"

"He probably just ran out of juice. C'mon, let's get this over with."

The three of us sat in Mrs. Dantes's kitchen sipping tea from perfect china cups on matching saucers. She'd even brought out a serving tray with cream and sugar and a plate of Italian cookies. This was a woman who took her hosting seriously, even if the guests were uninvited.

"What happened to your husband?" Kai asked.

I choked on my drink and shot a glare over my teacup. He could at least *try* to be tactful.

Mrs. Dantes, however, seemed unperturbed by Kai's question. "He was murdered about a month ago. This used to be such a lovely neighborhood. Families looked out for one another. What's this world coming to when a person breaks into someone's house and kills a harmless old man?"

"Were you here when it happened?" Kai prompted.

"No. I was shopping, same as I do every day. Only when I came back that day the police were here. They told me I couldn't go in. Can you imagine? Someone saying you can't go into your own home?"

"Did they tell you what happened?"

She shook her head. "They asked a bunch of questions about people Tony knew and what he'd been doing. When they finally let me in, they walked around with me and asked if anything was missing, but the only thing missing was Tony's body. Just a stain where he died."

She looked over her shoulder, as though she could see through the wall to the living room. "They did a good job cleaning, but I still see it."

Sweat beaded Kai's brow. He leaned forward and placed a hand over one of Mrs. Dantes's as though offering comfort, but there was no empathy in his eyes. "Where were the blood stains?"

"Next to the coffee table." Her dark eyes were glazed with tears, but she didn't look away from Kai. She didn't even blink.

"Alex, check it out."

"I already looked at the coffee table."

"Do it again."

Heeding the strain in Kai's voice, I headed back to the living room. I expected Mrs. Dantes to voice a complaint at this odd behavior, but she continued to stare mutely into Kai's eyes.

As I left the room, I heard him ask, "Did your husband have any family heirlooms, or an item that seemed precious to him?"

Her response was lost as I made my way to the coffee table. Kneeling beside it, I placed one hand on the table itself and the other on the carpet between my knees. I stayed like that for a good two minutes, trying to clear my mind, to open myself up, but I didn't feel anything that didn't belong to me.

Kai popped his head into the living room. "Anything?"

Shaking my head, I stood up. "Nope. What happened to Mrs. Dantes?"

"She's gone to lie down. We should leave." Kai was leaning heavily against the door frame.

"Are you all right?"

"Just tired. That lady was suspicious as hell, and stubborn to boot."

"And you were forcing her to talk." My lips pressed into a thin line.

"What did you expect? We had to get her to—" A knock at the front door cut him short.

We looked at each other in silence. The knock came again.

"Mrs. Dantes?" came a muffled voice. "Are you in there?"

"Do you have it in you to spell someone else?" I asked under my breath.

"Let's hope so."

With that glowing reassurance, I moved to the door and swung it open. Standing on the porch was a uniformed officer from the Golden police department. He had his hand raised to knock again.

"Hello. Is Mrs. Dantes here?"

If I could talk my way out of this, maybe Kai wouldn't need to use magic. "Yes, but she's sleeping. Can I help you?"

"A neighbor called. She said she heard Mrs. Dantes scream."

"That's my fault, I'm afraid. We came for a visit and surprised her when she got home."

"We?"

"My boyfriend and I," I confirmed. "He's in the living room."

"I see. Well, I'll need to confirm your story with Mrs. Dantes. Would you mind stepping aside?"

"Of course." So much for avoiding magic.

"Everything okay, honey?" Kai strolled in from the living room where he'd been eavesdropping. When he reached the officer, he held out his hand. "Hello, you can call me Bob."

The cop reached for the offered hand. Then his eyes glazed over. "Thanks for your time. Sorry to have disturbed you."

I shivered. It was amazing, and in this case useful, but it was also terrifying. If magic could change a person so easily, was anyone safe? Was I?

I shot a sidelong look at Kai. He leaned heavily against the wall, but his smile was easy, his voice smooth as honey. "No problem."

We waited for the cop to get back in his cruiser, report to dispatch that it had been a false alarm, and drive away. Only then did I dare to breathe.

I left the cozy house with its wild garden reluctantly. Despite the tragedy that had happened there, it was an amazingly restive place. Antonio Dantes had created a small piece of paradise in the middle of town.

When we got back to the Jeep, Simon was just sitting there, same as every other time.

"What the hell happened?" I snapped when I got to his window.

"Not now, Alex." It was Kai who spoke, angling himself into his seat. "Just get us out of here."

Being ordered around set my teeth on edge, but the exhaustion evident in Kai's movements made me snap my mouth shut on a snarky response and climb into the driver's seat.

WE DROPPED SIMON in front of Crossroads to collect his dubiously earned reward, stopping just long enough for him to jump out and Kai to climb up front. I was still annoyed about getting caught by both the widow and the cop after Kai had assured me Simon would be able to keep us hidden, but I didn't want to argue while I was driving. Kai didn't seem inclined to talk either, so we each brooded over our own thoughts on the drive home.

Once the Jeep was safely parked, I twisted in my seat. "What happened?"

With a sigh, Kai released his seat belt and swiveled toward me. "He ran out of energy. I was afraid it might happen. That's one of the dangers of working with a fae you don't know. There's no way to guess their limitations."

"Why didn't he just tell us he couldn't cover us for that last house? We could have skipped it. It's not like we found anything anyway."

"Telling us would have been an admission of weakness," he said with a scowl. "No fae would admit to that. He may have thought he had enough when we got there, that we'd be in and out before it was a problem. Or maybe he knew but was hoping we wouldn't notice when his spell wore off. If the widow hadn't come in when she did, we would have been none the wiser."

I shook my head, blowing my frustration out in a sigh. "I thought for sure we were busted when that cop showed up."

"The cop was easy compared to Mrs. Dantes. That lady had a will of steel."

I framed a mental image of Kai arm wrestling the old lady for control. In my imagination, she kicked his ass.

"What are you smiling about?"

"Nothing. Are you out of energy now, too? Do you have to like, recharge, or something?"

"Something like that. Unlike practitioners, fae draw energy from within. In simplest terms, we're made of magic. Similar to the way a practitioner can burn out by drawing too much energy without the strength to channel it, a fae can literally use themselves up. If we draw too much energy from our bodies, we can weaken, damage, or even kill ourselves."

"So you could have died today?"

"Hmph. Do you think so little of me?"

"You looked pretty worn out after dealing with Mrs. Dantes," I pointed out. "Besides, how should I know what your limits are?"

"Fair point," he conceded. "Prolonged manipulation spells like the one I used to make Mrs. Dantes talk are difficult. I'm nowhere near killing myself, but I am tired. I could use some food and rest to replenish my energy, and a shower wouldn't go amiss. So can we move this conversation inside, and maybe postpone it until I've eaten?"

Kai went straight to the bathroom to wash up. I spent a little time at my computer, checking emails and backtracking through my security footage to make sure there hadn't been any visitors while we were out. When I reached the recording of my conversation with James, I stopped rewinding and hit play.

On the camera, James knelt to take care of my cut foot. For someone who gave the impression of being aloof and imperious, he'd been incredibly gentle. I sat forward, focusing on his movements, cataloging his gestures.

"Whatcha lookin' at?"

I snapped the windows on my screen closed as quickly as I could. "None of your business."

Kai put his hands up and stepped back, "Okay, no need to get bent."

I raised an eyebrow. "Excuse me?"

He waved a hand. "Angry. Agitated."

"As in . . . out of shape?"

He looked down at his body, frowning.

"Never mind." I rubbed my temples.

Kai shrugged. "I only meant to agree. If you want to spend your time ogling pictures of your boyfriend, that's your business."

"He's not my boyfriend," I said before I could stop myself.

Kai grinned. "So you were ogling him."

I rolled my eyes. "Get bent."

Stomping to the kitchen under the pretext of preparing dinner, I did my best to forget the conversation—and all its dangerous possibilities.

Once we'd both eaten our fill, I curled up at one end of the couch, tucking my legs beneath me. Kai took the other end, one arm draped along the back. As soon as I settled down, Cat jumped into my lap and butted his head against my chin. He turned in a circle and plopped down, purring contentedly.

"Hey buddy," I cooed. "Finally got used to the new guy?"

Kai huffed, but didn't comment.

I cast a sidelong glance at Kai, then fixed my eyes on Cat and took a deep breath. "I have a question, Kai, and I need an honest answer if we're going to keep working together."

He licked his lips and sat up a little straighter. "Okay."

"That stuff you did to make people believe us. . . . Did you do something like that when you came to talk to me?" I had no guarantee he wouldn't just do it again if the answer was yes, but I was counting on the fact that fae couldn't tell an outright lie.

He was quiet for a long moment. "The amount of energy required to sustain something like that over our extended interaction is beyond me. If I'd made you believe me against your will at the beginning, you would have realized as soon as the spell wore off. You wouldn't have agreed to work with me after that."

As answers went, it wasn't exactly a no, so I tried again. "Have you cast any kind of spell on me?"

He pursed his lips. "After the way you reacted in the alley, I couldn't take the chance you'd reject me out of hand again."

The snakes writhing in my stomach coiled tighter. "So you cast a spell to make me trust you."

"I may have given you a little nudge to make you more open to what I had to say."

I nodded, my suspicions confirmed.

"I didn't alter your memories," Kai continued. "Just soothed your suspicion to ensure you'd hear me out. You made your own decisions after that."

I exhaled a long, slow breath that ruffled Cat's fur.

"No use crying over spilled milk, I guess." I narrowed my eyes at him. "But don't you *ever* do that again."

His eyebrows drew together. "I'm not sure what milk has to do with it, but you have my word that I will not use magic to manipulate you in the future."

The corners of my mouth pulled up. "We need to work on your colloquialisms."

Resting my head against the back cushion, I closed my eyes and thought through the day's experiences. We hadn't gotten enough to identify the killer. Kai could talk all he wanted about fae justice, but I'd been hoping for an easy ID that I could leave as an anonymous tip for the police. I had no desire to go head-to-head with a serial killer.

"If we had access to the police files," I mused, "maybe we could find some way to link the clues we've found to a person from one of the victims' lives. I'm sure the police must have looked into who Melissa was dating, or people who came into Angela's building around the time of her death."

"If the police knew of anyone who was at multiple crime scenes, you can bet that person would be at the top of their suspect list. It's not going to be that easy, Alex."

"Our best lead seems to be Melissa Row. We know she was sleeping with her killer. We have to assume the cops did all the basic stuff, like ask her friends and family who she was involved with. Plus, if they'd had sex right before she died there would be DNA, right? But for some reason, the police either haven't been able to find him, or couldn't connect him to the murder."

Kai shifted beside me. "Which leads me to believe the magic I sensed was used in cleaning up the evidence rather than committing the crimes themselves."

I opened my eyes and looked over at him. "What kind of fae would be able to do that?"

He pursed his lips, thinking. "There are a few options, depending on if they erased the evidence itself or masked it afterward. There's also the possibility that someone working the case is involved, either as the killer, or being manipulated by them. Maybe the evidence was there but it was ignored."

"Or tampered with." I pictured Agent Garcia's earnest face. She'd seemed genuine when she promised to catch Aiden's killer. But then, the secretary Kai shook hands with had seemed sincere when she thanked us for taking an apartment tour. There were no guarantees when magic was involved.

"If only we weren't so limited on resources." Kai ran a hand over his head, making his hair stick up crazily. "We don't even know how many people had access to the evidence."

"David could—" I stiffened. "Never mind."

Too late. Kai had already perked up. "Who's David?"

I shook my head. "Just a friend."

"And what is it you think he can do for us?"

"Nothing. Forget I mentioned him." I was kicking myself for bringing up David's name. I wasn't about to drag another friend into this mess.

"If he can help us . . ." Kai lifted his palms. "Unless you've got a better idea."

I ground my teeth. David *could* help. With his security firm, he could look into the officers working the investigation, find out who might have been able to tamper with the evidence. He might even be able to figure out who Melissa was hanging out with, maybe point us toward her mystery lover.

Dammit!

I slumped back, arms crossed. "I'll ask him to run background checks on the officers who worked the scenes."

"You think you can persuade him?"

I narrowed my eyes. "You are *not* going to magic him. In fact, you aren't even going to meet him."

I pulled out my spiffy new cell phone and dialed David's number.

"Hey, David, it's Alex. I need to talk to you, in person."

"Can it wait? It's pretty late, and I'm supposed to stay at Steve's tonight."

I pursed my lips. "Can you meet me for breakfast?"

"Sure. How about the IHOP on Twenty-eighth? I can meet you there at eight."

"Perfect, see you then."

Kai leaned forward. "Don't mention the victims being halfers or having artifacts. If the PTF finds out we knew and didn't tell them, the peace will be over."

Chapter 16

DAVID WAS SITTING in a corner booth, silhouetted by a window that looked out over the parking lot. Waving off the hostess, I strolled over and slid onto the vinyl cushion across from him. My hand landed in a puddle of syrup. Wrinkling my nose, I unrolled my utensil bundle in a clatter of pressed steel and wiped at the sticky mess until the thin, paper napkin tore.

"Thanks for meeting me." I plucked at the white shreds now stuck to my hand.

"I was actually hoping to hear from you."

I looked up. "Oh?"

"Maggie told me about your visitor the other night." He rolled a half-full mug of coffee between his hands, staring into the caffeinated swirl.

I drummed my fingers against the table. "Yeah, she mentioned that. Said she had you run his plates."

"Did she tell you what I found?"

"That he's a fae."

"A fae who registered *your* address as his residence. Tell me you're not actually letting that guy stay with you."

I examined the sugar packets in their little ceramic bowl. "It's temporary."

David leaned forward, resting heavily on his forearms, and pitched his voice low. "Does this have anything to do with the fae who came to your studio? Are you in trouble?"

"I've got it under control."

"How do you know this guy didn't use magic on you?"

"I said I've got it under control."

"I know you can take care of yourself, Alex, but you've got people who care about you. Don't forget that."

I glanced up, but couldn't meet his eyes. Instead, I shifted to look out the smudged window. White popcorn clouds raced across the sky on a wind that swayed the trees in the parking lot. "I know, David. And I appreciate it."

"Then tell me what's going on."

"I—"

"Ready to order?" A middle-aged woman with gray hair showing at the roots of her bleach-blond ponytail planted herself next to our table, pen poised above a creased notepad.

"Uh, yeah." I licked my lips. "I'll have a pancake combo, eggs over medium."

"Just the coffee for me." David lifted his cup.

"I'll be right back to top that off." Jotting a note, the waitress spun and swaggered back toward the kitchen.

David met my glance, but neither of us broke the silence until the woman reappeared, coffee pot in hand. With David's mug full and steaming, and the waitress gone for however long it took to fry pancakes, I leaned my elbows on the table, careful to avoid the still sticky patch of syrup.

"I need a favor."

"I'm listening."

"Could you do a background check on the cops working Aiden's case, the PTF agent who came to see me, and anyone else looking into these murders?"

His eyebrows arched. "When you ask for a favor you don't hold back. What do you need the info for?"

I shook my head. "Just doing what I can to get to the bottom of all this."

"And you think someone working the case is involved?" He frowned. "You're starting to sound like Aiden."

"Can you do it or not?"

He crossed his arms. "Of course I can do it, but I'd feel a lot better if you leveled with me about what was going on. Why are you looking into Aiden's murder on your own? Who's this Malakai guy, and why are you letting him stay with you? You've never had any love for the fae. What's changed?"

I shook my head. I'd been up half the night thinking of a hundred different ways to tell him the truth, but I couldn't. He'd find out soon enough. Once I registered, everyone would, and the PTF would take an extra-hard look at my friends. Better if he could honestly deny knowing. I schooled my expression and tried to convince myself it was for David's sake and not my own that I kept my mouth shut. Had Aiden told himself the same thing when he lied to me?

"I'm sorry, David. I don't have answers for you."

He ran a hand through his hair and sighed. "I'll run the checks."

"Thanks." I bit my lip. "There's one more thing."

He lifted an eyebrow.

"I was able to learn some stuff about the murderer. Not enough to identify him, but I was hoping you could help me piece the clues together."

"Clues?" He said it like a skeptic might say "aliens."

"I'm looking for a man who was sleeping with Melissa Row. He was in bed with her the night she died."

David set his palms flat on the table. "How could you possibly know that?"

I shook my head. "That's not important."

"Like hell it isn't!"

A few curious glances came our way, and I gestured for him to keep his voice down. "All right. The guy who's staying with me. . . . He's investigating the murders, too. Since he's fae—" I shrugged.

"He's got magic." He squeezed his eyes shut and pinched the bridge of his nose. "Shit, Alex."

I crossed my arms. "Are you going to help us or not?"

"I don't know. If you have information about the killer you should take it to the police."

"Unless the police have been compromised." I tipped my chin. "Think about it—if Melissa's murderer slept with her that night, why didn't the cops come up with any DNA?"

"Maybe they did and they just don't have a suspect to match it to."

"I'm not willing to take that chance."

He shook his head. "You really do sound just like Aiden."

I frowned. "Are you going to help or not?"

"What about Sol? Did you run your little theory by him?"

I shook my head. "He's out of town on assignment, incommunicado."

He sighed. "It'll take a while. Promise me you won't do anything reckless in the meantime."

I smiled and touched a hand to my chest. "Who, me?"

Our waitress stepped up to the table. "Careful, these are hot." She slid a plate of eggs and hash browns in front of me, followed by a stack of pancakes on a separate plate. "You folks need anything else?"

I met David's eyes. "We're good."

I PULLED IN BEHIND Magpie twenty minutes before my shift was due to start. Tugging my phone free of the detritus that always seemed to collect in my purse, I dialed Kai to let him know how my meeting with David had gone.

Eight rings, no answer.

Grinding my teeth, I reminded myself his lack of response was not entirely unexpected. While I'd been tossing back pancakes, Kai had headed to Crossroads.

My fingers itched to grab the steering wheel and make for the bar, but Kai had insisted he could get more info on his own.

Picking at a flap of chapped skin on the edge of my lip, I turned the ignition off and let the Jeep die. I'd have to wait until we met up later. In the meantime, I might as well enjoy my chance for a "normal day."

Sighing, I slid out of the Jeep and headed inside.

In the back room of the bookstore, I pulled out the frozen meal I'd grabbed for dinner and tossed the rest of my stuff in a locker. Emma wouldn't mind me borrowing space in the café's little fridge/freezer where she stored her milk and cream. Microwave meal in hand, I headed up front to relieve Maggie.

The person I found at the desk, however, was a stranger.

"Hi, can I help you?" She bubbled. She was five foot nothing and waif thin, her small frame covered in a conservative, high-necked dress that might have been in fashion for a Sunday school teacher decades ago. Straight, platinum blond hair held back by two silver clips hung almost to her waist, and dark brown eyes looked out of her alabaster face. She was pretty in a porcelain doll sort of way.

"Alex!" Maggie clapped me on the shoulder, making me jump. "Meet our newest recruit. Kayla, this is Alex."

"It's wonderful to meet you." She bobbed a little curtsy. "I hope you're feeling better."

"What? Oh, yeah, you covered while I was out last week. Thanks for that."

"My pleasure. It gave me a chance to show Margaret how helpful I could be."

"She was, too," Maggie added. "She's mostly trained, but not quite ready to be on her own. You know how crazy it gets sometimes. For now, I've got her overlapping shifts so the rest of us can take breaks again."

"Huzzah," I cheered.

Her smile slipped a little. She tugged me a few steps away from Kayla, dropping her voice. "Is everything okay?"

"Yeah, Maggie. Everything's fine."

Her lips pressed to a thin white line. "If you say so."

I patted her on the arm. "I'm fine."

She opened her mouth again, but the chime of the front door cut her off, and we both turned to see her husband Charlie stroll through the door.

"Good to see you, Alex." He gave me a smile, then turned to Maggie. "Ready to go, luv?"

In contrast to Maggie's dark, energetic, and let's face it, gorgeous body, Charlie reminded me of nothing so much as the Pillsbury Dough Boy. Shorter than Mags, slightly overweight, pale and freckled, the most striking thing about him was his hair—a shock of fiery orange that brought out the ruddy glow in his over-full cheeks. Though Charlie was far from the best-looking guy to ask Maggie out, I'd never met a nicer man. And most importantly, he made my friend ridiculously happy.

"Let me just grab my bag." Maggie cast me one last, searching look, shook her head, and trotted to the back room.

"She worries about you."

I turned to Charlie. His smile was still in place, but there was a tiredness in his eyes.

"When you disappeared . . ." He shook his head. "I've never seen her so worked up."

A lump caught in my throat. Maggie reappeared, coat and bag clutched in one hand, and I lost my chance to respond. Not that there was anything I could say.

I set my hand on Charlie's arm and gave it a light squeeze, a silent apology for the trouble I'd caused.

"Take care, Alex," Charlie murmured. "For all our sakes."

Maggie waved to Kayla as she passed the register. Then she slipped her hand into Charlie's, and the two of them left to enjoy the crisp autumn day while I got to know my new co-worker.

KAYLA WAS GOOD. She responded politely to customer inquiries, even when they asked questions that made me want to smack them upside the head. She was fast at counting change. She always smiled. Hell, she was a better clerk than I was.

The first fae I saw reminded me that Kayla was a halfer. Had Maggie told me what kind? The effects of my tattoo were still letting me see through glamours, but there was a new element to it. I could see both the fae and the glamour at the same time; two images superimposed. The result was a little dizzying.

I nudged Kayla to get her attention and tilted my chin in the direction of the fae. "What does that person look like to you?"

Kayla stared at the newcomer, looking like she'd just been given a pop quiz in ancient Greek. "Um, I'm not sure what you mean."

"Do they look strange at all?"

"His hair is a bit odd, but other than that . . ."

"Never mind," I waved the topic away. "Maggie said you're a halfer, right?"

"Um, yes. My mother is a pixie."

"Full-blooded?"

She nodded.

I gave a soft whistle. "Does she live here, or on the reservation?"

"The reservation."

"Have you ever been there?"

Her forehead creased, and she cocked her head slightly to the side. "Of course. I lived with my mother as a child."

"And your father?"

"He's a professor here. He teaches European literature."

"They're not together anymore?"

"They were never together," she replied matter-of-factly. "Well, obviously they were together, otherwise I wouldn't exist, but they were never a couple in the way you're implying."

"What, pixies don't have boyfriends?"

She gave me a strange look. "You don't know much about the fae, do you?"

I heaved a sigh. "I'm realizing that more and more lately."

She smiled. "Well, you're not alone. Even growing up on the reservation, there's a lot I don't know."

Unable to resist, I blurted out, "Can you tell fae and halfers apart from regular humans?"

Her lips twisted like she'd bit a lemon. "Sometimes, but not always.

I may have more fae blood than most halfers, but I didn't get much in the way of magic."

"What can you do?"

"I—" Her fingers twisted together like writhing snakes. "I'd rather not say, if you don't mind."

Too late, I remembered Kai's warning about such questions. "I'm sorry, that was rude. Forget I asked." I gave an apologetic smile that was met with one of her own, and we shifted the conversation to safer ground.

Two hours into my shift, I got in line at the café. Caffeine wouldn't help with my jitters, but I had a long shift ahead of me and I was already running on fumes.

Akshata, the evening barista, was busy behind the counter. "What'll you have, Alex?"

"Caramel macchiato." I flipped open my wallet to rummage for cash, and a slip of paper fell onto the counter.

Reaching down, I flipped it over and my heart nearly stopped in my chest.

I'd completely forgotten about the claim ticket in my mailbox. I'd had every reason in the world to get distracted after my ill-fated hike with Sophie, but now I was kicking myself. At the time, I'd assumed it was a clerical error, but I couldn't believe that anymore.

I slapped down some cash, grabbed my drink, and headed for the back room.

"Everything all right?" Kayla asked as I rushed past the register.

"I just need to make a call," I said over my shoulder.

My hands were shaking as I dialed the number on the back of the claim ticket.

"Smitty's," came a gruff voice.

"My name is Alex Blackwood. I have a claim ticket from your store."

"What's the number?"

I flipped the paper and read the number scrawled across the back.

Shuffling noises filtered through the line while, I assume, he matched the number to some sort of inventory. When he spoke again all he said was, "Oh."

"Oh?"

"We had a break-in recently. The item matching your ticket is one of the things that's gone missing."

My heart sank. If only I'd remembered sooner. "Can you tell me what the item was?"

"For that you'll need to present your ticket in person."

"How late are you open?"

"Five o'clock."

My shift wasn't over until nine.

I bit my lip. Maggie had said Kayla wasn't trained enough to be on her own, but if I called Maggie or Jake to cover, Maggie would never let me hear the end of it. It couldn't take more than twenty minutes to get to Smitty's from the bookstore. There and back, plus time for talking . . . maybe an hour. Surely Kayla could handle the store that long?

"We done?" The gravelly voice snapped me out of my thoughts.

"I'll stop by before you close today."

He gave a disinterested grunt, and the line went dead.

Now I just had to convince Kayla not to blab to Maggie.

SMITTY'S WAS A run-down storefront on Broadway. With bars on its windows and graffiti on its walls, it wasn't the type of place that inspired random passersby to stop and shop. A bell jingled when I walked in. From the halo of glamour around the man who approached, I could guess how the store stayed afloat, though it seemed his species wasn't the only thing he was hiding.

With my strange double vision I was able to see both the wrinkled old man walking toward me, wispy white hair flying off in every direction, and a crotchety-looking fae with eyes the size of saucers and the color of a midnight sky. The human body was thin and hunched, draped in a cheap suit, while the fae's real body lacked any cover at all, displaying a stick figure made of twisted reeds and a pair of sagging, wrinkled—

"Boobs?"

Heat flooded my cheeks as I choked on my own embarrassment. "Sorry, I just. . . . I wasn't expecting. . . . Um," My eyes darted madly around the shop.

She crossed twig-like arms, looking me up and down. "Mortals behave better when I wear a man's face." It was the same raspy voice from the phone. Oddly enough, it seemed perfectly fitted to both the old human man and the naked fae woman.

"Ooookay, but . . ." I cleared my throat and fixed my gaze on her face. "Why aren't you wearing clothes?"

She waved one spindle-fingered hand. "I'm wearing glamour.

That's enough. Now, you got business, or are you just here to gawk?"

"Sorry. Yes." I shifted my feet, keeping my focus on her luminous eyes. "I'm Alex Blackwood. I called earlier."

She nodded. "Got your ticket?"

I retrieved the ticket and offered it to her.

She hesitated, like she was afraid to touch it, then reached out and snatched the ticket from my hand. She silently clutched the thin slip of paper for the better part of a minute. Eventually, she looked up and said, "This ticket belongs to an item that was stolen, and you ain't the one who pawned it."

"The ticket was mailed to me."

She nodded. "You know who sent it?"

"I have an idea. Can you tell me what the item was?"

"A small silver box with engravings all over. The man who brought it in seemed awful concerned about it, very agitated. If he sent you the claim, he must've trusted you."

My heart twisted. "Did—" The words choked off, trapped behind the lump of emotion lodged in my throat. I gave a rattling cough and tried again. "Did he say anything when he dropped it off?"

"Nope."

My sigh turned into a growl as I raked a hand through my hair. The answers were so close, I could feel it. "Can you tell me anything else about the box, or who might have stolen it?"

"Police scoured the place top to bottom. Didn't find anything but a broken lock. As to the box, well—" Those saucer eyes swiveled, like the aperture of a camera shifting focus, and I shivered when her unnerving stare settled on a space just behind my eyes. "Whoever took it will have a hell of a time opening it."

"What do you mean?"

She paused, screwing her lips into a sour pucker. "I've heard the name Blackwood. I've a fair notion who you might be. If I'm right, you can maybe understand when I say that weren't no ordinary box. It was a seal. It's what's inside that's the prize. Though what that may be, I have no idea."

I didn't like the idea of my name being infamous. Would any fae know who and what I was as soon as I introduced myself? I'd have to ask Kai about that. With a smile and nod in lieu of thanks, I excused myself and backed out the door as quickly as was polite.

Crossing the street, I noticed a man watching me. He was sitting in a car across from Smitty's with the concentrated air of someone trying not to be noticed. If I had to guess, I'd put my money on a cop stakeout, or a thief casing the joint. Either way, he wasn't very good.

From the way he eyed me, I wished I had Simon's illusion ability to blend in, but it was too late for that. Whoever it was, he'd already seen me.

I climbed back into my Jeep, but didn't start it. Instead, I pulled out my phone and tried Kai again.

The call rang and rang without answer.

"Damn it!" I thumped my palm on the dashboard.

Every impulse screamed for me to turn the Jeep toward Crossroads and find Kai. But who knew if he was even still at the bar? His investigation might have taken him somewhere else by now.

I'd promised Maggie not to disappear anymore, and I'd already left Kayla half-trained and alone at the bookstore.

With a sigh, I turned the key in the ignition and drove back to work, swearing the whole way.

Kayla smiled when I asked how things went. Everything was fine, no emergencies while I was gone. Maggie would be none the wiser.

The clock crept toward five, and Kayla bid me goodnight.

I called Kai again and barely managed not to smash my phone when it went to voice mail. Where the hell was he? He'd said he probably wouldn't answer while at Crossroads, but surely he'd moved on by now?

If he'd gotten drunk and passed out I was going to kill him.

The last few hours of my shift dragged past in agonizing silence, broken only by an occasional customer and the hiss of the espresso machine behind the café. I checked my phone every ten minutes, but didn't bother calling again. The conversation we needed to have would be best in person anyway. I just hoped he was home when I got there.

As the night wore on, and my nerves frayed, I couldn't shake the feeling that I should be out there doing something, anything, rather than standing behind a counter playing human like there was nothing at all wrong with the world.

To pass the time, I busied myself restocking shelves and straightening displays. Then I exchanged a few words with Akshata. There were a lot of students, which translated to a lot of coffee, so she didn't have much downtime. I, on the other hand, spent the hour before closing catching up on paper work.

Finally, nine o'clock rolled around, and I chased the last of the stragglers out the door. Akshata stopped serving twenty minutes before close, so she was ready to go by the time I balanced the register and locked the safe. We walked out together. A streetlight burned at either end of the alley, but being sandwiched between other shops made the shadows in our section long and deep. Not the kind of place a woman wants to walk alone. I idled in my Jeep until Akshata's little Civic pulled out, then I started the commute back up the mountain.

It was a quarter to ten when I pulled up to my house, but I was wide awake, eager to talk to Kai. His car was parked off to one side, and lights shone through the living room windows.

The puffy, white clouds of the afternoon had stretched and darkened to blanket the sky and smother the stars. The moon was a pale glow behind their curtain. When I stepped out of the Jeep a blue arc jumped off the door to zap my finger.

I shook my hand, working to rub the tingle out of my fingers as I headed for the house.

Halfway to the door, the hairs on the back of my neck stood up. I was being watched.

Thinking of my run-in with Bryce, I whirled and brought my arms up in a fighting stance. The eyes staring back from the tree line, however, weren't human.

Chapter 17

THE BLACK FUR was no longer matted and the muzzle was closed over the razor sharp teeth I knew it held, but without a doubt, it was the werewolf that had attacked us in the meadow.

Terror poured over me like a bucket of ice water, and for one awful moment I couldn't move. Then some small part of my rational brain pushed through. I wasn't alone in the woods this time. The house was only ten feet away, and Kai would be inside. Surely magic could deter a werewolf.

Forcing a breath into my lungs, I spun and bolted for the door, screaming for all I was worth.

Kai swung the door open as I leapt to the porch, but I didn't slow. Charging straight into his chest, I knocked us both through the entryway and twisted to kick the door shut. Kai landed with a thump, then cried out as my full weight came crashing down on him. Ignoring his discomfort, I scrambled to my feet, reached for the nearest weapon, and spun to face the door. Heart pounding, umbrella at the ready, I crouched in a low stance and waited for the monster to come smashing through.

Nothing happened.

I risked a glance at Kai. He was propped on one elbow, rubbing his chest and staring at me like I was a rabid dog. "What the—"

"Shh," I cut him off. Inching to the window, I pushed the curtain aside and peeked into the yard. The place the werewolf had been was empty.

"What's going on?" Kai sat up, looking confused.

"There's a monster in the woods," I whispered.

"I know."

That floored me. I crouched by the window, opening and closing my mouth like a suffocating fish.

"He's gone, by the way. You can get up."

"How do you know?"

"I warded your house. Nothing magical can come within twenty yards of this place without my knowing it."

"Well, that's good to know," I snapped. "Why didn't you tell me?"

He shrugged. "I'm telling you now."

I straightened and put my umbrella back in the holder by the door. "So this ward will stop unwanted guests?"

"No, it's just a warning system."

"If you knew it was there, why weren't you worried? That thing could have killed you, or me for that matter."

"Unlikely. Besides, I thought you were friends with the local were-wolves."

Jaw hanging open, I tried to inflate the vacuum in my lungs. It was like I'd been sucker punched.

"How did you know that? How do you even know about them?" If Marc thought I'd betrayed their secret, they might be coming to kill me after all.

"Relax, Alex. I know much more about the paranatural world than you. Though I was surprised to see the types of friends you keep."

I took a deep breath, pushing back my initial panic. Of course the fae would know about werewolves. There was no reason for Marc to think I'd spilled his secret. Besides, he'd said he'd handle it himself if that was the case.

Had the rogue wolf escaped?

Shuddering at the memory of tearing flesh, I pulled out my phone. Marc had some serious explaining to do.

Marc picked up on the third ring, "Hello?"

"What's going on?" Not the smoothest greeting, but having my life threatened made me cranky.

"I have no idea. Why don't you tell me?"

"There was a wolf at my house tonight."

"What?" The single word came out with so much growl I barely understood it.

"It was the one from . . . you know, before."

Silence poured through the line, punctuated by deep breaths. Then he said, "I'll take care of it," and was gone.

I glared at the phone in my hand, resisting the urge to throw it across the room. Instead, I yelled at it. Not words so much, but my own version of growling punctuated by a few choice epithets.

"Feel better?" Kai handed me a mug of tea. He was smiling.

"Not really."

"Don't worry, a werewolf is unlikely to attack while I'm here."

"How can you be sure?"

He waffled his head from side to side. "Let's say it's an educated guess. Most paranaturals won't engage in unnecessary conflict that could result in human intervention." He gestured around us. "Even so far from the city, there's a chance word could get back to the PTF."

"So it's paranatural solidarity? Us against them?"

"More like self-preservation. The fae, and all those in the paranatural community, have a great many secrets we'd rather not see come to light. It's in everyone's best interest to keep a low profile."

"Yeah, well, according to Marc," I pointed out the front window, "*that* wolf ate all his human coworkers. So I don't think he shares your sentiments."

"Then I bet he was new. New wolves are unpredictable, barely capable of thought."

"Comforting." I flopped onto the couch. "Aiden's killer doesn't seem concerned with keeping a low profile either, but I'd say his reasoning is more calculated."

Kai shrugged to concede the point. "Not everyone wants to keep the peace."

"On a more positive note, David agreed to check the police and PTF officers involved with the task force to see if there's anything odd going on. He'll also try to track down Melissa's mystery man. Plus, I've got a new lead."

Leaning forward, I rested my elbows on my knees and waited for Kai to settle in the seat across from me. "I found a pawn shop claim ticket that Aiden mailed to me before he died."

"What?" Kai jerked straight, practically vibrating. "Did you claim what it went to?"

"Nothing so simple."

Closing his eyes, he shook his head. "Of course not."

"The pawn shop was robbed, and the box the ticket claimed was stolen."

"What was the name of the pawn shop?"

"Smitty's. Why?"

He ignored my question. "Did Smitty describe the box? Or say anything about it?"

"How do you know it was Smitty and not some clerk I talked to?"

"Smitty works alone," he said matter-of-factly.

"I take it you know her?"

He nodded. "She's a reader—like what you did at the murder scenes, but more. She can tell the history of an object by touching it. Any object. If she handled Aiden's box, she knew exactly what it was, where it's been, even who made it."

"What's her issue with clothes?"

Kai chuckled. "Spriggans can be a bit . . . eccentric. Smitty more than most. Maybe it has to do with knowing where every stitch of fabric came from."

"If readers can see the past of any object, why didn't you get one of them to help you?"

"Readers are almost as rare as imbuers. There wasn't one we could trust. Besides, if Smitty had touched Aiden's wall or Melissa's bed she wouldn't have seen what the victims experienced, only what the wall or bed did. Objects don't remember the same way people do."

"Humph. Seems like Melissa's bed could tell us who she slept with."

"It's a moot point. Smitty won't get involved, at least for any price I'm willing to pay, and there are no other readers in the area. Now, did she have anything to say or not?"

"Aiden dropped off a small silver box with engravings all over. It sounds like the box the fae who came here, and the PTF guy, were looking for. Smitty said whoever stole the box would have a hard time opening it because it was actually a seal to hold another item that was the real prize, but she didn't know what was inside. She recognized my name, and seemed to think I would understand her cryptic ramblings because of it. Any idea why?"

Kai had gone still while I spoke. His face was pale. "That's how she described it? An engraved silver box acting as a seal? You're sure?"

"Yes, I'm sure. Why?"

He shook his head. "Never mind. It doesn't matter right now."

"Then why do you look like you've seen a ghost?"

"Smitty recognized your name because it's the same surname my lord used when he started your line generations ago."

It was an obvious subject change, but I took the bait. "She knew I was a descendant of your boss?"

"Exactly."

A knot tightened my stomach. "Will any fae who learns my name?"

"Not *any*, but some."

Too bad Mom and Dad had never married. Then I would have been Alex Carter. Maybe I could change it?

"Why did my relation to your boss matter in this context?"

"Because my lord is the one who created that seal, which Smitty would have known when she touched it. She was probably fishing for information, hoping you knew what was in the box. Smitty trades more than pawn shop trinkets in that store of hers."

"So she thought I'd tell her what was inside?"

He scoffed. "No. She was watching your reaction, deciding what kind of profit there might be in pursuing the issue. Lucky for us, you didn't know anything."

I rolled my eyes. "Yeah, lucky."

I leaned back, resting my head against the back of the couch. "If Aiden knew it was my however-great-grandfather that made his box, that would explain his message about picking up my grandfather's gift. Maybe he suspected those fae goons were after him, so he pawned the box to keep it safe, then mailed me the claim thinking I could get it back to its real owner."

Kai nodded. "It's possible."

"So how did your day go? Did you make any headway identifying my mystery fae?"

His eyes lit up. "Perhaps." He leaned back in his chair, steepling his fingers. "I think I've found a way to draw them out."

"How's that?"

"While I was collecting tidbits of drunken gossip, I heard that Shedraziel has been sending lackeys into the mortal realm to acquire artifacts. Rumor has it, they're buying them from unsuspecting halfers. But if someone didn't want to sell . . . well, let's just say these aren't the kind of people who take no for an answer."

"So they killed the halfers and took the relics?"

"At least the ones who didn't agree to sell. That would explain Angela talking to her killer before she was attacked. They made her an offer, she refused, and . . ." he shrugged.

I shuddered at the memory of what came next. "Who's Shedra . . . um?"

"Shedraziel. She's, well, let's hope you never find out what she is. She's not who we have to worry about right now in any case. She can't come to the mortal realm, hence the lackeys."

"So her fae goons came to see if I had a box to sell." I pulled at my lower lip. "That's not exactly solid evidence they're killers."

"Or even criminals," Kai added. "Trafficking artifacts isn't a crime among the fae. I'll need more than that to move against them."

"So how do we find out if they're killers, or just over-eager antique collectors?"

"I made a show of getting drunk and let slip that I knew a halfer who'd come on hard times and was looking to sell a bunch of family heirlooms for a quick buck. Made a big deal about how, if I had the money, I'd buy them myself. That must have piqued someone's interest, because a little while later a man asked if I could set up a meeting between my friend and some associates of his, for a fee of course. I arranged to meet them tomorrow night, with my friend and the items in tow."

"At the bar?"

He shook his head. "No way Targe would let something like that go down at his place. We're meeting in a field north of town, mutually agreed upon as neutral ground."

"What's your plan? Wait to see if they murder us and loot our corpses?"

"I doubt they'd kill someone eager to sell."

"But we haven't actually got an artifact to sell them."

"Who says we don't?"

"You have one?" I cocked my head to one side. "What does it do?"

"You'll find out if I have to use it."

I got up and paced around the living room. "Even if they are the guys who came here, how do we find out if they're the ones who killed Aiden and the others?"

"Firstly, it's not we, it's me. My lord would never forgive me if I put you in harm's way. Your job is to identify whether they're the fae who visited you, then hang back where it's safe."

"I'm not helpless, you know."

"You want to fight them?"

"Well, no," I admitted. "Fine, I'll stay back and let you handle it."

"Good. There are three ways to get the information we need—trickery, torture, or some combination thereof."

I blinked a few times, wondering if I'd heard correctly. When he didn't elaborate, I asked, "Did you say torture?"

"Not my first choice, but yes, if necessary."

I shook my head fervently. "No. I'm not going to torture someone, no matter what they may have done."

"You won't have to. I already told you, you'll be hanging back for this part."

I bunched my fists at my sides. "I'm not going to stand by and watch *you* torture someone either."

"Even if they killed Aiden?"

I nodded, not trusting my voice.

"Then we'd better come up with a damn good plan A. But if push comes to shove, I'll do what I must for the success of my mission."

On that disturbing note, he walked down the hall and shut the door to his room.

It took a long time for sleep to come that night. When it finally did, my dreams were filled with burning fish-faced monsters, corpses waking up to give advice, and mountains of silver trinkets.

WHEN I ROLLED out of bed, the air was oppressive, smothering the house in silence and making my skin itch. Kai's door was closed. Only Cat waited in the living room, curled on the back of the couch.

The thought of our impending meeting with the fae and all its possible outcomes had my stomach tied in knots, so rather than try to choke down breakfast, I zipped into a soft hoodie and turned my feet toward the studio. My arms were feeling better, stronger, but nowhere near back to normal yet. Forging was out of the question. Still, working on Sol's chess set would keep my hands, and hopefully my mind, busy.

Wisps of breath puffed around my face as I turned my back on the faint smear of peach across the eastern horizon and walked toward the fading stars.

My fingers closed around the cold metal of the studio's doorknob, but I didn't twist.

I hadn't gone into my workshop, even just to look, since I'd learned about my imbuing ability. I was nervous about the prospect of creating anything after that revelation. Would it be different now that I knew what I could do? James's speech had made me feel better, but would I be able to create the same way now that I was aware it was magical?

Holding my breath, I pushed inside.

I stood in the doorway and surveyed the room I'd once thought of as my sanctuary. The forge was cold. Tongs lined the wall behind it, with the exception of the ones I'd used on Neil. Those were still on a shelf, waiting to be cleaned—something I wasn't sure I'd *ever* feel up to doing. All the other tools were in their places, hanging from pegs or stored on shelves. My workbench was strewn with sketches of half-formed ideas and scale models in a variety of materials.

I regarded the organic twists of metal that made up my most recent creation. The piece wasn't done, but far enough along that I could see the finished product when I looked at it. Tracing my fingers along a copper vine, I followed its loops and curves as it wrapped around the steel frame.

Curious, I cleared my mind as I had at the crime scenes. Opening myself up to my emotions was easier than I was used to. After my day of sharing other people's dying moments, my own emotions didn't seem quite so overwhelming.

At first, there was nothing. Perhaps I hadn't magically imbued this piece after all, or maybe I couldn't sense my own magic? Then I felt it. A sense of expanding, of change, of hope.

I stood like that for a long time, feeling my own ideas reflected back at me.

When I was in art school, a teacher told me that art was an extension of the artist, that truly successful artists put so much of themselves into their work the audience could connect with it no matter their background. That's why masterpieces maintained their impact despite differences in culture, technique, or time. Anyone who looked at such a piece would be able to see what the artist saw and feel what the artist felt when he made it.

Lifting my fingers off the metal, I sniffed and brushed at the tears collecting in my eyes.

So what if I had a little help? That didn't make my work any less valid. I was just doing what all successful artists strove to do. The whole point of art was to make people feel—something, anything—and I could do that.

Of course, Kai could do that with a touch.

I shook my head and took a deep breath. Why did magic have to make everything so complicated?

Settling at the workbench, I pulled out the chess set I was making for Sol. An army of wax pawns sat in a line on the board, waiting to be cast. Two bishops, one castle, and a knight stood behind them. I picked up the knight and rolled it lightly in my fingers, careful not to dent the soft material.

Kai's voice rang through my memory. *I'll do what I must for the success of my mission.*

What would I do to stop Aiden's killer? How far would I go?

Setting the knight back in its place, I pulled out a new ball of wax.

Bird song filtered through the studio as sparrows and finches greeted the dawn. The sky grew lighter, shifting from gray to pale blue. By the time the sun crested the treetops, a full army stood on my chess board waiting only for a king and queen to lead them to war.

Tucking the battlefield away on a shelf, I closed the studio and turned toward the house.

"Alex."

I spun toward the voice.

Marc stepped out of the trees like a wraith detaching from the shadows. A second man emerged behind him.

I took a steadying breath, the crisp air biting my lungs. "Out for a morning stroll?"

Marc gestured to the stranger. "Alex, this is Tim."

The name didn't register at first. Then I looked into the stranger's amber eyes and remembered Marc's story about the wolf who attacked me . . . Tim.

My heart leapt into my throat, and everything else disappeared. I stumbled back, tripped over a branch, and crashed to the cold, hard ground.

"It's okay, Alex." Marc crouched over me, blocking my view. "He isn't going to hurt you."

"Sorry."

I barely caught the whisper through the pounding in my ears, but the word carried a distinctive drawl.

"I shouldn'a come."

Marc gripped my shoulders.

I tried to pull away, but his hands were like iron.

"Alex, listen to me." He waited until my eyes met his. "I won't let anything happen to you. I brought Tim here to talk. That's all. Can you do that?"

I blinked, staring into Marc's starburst eyes. Could I sit with the man who'd been the monster that attacked and nearly killed me? Who'd forever changed the life of my friend? I tried to remember the way I'd felt after Marc's story. Tim had been attacked just like me. He'd been turned like he'd turned Sophie. I'd felt pity.

Pity was better than fear. Pity I could handle.

Marc crouched there, waiting for an answer. If I said no, he would take Tim away. I could choose not to face this.

Having that choice made all the difference in the world.

I waited until my pounding heart settled into a less frantic rhythm, then swallowed the dry lump in my throat and nodded.

Marc pulled me to my feet. "Thank you, Alex."

Nodding again, I led the way back to the house. Marc stayed between me and Tim the whole time.

The hiss of running water echoed through the living room. Kai was in the shower.

"New roommate?"

"A friend from out of town. He needed a place to crash, and I've got a spare room."

"Friend, huh?" He sniffed, then wrinkled his nose like he didn't like what he smelled.

I crossed my arms. "I assume you're here to explain what *Tim* was doing here last night?"

Tim sank into an armchair.

Marc sat down on the couch. "Tim and I had a chat after you called. Turns out, he's been to your place a few times now."

"I never meant to scare you." He sounded almost as panicked as I'd felt a moment before. "I just wanted to see you. I wanted to apologize for what happened . . ." His voice trailed off, and he hung his head, dark hair hiding his sun-leathered face.

I found myself rubbing the scars on my arm and forced my hands to still. "Then why come as a wolf and not a person?"

Tim hunched farther, collapsing around a black hole in his center.

It was Marc who answered, "He couldn't."

"Why not?"

"Tim isn't strong enough to control himself yet. When we lose control, we shift."

"And now?"

"Today I'm here."

I chewed the inside of my cheek and looked at Tim. He sat with his chin to his chest, curled up like he expected me to start beating on him at any second. I wasn't sure I could ever forgive what he'd done, but that didn't mean I couldn't get past it.

"Marc told me what happened to you, before—" My voice cracked, and I waved a hand to dismiss the rest of the sentence. "I take it you chose to stay with his pack?"

Tim nodded.

"Have you spoken to Sophie?"

When Tim didn't respond, Marc said, "He tried. Sophie goes into hysterics if Tim gets near her. We're keeping them apart for now. They're both young. Neither has the control they need to face what happened without letting it overwhelm them."

I smiled wryly, thinking of my earlier reaction. "I can understand that."

"We'll get out of your hair now," Marc said. "You shouldn't be seeing any more wolves skulking around your bushes, but be sure to call me if you do."

He looked at Tim as he spoke, so I got the feeling it was more for his benefit than mine.

Tim and Marc were halfway to the door before I worked up the courage to say, "Tim, I'm glad you've found a pack."

He looked over his shoulder, and I thought I saw tears before he turned away again. Nodding, he bolted out the door.

"Thank you," Marc said. Then he glanced toward the bathroom where the shower was still running. "Alex . . . He glanced at the floor, then looked up to meet my eyes. "Are you a halfer?"

I gripped the back of the couch as my knees turned to water. Was it that obvious? Did everyone know my secret?

"Werewolves have exceptional senses, especially smell. Fae smell different from humans. Halfers can go either way." He dropped his gaze. "You never smelled like a fae before, but it would explain why you didn't change."

I glanced at my arm where my hoodie covered the tattoo charm. Kai had said it made the magic in my blood stronger. "Do I smell like a fae now?"

Again, Marc's eyes traveled to the bathroom. "Hard to tell."

I took a deep breath and swallowed. "I just found out myself."

He nodded. "Anyone with fae blood is immune to the transformation. I had my suspicions, but I've never heard of a fae who could touch iron. I thought you were human."

"So did I."

After an awkward pause he asked, "Are you going to register?"

I wrapped my arms across my abdomen and shook my head. "There's something I need to take care of first."

He nodded and pulled the door closed when he left.

Marc wouldn't report me. None of the werewolves would. I was coming to realize that despite the PTF's strict policies, there were an awful lot of people keeping secrets.

Chapter 18

MY STOMACH, WHICH had started to growl while I was in the studio, was back to feeling like a steel ball in my gut. I wasn't used to dealing with so many emotions every day, and the results were twisting me up inside. Still, I'd need energy for what was to come, so I pulled down a bowl and a box of Shredded Wheat.

The shower turned off.

I stared at the little cereal squares swimming in milk and wondered if I'd be able to keep them down.

"I thought they'd never leave." Kai stepped into the living room. His sandy brown hair fell in a damp curtain over his eyes. I was amazed he could see where he was going. His bottom half was covered by baggy Toy Story pajama pants that cinched around his tiny waist. Kai had looked thin when fully dressed. Without a shirt, I could count his ribs.

"Good mor—" I choked on the word as he ran a hand through his hair, giving me my first look at Kai without his glamour.

His cheekbones were higher, his lips thinner, and the tips of his ears were pointed. When he opened his eyes, instead of chocolate brown they were swirls of black, brown, green, and gold, like tiny galaxies spinning beneath his lashes.

My stomach clenched, then settled. A lot had changed in the past week. The fae were no longer something I could avoid. I needed to accept that.

I cleared my throat. "I was thinking we could head back to Crossroads this morning, do a little more poking, maybe learn something about the theft at Smitty's. It doesn't hurt to hedge our bets in case the fae you set the meeting with aren't our guys."

He circled the counter and poured himself a glass of orange juice, then took a long sip. "Good thought, but you need to lie low until we ID those fae."

"Then give me a glamour so no one will recognize me."

"Well, aren't you gung-ho this morning? I thought you were all about getting back to your normal life."

"Back to. As in after *this* . . ." I spread my arms, "is over. The sooner the better."

He shook his head. "You still believe things can go back to the way they were? Even knowing who you are? Who you're related to?"

I gritted my teeth. Kai had hit the nail right on the head, and the concerns I'd been keeping in check tore through me. Once I registered, everything would change. I didn't doubt Uncle Sol would help in any way he could, but my fate would rest with the PTF. If they found out I knew and didn't say. . . . If they discovered I was related to a fae lord . . .

I pushed the thoughts away. One problem at a time. "I can't just sit around all day. I'll go nuts."

Kai opened his mouth, but my phone cut in.

I checked the screen and answered the call. "What's up, David?"

"Your suspicions were right. I have a friend on the force, Sarah Nazari. When I told her I had reason to believe some evidence might have been compromised in the serial murder investigation, she did a little snooping. Turns out some items went missing from the evidence locker."

"So someone on the force *is* involved." I wasn't sure whether to be pleased my suspicions were confirmed, or just plain scared. The implycations of the police being compromised made my blood run cold. "What did you tell her about me?"

"I might've implied you were a local white hat."

"White hat?"

"Someone who finds security weaknesses. I've got a few on staff."

"Do you trust her?"

"Absolutely," he said without hesitation. "Sarah takes her oath seriously, and she's no rookie. There's no way she'd mess with evidence of her own volition. And if the insider is being manipulated by a fae, I can't see why they'd bother with her since she isn't on the special task force."

"Is she going to report it?"

"Don't know. She was pretty upset by what she found, but nobody likes an I.A. investigation."

I bit my lip. If she was trustworthy, having someone with access to police files could really help, especially with the robbery angle. But the last thing I needed was a cop poking around in my business. No, better for Kai and me to handle it alone.

I shifted my grip on the phone. "Have you had any luck looking into who Melissa Row was dating?"

"'Fraid not. Most of her interactions were online. The woman hardly ever left her house. Whoever her lover was, they probably met in a chat room. Without access to her computer, there's no way to know for sure."

"Let me guess, her computer was among the evidence that's gone missing."

"Bingo. I'm still running background checks on the investigators. Nothing's jumping out so far."

I sighed. Another dead end. "Thanks for the help, David."

"Whatever I can do. Aiden was my friend, too."

I hung up the phone and tipped my head back, squinting against the glare of overhead lights.

While I was on the phone, Kai had poured and eaten a heaping bowl of Captain Crunch. Slurping up the last of the milk, he wiped his chin. "We were right about the cops?"

I nodded. "We're on our own."

"Well, if you're looking to be useful, there *is* something you can do."

I narrowed my eyes, suddenly wary. "What'd you have in mind?"

"I need to make some enchantments to get ready for tonight. If we're right, and those fae turn out to be the killers, I'm going to have my hands full."

I frowned. "That's not something I can help with."

"Sure it is. So far, you've only used your innate ability to imbue, but that's like breathing for a baby. There's so much more you could do, if you're willing to learn."

While curious, I wasn't sure I wanted *more* magic in my life. I shook my head. "I don't need to learn magic."

"You do if it helps us reach our goal. You have a responsibility to this mission."

The muscle under my eye started to twitch. Dad's voice echoed up the stairs where I crouched as a child. *We have a responsibility.*

"Alex?"

My eyes refocused.

Kai was staring, his brow creased. "You okay?"

I turned away, took a steadying breath, and paced to the window. A fine mist filled the air, condensing into shining beads on the glass. "How long will it take to teach me?"

"To use your magic? A lifetime. Luckily, I have something simpler in mind."

I SAT ON THE EDGE of Kai's bed. My once tidy guest room looked like a dumping ground for candy wrappers. "If I find ants in here, you're back to sleeping in your car."

Kai grabbed a plank of wood off the dresser and started scrawling symbols on it with a piece of chalk. Finishing with a flourish, he dropped the wood on the bed next to me and rubbed his hands together. "Time to make some enchantments."

A steady pounding at the base of my skull promised a headache was on the way. "And how do I do that, exactly?"

"Well, you won't be making the actual enchantments, goodness knows what we'd end up with. I just need you to lend me some energy."

I pursed my lips. "Fae die if they use up all their magic, right?"

He nodded and pulled a length of string out of small black box.

"Since I'm only a halfer, I don't imagine I've got much magic to start with. What happens to me if you suck it all out?"

"I won't." He set the string beside the symbol-scrawled wood.

"But what if you did?"

With a sigh, Kai asked, "Have you ever seen a backlash survivor?"

Backlash happened when a practitioner drew more energy than they could safely channel. It burned them out from the inside. Hardly anyone survived such an overload, and those who did were said to be walking shells of their former selves. Bodies without a soul.

"I've heard stories," I whispered.

"Well, I imagine it would be like that. You'd survive, but something inside you would die."

"That doesn't sound like something I want to mess with."

"You'll be able to stop the flow of energy at any time. I can't take your magic, Alex. You have to give it."

I bit my lip. "That makes me feel a little better."

"Good. Let's get started."

It took a while to get me up to speed, but once we were on the same page, the magic transfer was a piece of cake. In fact, it was scary how easy it was to give someone my magic.

Along with the wood and string, Kai chanted over several seemingly useless pieces of junk he collected from around his room. The words were guttural and slurred, in no language I could recognize.

Hours passed, and I grew more and more lethargic. By the time Kai was satisfied with his arsenal I could barely raise my head. My muscles sagged like I'd run a marathon on an empty stomach.

Sitting on the floor across from me, Kai looked to be in about the same shape.

I rested my head against the mattress. "I can't move."

"A few hours' rest and a decent meal, and you'll be good as new."

"How long do we have until the meeting?"

He glanced at the nightstand. "Six hours."

With a grunt, I heaved to my feet, stumbled across the hall, and toppled into bed.

THE GENERIC CHIME of my phone's default ringtone shattered my dream and scattered the memory of it beyond recall.

Rolling over, I struggled to untangle my covers and reach the nightstand. There was a muffled hiss when my elbow came down on something soft and warm. Cat slunk off the bed and glared from across the room.

I finally managed to wrap my fingers around the ringing phone. "'Lo?"

A deep sigh. "At least you answered this time."

"James?" I sat up, rubbing gummy chunks out of my eyes. "What's up?"

"Were you sleeping?"

"Just a nap." I looked at the clock. Quarter to eight. Tuesday. Suddenly, I was wide awake. "Crap! I totally forgot to call you about tonight."

"I take it I'll be dining alone?"

"I'm so sorry, James. Something came up."

"Nothing dangerous, I hope?"

My mind raced ahead to a dark field full of murderous fae. "No, nothing dangerous."

"This makes two weeks in a row you've stood me up. I hope you're not avoiding me."

The silence stretched while I struggled to find my voice. Was I avoiding him?

A phantom touch tickled my cheek. *The girl he seems to care for . . .*

I shook my head to clear the thought.

"I'm here if you need me, Alex." James's voice rang in my ears like a gunshot.

Swallowing past what felt like a mountain in my throat, I disconnected the call and fell back on my pillow with one arm draped over my face.

Cat butted his head against my side.

Lifting my arm, I stared into his big green eyes. "I may not have any friends left when this is over. Not that it matters, I guess. Even if this thing with Kai ends tonight, my life will never go back to normal. I'll register with the PTF, and maybe get shipped to the reservation for not coming forward right away. Or worse, maybe they'll dissect me because of my immunity to iron, or try to use me as leverage against the Lord of Enchantment." I sighed, scritching Cat's stomach as he rolled to expose it. A parade of lost friends and aborted relationships marched through my thoughts, scored by my mother's words: *Don't get attached*. "Probably best just to cut ties now."

My stomach let out a long gurgling rumble, so I gave Cat one last pat and rolled out of bed.

Kai's door was shut.

My stomach grumbled again as I pulled out a carton of eggs and a loaf of bread. I couldn't remember the last time I'd been so hungry.

I decimated a pan of scrambled eggs and four pieces of toast before Kai's door finally opened.

He poked his head into the living room and sniffed. "Is that bacon?"

Smiling, I moved the sizzling strips over to a paper towel and turned off the stove. "Only if you hurry."

The bacon was gone in seconds, and the rest of the loaf of bread followed.

Gravel crunched outside, and I froze with the last piece of jellied toast halfway to my mouth. "Were you expecting company?"

Kai shook his head, cheeks bulging from the bite of egg he'd just shoveled in.

Trotting to the window, I peeked out to see who this latest invader might be. A tall woman stepped out of a black SUV with the word POLICE printed in glowing white letters on its side.

"Shit. Now what?" I tugged the curtain until I was looking through the thinnest slit possible. The officer's fitted uniform blended with the night around her, making her look like a floating head until she stepped under the glare of my porch light and knocked on the door.

I waited a breath, then straightened my shoulders and pulled it open. "Can I help you?"

She was six feet tall with curves like a gymnast, and she watched me like a hawk eying a mouse. Not an ounce of fat softened her sharp features, and her raven hair was pulled back in a severe braid that tugged the bronze skin on her forehead tight. It was hard to place her age; her brown eyes seemed older than the lines on her face would warrant.

"I hope so," she said. "My name is Sarah Nazari."

I frowned. Then the name clicked into place and my mouth went dry. David's cop friend. But what was she doing here?

"May I come in?"

"What's this about?"

"It's all right, Alex." Kai pulled the door out of my grasp and opened it wide, gesturing for Sarah to enter. "Please, come in."

Sarah's lip curled back from pearly white teeth, but she stepped past Kai and crossed the living room in three long strides.

"Do you—?" I pointed at Sarah's back.

"No," Kai said. "But I know enough."

"Care to share?"

He smiled and closed the door.

I stepped behind a chair, digging my fingers into the back cushion. Between Kai's smile and Sarah's frown, I felt like the only person in a comedy club who'd missed the punch line.

Sarah's eyes traveled over my walls and shelves, cataloging. "David had me look into your suspicions that the task force investigating the series of recent murders might have been compromised."

"He told you who I was?"

"He told me enough." She crossed her arms. "I am a cop after all."

I wracked my brain, trying to remember what David had told her about me. White hat? Some kind of security expert? Cold sweat broke out across my back and palms. If she put me in front of a computer it wouldn't take long for her to know that was a lie.

Kai reclined on the couch, crossing his ankle on the coffee table. "Happy to have you on board."

She frowned. "I'm not thrilled to be working with you." Her eyes shifted between us. "Either of you. But I want the killer caught, and you clearly have information about these cases. And while I don't believe for a second that any of the officers on the task force would tamper with evidence, David also mentioned possible fae involvement." She looked pointedly at Kai. "Which means all bets are off."

"Indeed." Kai offered her a toothy grin. "We think it likely that one or both of the fae who paid Alex a visit here last week are involved."

Sarah uncrossed her arms and perched on one of the bar stools. "What do you know so far?"

I glanced at Kai, hoping for some clue that would explain his easy acceptance of this woman, but he just offered a lazy nod.

I shook my head but said, "The murderer has been targeting people who own specific items. My friend, Aiden, took his to a pawn shop and mailed me the claim ticket before he died. Then two fae came here asking about a box that sounds like the one Aiden had. I chased them off and they haven't been back, which I thought was weird until I found out the pawn shop Aiden used was robbed and the box was stolen. It's not a huge leap to think the fae who came here killed Aiden for the box, then stole it from the shop when they realized I hadn't picked it up yet."

Sarah narrowed her eyes. "How do you know what the killer was after?"

Kai sat forward, his feet once more firmly on the ground. "Alex, tell the officer what you saw in Angela's apartment."

I stared until my eyes felt like they were going to fall out of my face. Had Kai lost his mind? I wasn't going to out myself to a cop.

"She already knows what you are," Kai said as though reading my mind.

My stomach dropped, and I would have followed if not for the death-grip I had on my chair.

"Relax, Alex. She's not going to tell anyone." He turned that toothy grin back on Sarah. "She can't."

My breaths were coming fast and shallow. "How—"

Sarah studied the floor, every muscle coiled like a spring waiting for release. "You've met Marcus."

It took a moment to realize that was all the explanation I was going to get, and all I needed. "You're a—"

"Don't," she snapped. "Don't even say it. Let's just agree we both have secrets we'd rather didn't get out."

That's why Kai had been so quick to accept Sarah. He'd known she was a werewolf as soon as she crossed the ward, just like Tim.

Kai picked up the conversation like Sarah and I weren't standing ten feet apart pretending the other didn't exist. "We know the killer is after magic artifacts because Alex watched him kill Angela Espinoza, and he made her tell him where she'd hidden her treasure first."

My hands clenched at the memory.

Sarah's eyes snapped up to meet mine. "What does he mean, you watched?"

"I didn't watch." I rubbed the goosebumps that had sprung out on my upper arms. "I relived the memory of Angela's murder."

"You saw the killer?"

I shook my head. "He was behind her when she died."

Sarah pinched the bridge of her nose. "It's a good working theory, but it's all circumstantial. We need physical evidence that can place these fae at any or all of the crime scenes."

"You can help with that." Kai pointed out. "Scent them out. The same magic was used at all the murders, I just don't know who was using it. Melissa Row's house is closest. If the fae from Alex's studio were also present at the pawn shop and Melissa's house, that would make them look pretty guilty."

"It wouldn't be admissible."

"It doesn't need to be," Kai assured her. "If this is a fae matter, there's no reason to bring human law into it."

Sarah pursed her lips, thinking. "And if I confirm their presence at all three locations?"

"Then I would have all the evidence I need."

"I can tell if they were present, but not who they are. How will you find them?"

"I have a meeting scheduled with some fae buyers tonight. Alex is going to see if she can ID them as the fae who came here."

"So if the fae you meet tonight were Alex's visitors, and I tell you they were also at the pawn shop and a murder scene, what will you do?"

Kai shrugged. "As I said, that would make it a fae matter. No need to drag the humans into it."

Sarah looked at me. "You're okay with that?"

"I want to catch the people responsible for my friend's murder. Preferably before anyone else dies."

She shook her head, but said, "All right. I'll get the scents from the studio and see what I can match up. Fae killing fae isn't a matter for the police, but promise you won't act unless I confirm they were at all three locations."

"I won't do anything permanent until I get your call," said Kai.

"Good enough, I guess," Sarah muttered. "When's your meeting?"

"Ten o'clock. Here's my number." Kai scrawled it on a slip of paper. "Make sure to call by then."

"One last thing." Sarah focused on me. "If this comes back to bite you in the ass, and it probably will, leave me out of it. If I'm exposed, you'll be facing more than homicidal fae."

I bridled at her tone. "I don't like being threatened."

"Neither do I," she countered. "The fact that you know about me at all is a threat to my career, my life, and my family. When I found out who you were, I almost didn't come. But Marcus vouched for you, said you're a good person. His assurance carries a lot of weight, but he's been wrong before. You wanna keep breathing? Prove him right." With that, she strode out the door.

Great. It seemed Sarah was one of the wolves who'd have been happier if I'd bled to death, or been killed because I knew too much. Hell, she probably volunteered to do the deed.

I turned to Kai. "If she's so worried about being exposed, why help at all?"

Kai shrugged. "She's a cop. I guess she wants to see justice done, and she knows the police don't stand much chance of accomplishing that if there are fae involved."

"Isn't that what the PTF is for?"

"Sure, in theory, but she'd have to provide evidence to back any claim she made. She can't do that without revealing herself. Besides, this is a win-win for her so long as she keeps her hands clean. A murderer is taken off the streets, and there are a few less fae in the world."

"Why don't werewolves like the fae? I mean, I get why they don't consider themselves fae since they start out human, but it seems like more than that."

"The wolves blame the fae for their curse, as they like to call it. It's ancient history."

"Did you? Curse them I mean."

"No," he said tersely. "Now, let's get ready. With any luck this will all be over tonight."

I OUTFITTED MYSELF in as much steel and iron as I could on short notice; insurance in case the car wasn't such a safe place after all. To that end I was wearing steel mesh gloves, steel-toed boots, and a steel choker that covered my neck. I also had a couple three-foot iron rods to defend myself.

Taking Kai's car in case they recognized mine, we arrived for the meeting an hour ahead of schedule. The parking area we pulled into was packed dirt marked off with old logs. To one side was the trailhead for a hike that wound into the foothills north of Boulder.

I waited in the car while Kai jogged a circle about twenty yards out from where the meeting would take place. Stopping periodically, he crouched in the grass for a moment only to stand up and continue on. The clouds threatening rain overhead blotted out any chance of moonlight, so it was difficult to track him while he worked. I was amazed Kai could see well enough to run without tripping, let alone whatever he was doing in the field.

When he completed his circuit, he returned to wait with me in the car. The dashboard clock turned to 9:48.

I drummed an erratic beat against my thigh. "Sarah should be done by now. What's taking so long?"

Kai shrugged and leaned back in his seat. A few drops of rain speckled the windshield.

Five minutes before the appointed time, a van pulled up on the far side of the clearing.

Kai checked his phone, shook his head, and set it back on the dash. "What if she doesn't call?"

"We follow the original plan."

I narrowed my eyes. "The capture-torture plan?"

A man got out of the van and stepped around so he was backlit by the headlights.

"Do you recognize him?" Kai asked.

I squinted through my window, but the bright lights combined with the distance and general gloom made it impossible to see the man's features.

I shook my head. "I can't tell from here."

Kai frowned. "You'll have to get out of the car."

His phone buzzed, vibrating on the dashboard, and we both jumped. He snatched it up. "Hello?"

I leaned close, but couldn't catch Sarah's half of the conversation. The knots in my stomach were twisting tighter by the second.

The man in front of the van took a step forward. "Are you going to make us wait all night?"

Kai disconnected the call. "We're good to go."

"Sarah was able to verify the fae from my studio were at Melissa's and Smitty's?"

"And Aiden's. That's what took so long. She wanted to make extra sure by checking the freshest scents. She smelled you, me, and two other fae. That's good enough to green light tonight's little escapade."

I licked my lips. We were really doing this.

Together, we stepped into the night.

"Stay behind me," Kai said. "If they attack, you run."

We made our way to a point between the two vehicles. Then Kai yelled, "That's as far as we come. If you want to do business, you'll meet us halfway."

"Fair enough." The man waved one hand, and a second figure emerged from the van.

I was pressed close to Kai's back, squinting over his shoulder as the men approached. They were definitely fae. Both caused the double vision I was still struggling to control.

The first had antlers like an elk, a long face, and broad shoulders with willowy arms that hung almost to his knees. As he got closer, I focused more on his human glamour. Nothing remarkable, just an average guy. Mr. Smith had struck me the same way, but that was the problem with trying to identify an average-looking person; there were a million just like them. I couldn't be certain this was the same man.

My gaze shifted to his companion, and a mouth full of needles grinned back at me. Across the second fae's cheek was a long black scar. Cold sweat coated my skin and my breath came in short, painful bursts. I hadn't realized until that moment how afraid I was to see that terrible face again.

Twisting my fist in the back of Kai's shirt, I hissed, "It's them."

Chapter 19

"MS. BLACKWOOD, how lovely to see you again," said Mr. Smith. "We rather hoped you'd be joining us."

Kai's back stiffened under my hand.

"Did you think we would fail to recognize a dog of the Realm, Malakai? Even a pup, like yourself?"

Out of the corner of his mouth, Kai hissed, "Run." Then he sprang forward and all hell broke loose.

I barely had time to glimpse the tiny dark shapes pouring out of the van's side door before my vision was filled with the flat-faced grin of Mr. Smith's companion, Neil.

"I've been looking forward to this," he hissed.

"That makes one of us." Fists at the ready, I backed toward the car and my iron rods.

"You caught me off guard before. You won't be so lucky this time."

I'd been watching for the shift in balance that announced where he was going to move, so when he lunged for me I was already pivoting. Unfortunately, Neil wasn't human, and the basic rules of fighting a human didn't apply. He redirected his path in one liquid movement, as though he had no bones in his body, and tackled me like a linebacker.

I lost all the air in my lungs when I hit the ground, and with Neil perched atop my chest, I couldn't recover it.

"Too easy," he purred, pressing a finger against my lips.

When I gasped, it wasn't air that flooded my mouth.

Perched directly over my nose and mouth was a sphere of water held together by glowing light. The same light shone from Neil's eyes.

I whipped my head from side to side, searching for air, but the glowing orb stayed in place. Fingers scrabbling in the dirt, I willed myself to stay calm as my body went rigid with the effort not to cough and suck in more of the deadly liquid. Panic would only kill me faster.

One of my arms was pinned beneath Neil's leg. He held the other in a grip that had my fingers tingling. Not a lot of options.

Spreading my feet for purchase, I braced against my shoulders and jerked into a bridge as hard as I could, twisting at the same time. It didn't dislodge him, but Neil's knee lifted enough to slide my arm free. With all the strength I could muster, I swung my hand to deliver a resounding open-palmed slap across his face.

Under normal circumstances it would be silly to slap a man who's trying to kill you, but not when that man is a full-blooded fae and you're wearing steel-mesh gloves.

With a shriek that was more surprise than pain, Neil rolled off me. The water bubble over my face burst, drenching my head and shoulders. Scrambling to my knees, I coughed up as much liquid as I could.

Neil sprang to his feet. My own progress to standing was more labored, but the corner of my mouth pulled up when I saw the bright handprint across his previously unmarred cheek.

"Not so easy after all," I croaked.

He began to circle, and I pivoted to keep him in view. Neil darted in for a jab, but jumped back before I could counter. Lunge, retreat. Lunge, retreat. He was testing my defenses.

I studied his moves, trying to gauge when he would attack in earnest. As we danced, I kept us moving toward the car. The gloves had given me the edge I needed to hold him at bay, but steel didn't do as much damage as straight up iron.

We were ten feet from the car when a scream tore through the night like a crack of thunder. Neil and I both spun toward the sound.

A pillar of flame rose from the field to my left. At the center, I could just make out the shape of a man flailing wildly as he burned alive. I took half a step toward the inferno, heart in my throat. Then I saw the antlers.

I glanced sideways. Orange light danced over Neil's stunned features. Would he try to save his companion?

I dashed for the car.

I'd only taken three steps when the warning pressure of a tackle brushed my back. This time, I waited until there was enough contact that he wouldn't be able to shift away, then I dropped to the ground and rolled. My tight circle brought me up within reach of the car. Neil's extra momentum sent him tumbling over me, and he landed with a heavy thud against the rear panel.

Yanking the door open, I grabbed two of the rods propped against the seat. I hadn't had any real training with weapons, but I'd take as much iron between me and the angry fae climbing to his feet as I could get.

The warm light of the fire was fading, leaving only the harsh yellow glow and stark shadows of the headlights, and an acrid scent that singed my throat with each panting breath.

Sparing a look to the side, I caught a glimpse of Kai wielding a long silver sword at the heart of a writhing mass of black bodies. Probably shouldn't count on help from that corner any time soon.

Neil faced me again, more warily. I'd surprised him twice, and now that I was armed, I was on the offensive. We took turns feinting, dodging, looking for openings. He caught a solid blow to my upper arm, claws tearing through my sleeve and coming away red. The cuts weren't deep, but my arms were still healing and the rods weighed them down. If the fight dragged on, my diminished strength would become an issue.

Skin bubbled where my weapon connected with Neil's bare wrist, and the smell of burning flesh grew more pungent. Another blow glanced off his knee, causing him to limp, but his clothing protected him from the worst of it.

I brought my weapons up as Neil darted in on my left, but at the last second he performed another impossible, boneless shift that brought him crashing into my right side. I tried to twist away, but he wrapped around my torso, and together, we fell. I hit hard, grunting when my shoulder lodged in the packed dirt. Neil's weight pressed me farther into the earth and squeezed the air from my lungs.

The grass I was laying on shriveled and curled as glowing beads of moisture formed on their leaves and rolled toward me like ball bearings toward a magnet. The droplets disappeared when they touched Neil. Then his whole body started to glow.

His flesh seemed to soften and spread, and I shivered as the arms trapping me flowed outward until I was wrapped in a thin coat of water down to my wrists. Neil's legs wove between mine as only liquid could. Finally, water swelled over my head, trying to push past my lips, to find its way to my already aching lungs.

I jerked my head from side to side, but the water didn't relent. My sinuses burned as the liquid pushed farther in, pressing against the last desperate pressure of my remaining air. My heartbeat pounded in my ears, echoing strangely, muffled by my cocoon.

With only my wrists to work with, I couldn't make any meaningful contact with my weapons. The way Neil's limbs had morphed, I wasn't even sure what bits were where. All I knew for certain was that his mouth was near my ear.

"How long can you hold your breath?" He taunted. "I hear drowning is like being burned from the inside out."

Dark spots swam in my vision as the last of my air trickled from my lips in a thin stream of bubbles. As that darkness expanded and the fire in my chest grew unbearable, I did the only thing I could think of. I rocked forward until our collective weight shifted past the balance point and I toppled onto my stomach with Neil's weight on my back.

My shoulder dislocated with a sickening pop as we rolled over it, and I scrunched my eyes closed against the wave of pain that washed through me.

Whatever part of Neil was holding me was now trapped between my body and the iron rods, with our combined weight holding us in place.

Lips pressed tight, I clung to the shredding threads of consciousness as the vacuum in my chest threaten to pull me inside out. James's face floated in the abyss of my thoughts. Then Maggie and David joined him. Behind them, Aiden's smile drove a dagger through my heart.

I'd failed them all.

Salty tears mixed with my prison as seconds ticked by like centuries. My body shook to the frantic pounding in my ears, and the last of my strength drained away. Water flooded my mouth.

Then the pressure around me collapsed in a shower of rain and the acrid smell of burning flesh came wafting back.

Water gushed from my nose and mouth in shaking gasps as my abdomen cramped. Above me, Neil's body jerked against my back, each impact sending a jolt of searing pain through my shoulder. The high-pitched screech I remembered from my studio pierced my ears from inches away.

Then the resistance between my chest and the rod beneath fell away and I dropped the last few inches to the ground. Neil rolled off my back with a shriek, writhing on the ground beside me.

Ignoring the protest of my body, I lurched onto my knees, wrapped both hands around a single rod, lifted it to the dark sky, and brought it down on Neil's screaming face.

The horrible wail cut off abruptly.

I flopped onto my back, still gasping for air.

When the ringing in my ears cleared, the world was silent. Perhaps I'd gone deaf. Or maybe Kai was dead and a hoard of tiny black monsters was about to tear me limb from limb. Somehow, I couldn't work up the energy to care. I'd won my fight. I'd assume Kai had managed his until someone showed up to tell me different.

"You . . . planning . . . to lay there . . . all night?" Kai gasped in a ragged voice.

"Yep," was all I could manage. Now that I wasn't about to die, the throbbing in my shoulder was unbearable. My eyes and throat burned from smoke and water, and my lungs rattled with each breath.

"Okay then." Kai flopped down beside me. Together we lay in the field of carnage, silently waiting for whatever came next.

It was my patience that gave out first. "Can you help me up?"

Kai grunted, but crawled to his feet. I kept my left arm tucked against my chest as Kai hoisted me up.

Neil's corpse lay half-hidden in the dry grass. His face was caved in. His skin had peeled back from the impact wound in charred strips to reveal his skeletal grin in all its needle-tipped glory. His arms ended in blackened stumps below the elbow.

Turning, I found his severed hands on the ground. A good two inches of his arms had been burned away by the iron rods he'd been trapped against. *My* iron rods. *My* weight trapping him as the metal ate through his flesh and bones.

Shock can be a wonderful thing.

I stared at my handiwork without registering it. Somewhere in the back of my mind I knew this scene would haunt my nightmares, but for now, I looked on with calm detachment. Then I pulled my eyes from the gruesome sight to get my first look at the rest of the battlefield.

Where I'd seen the burning pillar was a twisted, blackened form that might once have been a person. All around the intervening space were strewn the naked bodies of tiny black monsters with large ears, long tails, and vicious-looking claws.

"What are they?"

"Gremlins. A lesser breed of fae, often used as cannon-fodder."

"Tonight didn't work out how I expected."

"No." Kai was staring at his hands like they belonged to someone else. "I'm glad you survived."

I prodded the emptiness where my emotions should have been waiting to ambush me, but found only a hazy dread and profound exhaustion. "Let's go home."

When we reached the car, I glanced back toward Neil's corpse. "My rods—"

"Do you want to go back?" Kai asked. "Because I'm not touching them."

Shaking my head, I collapsed into the passenger seat and looked out over the field.

One corpse with missing hands and a crushed head, another charred to a crisp, and who knew how many little Gremlin bodies hidden in the tall, dry grass. Even something as simple as a bar fight was grounds for the PTF to exile or imprison a halfer. No way they'd let me walk if I got tied to something like this. "Sarah was right. This is going to bite us in the ass."

He shook his head. "No one will ever know we were here."

I gestured to the carnage. "Have you seen this mess?"

"Watch and learn."

I rolled my eyes, but sat back as Kai walked past the car to one of the spots he'd visited earlier and set his hand on the ground.

First thing tomorrow, I'd get my affairs in order, then call Uncle Sol and explain what had happened. I just hoped he was back in town.

A white glow spread under Kai's hand.

Against my shoulder's protest, I twisted to watch as the light shot out in either direction to find the next points Kai had marked on his earlier circuit, then the next, and the next. When the light came together at the far side of the meadow, a blazing circle encompassed the entire battlefield.

Kai stood and wiped his hands on his pants, then spread his arms to either side and said a bunch of gibberish I could barely make out. His palms came together above his head with a resounding clap. The light of the circle raced inward, closing the area in a shimmering dome. When the light sealed at the top, a bright flash turned the world white.

I rubbed my eyes to clear the after image, but my vision was patchy when Kai climbed into the driver's seat.

No trace remained of the van the fae arrived in. I could only assume the bodies were gone as well.

"That's what you were setting up earlier with all those enchantments? A clean-up spell?"

"That, and to boost my power," he said, turning the engine over. "Much as it pains me to admit it, I'm not normally strong enough to take on all those gremlins and a forest fae by myself."

"You made yourself stronger?" My words were starting to slur as the adrenaline wore off and the last of my energy faded.

"Temporarily."

"Handy." I let my head fall back against the seat, my eyes sliding closed as pain lanced through my shoulder. Covered as I was in blood and gore, a trip to the hospital was out of the question. Luckily, I knew how to track down a practitioner with excellent discretion.

I wriggled my phone out of my pocket, clenching my teeth against the pain. The screen had a spiderweb crack in one corner, but Marc's number was displayed clear enough. "We need to swing by Luke's to get my arm checked out. Then you can head back to faerie land, and I can—"

What? Try to salvage what remained of my human life? Move to the reservation and become fae royalty? Turn myself over for testing as the first halfer immune to iron and become the PTF's guinea pig?

"We're not done yet."

My eyes snapped to Kai's profile. "We got the bad guys."

"My mission was to stop the murders *and* recover the stolen artifacts. As it stands, all I know is that the killers were working for Shedraziel. I just hope they stored their treasures here in the mortal realm, waiting to take them back in a single trip. The alternative does not bear considering."

"You mentioned that name before. Who is she?"

His jaw tightened. "An enemy of my lord."

"Well, I was in this to get justice for my friend and stop a murderer, and honestly, it was more than I bargained for. I'm sure once the shock wears off I'm gonna be totally flipped out that I just killed a guy. So best of luck and all, but count me out."

LUCKY FOR ME, Luke's house was only a short detour on the west side of Boulder, and Marc didn't ask any difficult questions when I called for the address.

Luke took one look at me, shook his head with a heavy sigh, and ushered me to a back room that looked like a cross between a professor's study and an apothecary shop. With clinical efficiency he checked me over, head to toe, and announced I'd live. Most of my wounds were superficial and would heal on their own, but he set my dislocated shoulder and gave me some pain killers. Then he shooed me out the door with a litany of advice he seemed convinced I would ignore.

The drugs did their job, the rest of the night was a blur. Kai helped me strip off my grimy clothes and climb into the shower so I didn't fall straight into bed and ruin a perfectly good set of sheets. Under normal circumstances I wouldn't allow a man I barely knew to undress me, but I was too exhausted to care. Kai was at least as tired as I was, and moved with the speed of an arthritic old man. Once the worst of the grime was off us both, we went our separate ways without a word. The welcome oblivion of sleep rolled over me as soon as my head hit the pillow.

When I finally emerged, bleary-eyed and achy, into the bright glare of a mid-morning sun, Kai was at the stove flipping blueberry pancakes onto an already precarious tower.

"Good morning," he called. "Help yourself."

I headed straight for the coffee maker and filled a mug, dumping in lots of cream and sugar.

After stacking the last pancakes on the overflowing plate, Kai joined me at the table and we both tucked it. The pancakes were light and fluffy, but I found it hard to enjoy them. That morning should have been a celebration. We'd ended a killing spree and gotten justice for my friend. But as we ate in silence with our eyes on our plates, I knew I wasn't the only one feeling uneasy.

It was Kai who broke the silence first. "How are you feeling?"

"Not bad, all things considered."

"How's your arm?"

"Sore, but I can move it. Luke said it should heal fine."

"That's good." He didn't look at me, staring instead at the napkin he was wringing to death in his lap. "I apologize, Alex. I should never have put you in such a position. If you hadn't handled yourself so well, last night could have ended very differently, and I'd be facing my lord right now with sad tidings indeed."

"Everything worked out okay."

"Yes, but that doesn't make it all right." He raised his gaze, and I pulled back from the intensity there. "I've done you a disservice. This is the first time I've run a mission on my own, and it was my unique position, not my competence, that got me the assignment. A more experienced knight would not have put you in such danger."

I frowned. "But James said you were a knight when he met you before."

"A knight in training. I . . . ." He shifted in his seat, fists clenching. "I am still considered a child among my people."

"How old are you?"

"I'll be 87 this spring."

I rocked back with a whistle. "I know the fae age differently, but how can you still be a kid when you're that old?"

"Anyone who hasn't lived to see at least one century is not an adult by fae standards."

"You must think of humans as babies."

"Some do," he admitted. "Others think of them more as animals. It's one reason the fae have such difficulty following the rules laid out by your people. They chafe at taking direction from an infant race."

"So this mission was what? Your chance to prove yourself? Some kind of test?"

"Yes and no." His gaze slid to the floor. "Before we continue, I must ask that you turn off your cameras."

"Why?"

"What I'm about to tell you is a secret even among my own people. There can be no record."

I pursed my lips. "You know the cameras don't record sound, right?"

"Even so."

"All right." I punched a code in to disable the cameras, returned to my seat, and motioned for him to continue.

"You were right to question my closeness to Aiden. While it's true we were related, it was many times removed. I would not have sought retribution for his passing if not for the intervention of my lord. He summoned me to his chamber and told me I was to put an end to the caretaker murders and recover the stolen artifacts."

Kai took a deep breath and leaned forward, resting his elbows on his knees. "I've played the role of backup on many such missions, but this assignment was different. My lord proclaimed that I had to undertake the matter as a family member seeking justice. I could request no assistance from my fellow knights, and no one was to know the mission was at my lord's behest."

"Didn't you ask him why?"

Kai's frown deepened. "One does not question a fae lord."

I snorted and crossed my arms. "If I ever meet this guy, you can be damn sure I'll have some questions for him."

Kai pressed his lips to a thin line, but didn't argue. "Before I left, he told me to secure your assistance. Beyond that he said only that recovering the artifacts was paramount and I must not fail."

I ground my teeth willing the muscle under my eye to stop twitching. "So the old man sent you to turn my life upside down because he didn't want anyone important involved." As if I needed another reason to be pissed at my mysterious fae relative.

Kai's eyes refocused. "That's not the only reason, Alex."

"But it was a factor."

He sighed. "We were both called upon because of our unique situations. You were a blood relative not yet tied to the court, and you have a powerful skill well suited to this type of investigation."

"And your situation? Why send a kid if the work was so important?"

Kai cringed as though I'd struck him, and I berated myself for lashing out. It wasn't Kai's fault we were in this mess.

"Many years ago, I had the distinction of being of service to my lord. I was not the only child selected, and I will not tell you what was required of us. The result was the creation of a seal in the form of a small silver box. We were each granted a commission in exchange for our silence. I chose to become a knight. No one was ever to know the artifact within that seal existed. If the other lords learned the truth, they would go to war to see it destroyed, and while my lord is strong, he cannot stand alone against the other Realms."

"If it's so dangerous, why keep it?"

"The artifact is amazing; the strongest ever made. My lord put so much into its creation that he could not bear to see it destroyed. Instead, he chose to hide the artifact in the guise of a more common item. Only a reader like Smitty would see the box as a seal rather than the trinket it appears to be."

I rubbed my temples, trying to ease the ache behind my eyes. "And Aiden was the caretaker of this uber-dangerous sealed artifact?"

"So it would seem," he said solemnly. "Tell me Alex, what do you know about dragons?"

Chapter 20

"DRAGONS?" I RAISED an eyebrow. I couldn't tell if he was joking. "Giant lizard-monsters that breathe fire and fly?"

"Most human stories are based at least loosely on actual fae creatures. I should think you'd have learned that by now."

He was right, of course. Human beings were like children stumbling through the dark, trying to convince themselves the monsters under the bed weren't real. Unfortunately, they were. Not just the fae, but werewolves and who knew what else. Still. . . . "Dragons? Really?"

"Dragons were once the most powerful race among the fae. They are the progenitors of several younger races, including shifters and elementals."

"Are they still around?"

"Only a few," he said sadly. "The fae seem ever at war with someone. The war on your world was a schoolyard skirmish compared to that waged against the dragons."

I shuddered. So many people dead, or missing like my father. Wastes created by the conflict, dead zones where nothing would grow. It was hard to imagine worse.

"Many hundreds of years ago, the fae were cut off from our rulers, the first and strongest of our kind. This left a power vacuum in which every lord was fighting every other. Many fae believed the dragons would claim dominion over the other races, being older and stronger than most. The dragons had little interest in governing the lives of others, but like humans, fae seldom trust what they don't understand. The ambitious fae lords could not believe the dragons would abstain from power, so they created a weapon to level the playing field and went to war.

"I was not alive, so I cannot give specifics, but it is a story every fae child knows. The fae realized too late that the weapon was an abomination, that if the fighting continued they would inevitably destroy themselves. Much like humans with their atomic bomb, the weapon brought an end to the war, but at a terrible cost. The dragon home world, and the seat of the Elemental Court, was destroyed."

"What did the weapon do?"

"Have you ever seen one of the wastes left behind by the war here?"

"Yes," I whispered. "There's one east of here. It's terrible."

"Everything requires magic to live, even if it cannot draw on that magic in any tangible way. Magic is the energy that binds all living things. The wastes are places where all the magic has been used up, created when fae and human practitioners clashed. Those dead zones will eventually fill in, drawing energy from the surrounding world to heal, but it will take many years. Several mortal lifetimes at least."

I nodded. "The wastes are like sinkholes for magic."

"Exactly. And since the fae are creatures of magic, the magical void of a waste would pull the energy from our bodies until we were sucked dry. It would kill us in a matter of minutes, hours at most."

I rubbed at a deep crease on my forehead. "But it's not just the fae, is it?"

"No. Human practitioners draw and channel magic to cast spells. They would feel it first, as though a piece of their soul was missing. Even regular humans would eventually sicken and die. A waste will, eventually, kill all life foolish enough to remain."

"So the weapon used on the dragons made a waste?"

Kai nodded. "On a much larger scale. The weapon is a magical black hole. Once opened, it draws in all the magic around it. It never fills up. When the weapon was used on the dragon home world, it devoured all magic in a ten mile radius within the first hour, starting with the fae who opened it. After that, no one could get near enough to close it. The artifact ate that world, draining the energy from fae, animals, plants, everything. Some few managed to flee through portals ahead of the cataclysm. Now all the dragons that remain, once the most powerful and feared of the races, are refugees and vagabonds scattered throughout the realms."

Fingertips trembling against my lips, I whispered, "That's what's in Aiden's box? A black hole for magic?"

"I believe so. It would explain my assignment, and its secrecy. Most fae believe the box was destroyed along with the dragon's world, sealed away when the last portal was devoured. With no other magic to feed on, the weapon would eventually eat itself. But the box was retrieved from that dying world before the last gateway collapsed. I was chosen for this mission because I'm the only person with the right to investigate who also knew of the weapon's continued existence, having helped create the seal that contains it."

"If it's sealed, what's it matter who has it?"

"Any seal can be broken. It buys us time, that's all. We must recover the weapon before the seal is breached, or the artifact is taken out of this realm and beyond our reach."

I clenched my fists until nails bit into my palms. "That's the real reason you didn't want me talking to the police or PTF, isn't it? All that stuff about breaching the treaty and reigniting the war was just to convince me. You didn't want anyone getting their hands on your magic A-bomb."

"The threat that someone was trying to rekindle the war was very real. As was the fact that the official investigation was compromised. Everything I told you was true, it just wasn't the whole truth."

I sighed, shaking my head. *The fae couldn't tell outright lies, but that didn't mean you could trust them.* I'd grown comfortable with Kai, started to like him even, but he'd had his own agenda from the start. How could I believe him now? But if he was telling the truth, could I afford not to help? A device like that needed to be destroyed.

"What will you do if you find it?"

"Return it to my lord," he said without hesitation.

"So he can use it on the next world that stands up to him?"

His gaze flicked away. "I don't know what my lord intends to do with the box once it's recovered. However, he is the only fae capable of destroying it safely. Perhaps this theft will convince him the artifact is too dangerous to retain. The very fact that someone has learned of its existence is disturbing, and may indicate a larger problem in his court. But whatever the case, there's no question as to the horror Shedraziel will wreak if she obtains the artifact's power."

"How could he even make such a terrible device? What kind of monster would do that?"

"It was a time of war."

"That's no excuse." My stomach twisted, imagining an entire world reduced to a barren waste that would never heal. A lifeless land where nothing could survive. I didn't want to be related to the kind of person who could do that.

"Will you help, or not?"

How could I give a weapon like that to a man who'd already committed genocide? But the alternative was leaving it in the hands of a person who'd ordered the torture and murder of innocents to find it. I gritted my teeth. "I'll help."

If I got the chance, I'd drop the damn box in a volcano.

Kai nodded solemnly, as close as he'd come to saying thank you.

"But—" I crossed my arms, "—if this box is as dangerous as you say, we need to find it fast, before Smith's boss sends more goons to retrieve it. That means getting help. We'll find it a lot faster with the resources of the PTF."

Kai's brow furrowed. "I just told you this is a secret even among my own people, and you want to inform the agency most likely to use it against us?"

"We don't need to tell them what it is. Agent Johnson is already looking for Aiden's box. We just need to point him in the right direction."

"You trust this Agent Johnson?"

"With the fae gone, the authorities should be trustworthy again."

"What do you propose telling him?"

"Whatever you think might help him find where those fae were hiding the artifacts."

"Hmm." Kai's lips twisted in a sour expression. "While I don't relish the idea, even human hands are safer than Shedraziel's."

"So you'll talk to him?"

"No."

I opened my mouth to protest.

"But I'll tell you what information to pass on about our departed smugglers."

"Wouldn't it be better coming from you?"

"I avoid the PTF when I can. Besides, there are other stones to turn. I'll go to Crossroads and see what I can get out of Targe and the patrons there."

I nodded. "So what should I tell him?"

I CALLED UNCLE SOL first, the one PTF officer I actually trusted, but the call went straight to voice mail. I had similar luck with Agent Johnson, whose answering service picked up after six rings.

"This is Alex Blackwood. You came by last week to talk about an item that went missing when my friend, Aiden, was killed. I've got some new information about the fae who came looking for it. I also learned about an enchantment that's protecting it. It's dangerous to mess with if you don't know what you're doing, so maybe we can work together to get to the bottom of this? Please let me know as soon as you get this. Thanks."

Kai had spent a good hour going over what information to give the PTF and what to leave out, but he'd refused to tell me more about our mysterious enemy except that if she got her hands on the weapon she wouldn't hesitate to use it.

I paced a circle around the living room, Cat's eyes swiveling to watch from the back to the couch. Tapping the phone against my thigh, I made the circuit twice more. Then, for fear I'd wear through my carpet before Johnson called back, I pulled out some anodized aluminum jump loops and started weaving a strip of simple European 4-in-1 chain mail. When that was done, I layered blue rings into the pattern, transforming it into a tight dragonback hybrid. I ran a finger over the cool links.

What would a dragon's scales really feel like?

Just as I was contemplating a new design, Cat jerked his head up and meowed. Gravel crunched outside.

I hadn't expected Kai back so soon. Maybe he'd gotten lucky.

Stretching the stiffness out of my neck and back, I went to meet him at the door, but it wasn't Kai's car that pulled up. Agent Johnson stepped out of a shiny black SUV.

He must have come straight from an assignment, because he was wearing PTF-issued riot gear. A pullover shirt with a high collar buckled into loose fitted pants tucked into boots. The fabric was black, but had a tell-tale sheen where thin bands of metal wove through it. From one gloved hand dangled a helmet that would complete the outfit. No fae could touch an agent without being burned, and wrapped head to toe in iron, it was believed most spells wouldn't work on them—a magic Faraday cage.

He dropped a cigarette butt into the gravel, stubbing it out with the toe of his boot before approaching my door.

"Agent Johnson," I greeted. "I wasn't expecting you to come all the way out here."

"I got your message and thought it best we speak in person. I would have had you come to my office, but I have reason to believe not everyone working your friend's case can be trusted."

So he'd noticed the inconsistencies in the investigation as well. "Please, come in."

"Where's the fae who's staying with you?"

"He's out right now."

"Good." He pressed a set of prongs into my side.

Every muscle in my body seized in a moment of intense pain, then the world went dark.

THERE WAS MUSIC. It was getting louder. My cell phone. Someone was calling me.

My body didn't respond when I tried to move.

I opened my eyes, and immediately wished I hadn't when nausea twisted my stomach. The world was on its side, and my immediate view was of the dust bunnies under my couch. My mouth tasted like I'd been sucking sawdust, and my cheek was cold and wet in a puddle of drool. Rolling my head to separate my skin from the sticky mess, I found Cat looking down from an end table, head cocked to one side in silent query. Beside him was the panic switch David had given me in case of emergency.

Gingerly, I tried to sit up, but my hands stayed resolutely behind my back. I succeeded only in flopping onto my face.

"Oops, careful now. Wouldn't want you to drown in that puddle you've been working on." Rough hands rolled me back to my side.

My shoulder screamed.

Grinding my teeth, I focused past the tingling numbness in my arms. My wrists were secured with heavy tape. A quick test confirmed my ankles were similarly bound. It was hard to think through the cobwebs in my head, but I was obviously in trouble.

A pair of shiny black boots stepped over me, and Paul Johnson, an officer of the Paranatural Task Force, one of the good guys, leaned over me with a knife.

My stomach clenched. Either the fae we killed weren't working alone, or their reinforcements had already arrived and taken control of the human puppet show.

"Please," I croaked through a throat like sandpaper. "You're not yourself. You don't know what you're doing. I can help."

"What do you mean, I'm not myself?" He sounded more amused than skeptical at the idea.

"You're being manipulated. The fae behind the killings have been messing with the humans investigating. You said yourself you didn't think everyone on the case could be trusted. They must have gotten to you."

"Hmm." He sat down on the couch, effectively hiding his face. As much as I craned my neck, I could only see from his boots to his knees. "That's an interesting theory, but I'm afraid you're quite wrong."

His chuckle made my blood run cold. I knew that voice. I'd heard it in Angela's apartment.

"It was you?" Maybe it was an after-effect of the stun gun, or just my own disbelief, but I couldn't wrap my head around the idea. "But the killer used magic. It couldn't be you unless—Are you fae?"

One shiny boot kicked out with enough force to roll me over my bound arms and onto my other side. The screaming ache in my ribs when I tried to fill my lungs told me I'd be lucky if they weren't broken.

"Don't you dare accuse me of being one of those filthy monsters!"

He was up and pacing. When I saw his face, the last of my doubts disappeared. In his eyes burned the insanity of a righteous zealot, someone who believed in what they were doing beyond all reason. This was a man who would kill without hesitation. How had I missed it?

He took a deep breath and smoothed his hair back.

"I'd like to be civil about this. Tell me how to break the enchantment on your friend's box, and I'll make it as painless as possible."

He planned to kill me either way. Angela's final thoughts echoed in my head. *Only one choice left to consider—fast or slow.*

I shivered at the memory of blades slicing through my neck.

Fuck if I was gonna just roll over. Maybe Kai would get home, maybe whoever called would decide to pay me a visit, maybe hell would freeze over. At least I could learn the truth before I died, for all the good it would do me.

"So you killed all those people? Why?"

He scoffed, "To get their magic baubles of course. You must have figured that much out by now. How else could a human hope to fight a faerie?"

"But why kill them? You work for the PTF, you could have reported them and confiscated the artifacts."

"And send the items into the system to be catalogued and shipped off to gather dust until the next war? I'd never get my hands on them."

I strained against my bonds, trying to keep my voice even. "Why do you want them?"

"The faerie filth don't belong here." His voice carried the rhythm of a well-worn phrase. "This is our world. I'm going to see that they leave and can't ever come back."

"You're going to start a war."

"We're already at war," he shouted, spittle flying. He began to pace. "People pretend we've got the fae under control since they signed a piece of paper promising to be good little monsters, but I know better. Every day I see evidence that the fae are ignoring their agreement. They walk through our streets looking like people, twisting the minds of honest folk to get what they want. They can't be trusted. If not for them—" His fists clenched.

He turned so I couldn't see his face, but I caught the hitch in his voice. "What did they do to you?"

He shook his head and stood a little straighter. "It doesn't matter. Not anymore."

"If you start a war, innocent people will suffer."

"The innocent have nothing to fear. Not once I get this box open." He pulled out a small silver box covered with intricate markings and caressed it fondly.

"You have no idea what that box is capable of," I warned.

"On the contrary, I've been looking for this little beauty for some time. I know exactly what it's capable of." He held the box up reverently. "This is our salvation."

I shook my head, staring at his rapt expression. Kai had been adamant, the weapon's continued existence was a well-kept secret. A reader like Smitty couldn't even figure it out. How could a human, of all people, know what Aiden's box truly held?

I licked my lips. "How did you learn about the box?"

He rolled his eyes toward me and a wicked smile curved his lips. "You think I'm the only soldier in this war?"

A shiver ran through me as I stared into that glassy leer.

"If all you wanted was Aiden's box, why kill those other people?"

He snorted. "People? Those weren't people. They were freaks. The cast-off by-blows of monsters that couldn't keep to their own species. But they were a necessary step. Everything I did brought me closer to this." He stroked the box like an adoring parent.

I cast about for another argument, anything to drag this out. "How could you stand to sleep with Melissa if that's how you saw her?"

His head snapped up, and the color drained from his face. "How did you know about that?"

"I . . . heard it from a fae who knew her."

Eyes narrowed beneath his knit brow, he glared at me. "She was repulsive. It sickened me to touch that creature, but I needed her. Part goblin. They're amazing at tracking down hard to find items."

"You used her to find people with fae artifacts." But Melissa died over a month before Aiden, and two others were killed between them. "Why kill her before you got your hands on the box?"

"She'd become a liability. Some faeries tried to buy her services to help them track down artifacts. Probably the ones who visited you. She turned them down, but it was only a matter of time. Lucky for me, your friend was on the list she made before she died."

"But Aiden hid the box."

"Irritating little prick." His face flashed an ugly scowl, but cleared in the next breath. He shrugged. "No matter. I've got it now."

"But you can't open it."

"Not alone, but I can be very persuasive." He set the box on my end table and pulled a wicked looking knife from a sheath at his waist. "Last chance for mercy."

Light glinted off the blade. I couldn't look away.

Even if I wanted to save myself, I didn't know how to break the seal. I opened my mouth with no idea what to say, and a scream erupted as cold steel found a home in my thigh.

"Too late." He smiled. "That's all right. It would've been too easy if you'd told me. Too good a death for a faerie-lover like you." He twisted the knife, and another scream ripped out of me as the muscles in my leg tore apart.

When I faced Tim in the meadow, it had been all adrenaline and action. I'd known I was going to die, but I'd been on my feet, fighting it. This was slow, and certain, and a hundred times worse. The beast Tim had been was nothing compared to the monster kneeling over me now.

Sweat coated my skin, my breath came in ragged gasps through gritted teeth. "You can't control it," I panted. "It'll destroy us all."

"This little beauty destroys magic. Only the freaks need to fear it. We'll finally purge the world of all the filth. No more faeries, no more halfers, no more damned practitioners. Send them all to Hell where they belong." He jerked the knife out, and I screamed again.

"There's no point protecting them. They don't belong here. Do yourself a favor and tell me what I need to know to set the world right."

I shook my head with a sob, tears blurring my vision. "I don't know!"

This time, when his boot hit me, bones cracked. I curled into a ball to protect my middle, and the next shot landed on the wound in my thigh. I gasped. I didn't have enough breath to scream.

"Tell me," he shrieked, raining kicks on my battered body.

With my arms and legs bound, I couldn't protect myself, so I hunched as much as I could, scrunched my eyes shut, and let the pain wash over me.

"Fine," he huffed, out of breath. "I'll get it out of your faerie friend when he comes back. That'll be more fun anyway."

I blanched at the memory of laying on the floor with this man on my back. Except it wasn't me, it was Angela. He'd burned his knee into her back wearing iron-laced PTF riot gear, and he'd do the same to Kai.

"Please," I begged, "stop."

"Ready to talk?"

"It's not what you think," I sobbed. "That artifact will kill the fae, but it will destroy our world, too. That's what it does."

"You're just trying to save your freak friends," he spat. "At least killing you will keep the cops chasing their tails. Dumb as they are, they would have made the halfer connection eventually. A metalsmith is the perfect victim, indisputably human."

I laughed at the irony, but the sound became a wheeze as the pressure in my chest shifted. Above me, Johnson raised his blade and started an arc that would take the tip straight into my neck. At least it would be quick.

Chapter 21

A STREAK OF GRAY flashed above me as Cat launched himself at Johnson's unprotected face, a furry ball of biting teeth and ripping claws. The knife clattered to the floor. Johnson wrapped both hands around Cat's middle and tried to pull the furious beast loose. Smoke curled off Cat's fur and the smell of burning flesh filled the air.

Cat's hiss became distinctly more human as his body seemed to twist and melt, morphing into a full-grown man. Pointed ears peeked out from a cascade of silver hair. Johnson was doubled over with his hands around the waist of a six-foot, angry, naked fae.

A knee shot up and caught Johnson in the chin, breaking his hold and sending him reeling. The man who'd so recently been my cat rained blows on the disoriented PTF agent, moving the fight away from me. Every time the fae made contact with Johnson's iron-laced clothing there was a hiss, and the burning smell grew stronger. Johnson landed several blows as well, each resulting in a blistering burn on the fae's unprotected flesh. Cat, or whoever he was, wouldn't last long.

Resolutely ignoring the pain that lanced through me, I scooted to Johnson's discarded blade. It took several tries to locate the knife behind my back and coax my numb fingers to grab it. Sawing clumsily at my bonds, I nicked my wrist and lost my grip.

Cursing through clenched teeth, I groped for the blade's handle, now slick with blood. Again and again, the blade caught my skin, but I gritted my teeth and kept sawing. I wouldn't die on the floor like some sacrificial lamb.

After what seemed like an eternity, the tape gave way and I

brought my aching arms around to work on my ankles.

Johnson had Cat backed into a corner. With nowhere to maneuver, and the constant burns taking a heavy toll, Cat had to be nearing his limit.

Cutting the remaining restraints, I rolled gingerly to my knees, but froze as a wave of nausea washed over me. Every breath sent fire racing through my chest. My arms and legs tingled, and I recognized the eerie chill spreading through me as a symptom of blood loss. The pattern on the rug beneath my trembling hands swam, and the light around me dimmed.

This was impossible. I couldn't even move. How could I fight?

The smell of burning hair and singed flesh cut through my thoughts and brought my attention back to the corner where Cat still struggled.

As much as it hurt to move, I had to try. Cat had saved me. Now it was up to me to save us both.

Biting my lip until I tasted blood, I tested my ruined leg. The world disappeared as another wave of nausea hit me, and it was all I could do to keep from crying out. The muscles Johnson had eviscerated in my thigh would not hold my weight, and no amount of resolve would change that.

Dragging my useless leg, I crawled to the corner where Johnson was closing in on Cat. Every movement sent bolts of pain shooting through me, and I prayed he didn't hear the whimpers that escaped my pinched lips.

Johnson's back loomed above me, blocking Cat from view.

To hell with it.

I swung the blade at the back of Johnson's knee, slicing steel filaments and tendons alike. It wasn't deep, but it didn't need to be.

Johnson howled and twisted to lunge for me, eyes wide and wild.

I had nowhere to run, and no time.

Then Cat's arms wound through Johnson's to bring him up short. Both men hit the floor, and Cat shouted, "Do it!" as ribbons of smoke curled off his skin.

Without thinking, I slammed the knife into Johnson's chest as hard as I could.

He screamed once, but the sound was quickly overwhelmed by a gurgle of blood. With one massive shudder, his head flopped back and his eyes clouded over.

I stared at my hands, still gripping the knife buried deep in a dead man's chest. The second man I'd killed in as many days. My fingers stuck to the handle and came away wet, my palms crimson. I looked down at them in stupefied horror until a quiet moan brought me back to my senses. Cat was still burning.

Shifting to the side, I rolled Johnson's body until the handle of the knife hit the floor. The strain on my ribs was enough to make me cry, and the sight before me made it impossible not to.

The fae who had saved me lay prone on the floor, breathing shallowly, his skin raw and blistered. His flesh hadn't charred as Neil's had, but it was a tight, shiny red, interrupted by patches of oozing blisters.

Choking down a sob, I found an undamaged patch of skin on his cheek to gingerly lay my hand.

Silver lashes fluttered open, and the eyes that sought me were iridescent yellow-green with vertical pupils. Cat's eyes.

"Is he dead?" His voice was so quiet I could barely make it out.

I nodded.

The beautiful eyes closed. "The police are on their way. Don't tell them about me."

"How—" Then I remembered my ringing cellphone, Cat sitting by the panic button. He'd saved me twice.

His body again seemed to melt and twist, this time shrinking back into the familiar shape of Cat. Chunks of fur were missing, and the skin beneath was burned and blistered, just as it had been in his human form. He lay unmoving, and I held my breath until I saw the shallow rise and fall of his chest.

From the end table, the small silver box that had caused so much trouble seemed to wink at me as the light caught its surface. I could try to hide it, but not without leaving a trail of blood and questions. Better to leave it in plain sight. Just a harmless bauble to decorate my living room.

My gaze drifted to the blanket draped over the back of the couch, but I couldn't bear the through of crossing that distance again. Instead, I tore off the bottom of my shirt and pressed it to my thigh to slow the bleeding. Shivers wracked my frame as I fought the urge to lie down.

It was a long wait for the sound of a car engine that told me help had finally arrived.

THE CEILING THAT greeted me was not my own. In place of the familiar water stain that reminded me of a tree, were industrial tiles and florescent lights. There was a beep of nearby machinery, and the unmistakable smell of antiseptic. I was in a hospital. My limbs felt heavy, and the fog in my brain meant I'd been given some kind of medication.

"What am I going to do with you?" Beside the bed sat a single chair. Its occupant was mostly hidden behind a newspaper, revealing only a pair of immaculate gray slacks and shiny black shoes.

"Hi, Uncle Sol."

"Hi?" He folded the paper so I could receive the full force of his glare. "That's all you've got to say is, hi?"

I smiled. "It's good to see you."

So much of my life had been turned upside down, it was wonderful to see that leathery face with its familiar disapproving scowl. The crow's feet around his light brown eyes and gray streaks in his hair were more pronounced than I remembered, and the ever-present creases on his brow were more distinct. It looked like I wasn't all he'd had to worry about lately.

"Lucky for you, I got back last night. I came as soon as I heard." He sighed. "You wanna tell me what happened?"

So I did. The words were stilted at first, but gained momentum as I spoke until they tumbled out like a flood. I told him about Aiden and the rest of the victims being unregistered halfers who owned fae treasures; I told him about agent Johnson being the serial killer, intent on purging the world of magic; I even told him about Kai's revelation that I wasn't as human as I'd thought. What I didn't tell him was that sitting on my end table was a fae artifact that could tear the world apart, or that I was related to the fae lord who made it. I wasn't certain I wanted to give the box back to my grandfather, but I was damn sure it shouldn't fall into human hands.

Sol listened patiently to my explanation, occasionally nodding or frowning, but never interrupting. When I told him I was an unregistered halfer, I expected him to be furious, disbelieving, or at least surprised, but he took it in stride with the rest of my story. By the time I finished, my mouth was dry and I felt as though I'd been wrung out.

"How could someone who hates paranaturals so much work for the PTF?" I asked. "It's your job to maintain the peace, and he wanted to start a war."

"We have a screening process, but the selection committee isn't infallible. The fact that people with prejudices like Mr. Johnson's are employed with the PTF is unfortunate, but hardly surprising. If someone wanted to go after paranaturals, what better way than to work for the agency that monitors them?"

I bit my lip. "So what happens now?"

"Since Johnson's death was clearly self-defense, I don't think you'll have much trouble, but I've arranged a lawyer just in case." He patted my good leg. "I'll stick around until this is cleared up."

"I meant—" I bunched the blanket in my fists and swallowed past the lump in my throat. "What happens now that we know I'm a halfer?"

He peered at me over the rim of his glasses and frowned. "Nothing."

We stared at each other for a beat. Then I stammered, "Isn't there some kind of quarantine period when a person registers? Tests and things?"

"There isn't a test currently in use that can identify you as fae, and we're not going to give them reason to make one."

"Wait, did you know?" I was halfway to sitting before the screaming pain in my ribs made me reconsider.

"You and I will discuss your situation later. For now, don't mention it to anyone. When the officers take your statement, tell them Mr. Johnson tried to kill you because he saw you as a fae sympathizer, and the death of a pure human would help keep the investigation off-track. Your connection to Aiden and that you had a fae staying with you are established facts, and more than enough reason for someone with Mr. Johnson's prejudices to want you dead."

"You want me to lie?" I couldn't believe my ears. Uncle Sol, a high-ranking official with the PTF, was telling me to hide the fact that I was a halfer.

"Have you got any idea what would happen if the PTF learned there were fae who could handle iron?" He shook his head. "Just keep your head down until this blows over. You've been drawing a lot of attention from the wrong kinds of people lately, and I can only do so much."

"It's not like I meant to," I grumbled. "I was just minding my own business when my life went haywire."

"I know, kiddo." He stood with an exaggerated groan and pop as he cracked his back. "Don't make a habit of this. The chairs here aren't very comfortable."

"Thanks for being here, Uncle Sol."

"He patted me on the head. "The police are waiting outside. You ready to face the music?"

"Not really," I admitted, "but I might as well get it over with."

"Atta girl." He smiled and pushed open the door.

IT DIDN'T TAKE AS long as I expected to relate my story to Detective Garcia and the two other cops who came in for statements. Everyone seemed to accept that Johnson was the serial killer and I was acting in self-defense, which made me wonder what Uncle Sol had told them before they came in.

I didn't have to fake the hitch in my voice when I got to the part about waking up bound on the living room floor, or the way my hands shook when I gestured to my bandaged leg.

Garcia shared a look with her companions and flipped her little notebook closed. "That's enough for now, Ms. Blackwood. We'll be in touch."

My head flopped back against lumpy pillows, and I breathed a sigh of relief. Then the door opened again.

Just shy of six feet with dark brown hair and eyes, my next guest marched into the room like a man on a mission. He introduced himself as local PTF agent Ben O'Connell.

An uneasy foreboding settled in the pit of my stomach. This was the man I'd spoken with when I called to report my unwanted fae visitors to the supremely unhelpful local office. More importantly, Agent O'Connell was the man who'd been trying so hard not to be noticed outside Smitty's Pawn Shop. I was glad Sol wanted me to keep my fae nature a secret. From the daggers O'Connell was glaring, I couldn't imagine this man knowing the truth about me would be anything but disastrous.

I greeted him with a forced smile and said, "How can I help you?" Customer service habits die hard.

"You can confess to murder." He pointed a finger at me like he wished it were a gun. "I wanted to tell you to your face that I don't believe what you're accusing Paul Johnson of. He was a good man, and he happened to be a friend of mine. I'm gonna do what I can to clear his name and prove you murdered him."

My mouth fell open. "What possible reason would I have to do that?"

"I don't know yet, but I'm damn well gonna find out." With that, he stormed out of the room, slamming the door.

I knew all too well how upsetting it could be to learn a friend wasn't quite who you'd thought, and finding out Aiden was a halfer didn't hold a candle to O'Connell finding out his coworker was a homicidal psychopath. Still, being the target of his rage made my skin crawl. He couldn't discredit my self-defense plea since it was true and I had plenty of evidence to back it up, but that didn't mean he couldn't cause me a world of other trouble.

DESPITE MY EXHAUSTION, sleep was elusive. I shifted, unable to ease the pain in my thigh or the ache in my chest, as shadows stretched across the ceiling and the orange-tinged sky faded to black. Finally, I called a nurse to pump me full of painkillers. When my vision fuzzed around the edges, I slumped against my pillows and tried to relax, drifting in and out of consciousness in a clouded daze.

Well after midnight, my eyes popped open for the millionth time, though my pain seemed blessedly quiet.

The door to my room stood open, and a man slipped inside.

My mind jumped immediately to O'Connell, and my heart started to race.

Don't be stupid. It's probably just a nurse.

Then the figure stepped fully into the room, and the dim light from the window fell over James's features.

He moved so smoothly he almost seemed to float as he crossed the room in less time than it took me to blink.

The bed dipped as he settled on its edge, and I rolled slightly toward the weight. Blinking heavy eyelids, I struggled to get my hazy mind to focus. "Is this a dream?"

The corners of his mouth lifted. "No."

"Visiting hours are over."

"Shall I come back another time?"

I shook my head. "It's nice to see a friendly face."

He brushed a strand of hair away from my forehead. "I needed to see with my own eyes that you were all right."

"Sorry for worrying you."

He frowned, lines etching deep around his mouth and eyes. "Why did you take on so much? Colluding with fae? Chasing a murderer? There are easier ways to kill yourself."

I closed my eyes and rolled my head from side to side, replaying events, assessing each choice. "Honestly, I'm not sure how it all happened. Just, one thing led to another and another, and every time I thought it was over something happened that kept me moving forward."

"If anything like this happens again, promise you'll tell me."

My eyes popped open. "God, I hope nothing like this ever happens again."

He shifted slightly, making the springs creak, and lifted my hand in both of his. "The thought of losing you—" He shook his head. "I care about you, Alex. More than I was willing to admit."

James's words settled around my heart like a warm blanket in a blizzard of rampant emotions as all the what-ifs I'd pushed aside over the years came pouring back.

The regret I'd felt in Aiden's dying memory burned bright in my mind. He'd loved me, but suppressed his feelings so we could be friends, safe and simple. Now he was gone, and we'd never get a chance to see what might have happened.

Keeping myself closed off wasn't brave, and it wasn't smart. It was cowardice, plain and simple. Maybe a relationship with James would crash and burn. Maybe not. I wasn't sure which was more terrifying, but I wouldn't know unless I tried.

Acting before my treacherous brain could think better of it, I pushed off my pillows. James looked as surprised as I felt when my lips sealed over his.

The kiss was soft at first, a question. Then it grew deeper as we both relaxed into it.

After what seemed an eternity and entirely too short a time, I pulled away. "My life is a mess."

Gently, he lowered me back to the pillows. Electric tingles danced over my skin where his hand lingered near my collar bone. "Whose isn't?"

I was grinning like a fool when he left, and well into the night.

DAVID WALKED through my door five minutes after an intercom chime announced visiting hours were open, a takeout cup in each hand. The scent of pumpkin spice latte managed to push back the pervasive smell of sanitizer that went hand-in-hand with hospitals, and my mouth began to water.

"I could kiss you."

"How ya holdin' up?" He handed me one of the drinks, and I took a long, slow drag of burning heaven.

"Do you have any idea how many things in this room beep, ding, and buzz?"

He smiled and sipped his drink.

"All night," I continued. "They never shut up."

"It's a hospital, Alex."

"And this bed!" I held up the remote a nurse had given me. "I've pushed every button on here at least fifty times. It doesn't get any comfier." I flopped back into the too-soft pillows. "I'm gonna go crazy if I stay here much longer."

He pulled a deck of cards from his back pocket, "I figured as much."

We spent three hours playing everything from Go-Fish to Texas Hold'em as clouds drifted across the pale blue sky outside my window.

"Two." David set two cards face down between us. "I got a call from All-States today."

I dealt him two new cards. "Who?"

"Aiden's cremation place."

I stared at my full house, not really seeing it.

"It's done," he said. "The ashes should arrive next week. Fold." He dropped his cards face-down on the bed. "We need to decide what to do with them."

I collected the cards and shuffled the deck. "We should take him back to Mexico. In the spring."

David tilted his head, then nodded. "He was happy there."

I dealt out a new hand.

David picked up his cards and rearranged them. "You could have died, Alex." His voice dropped to a raw whisper. "You nearly did."

"That panic button saved my life."

"You saved your own life. The police said you took him out before they even showed up." He shook his head. "Johnson's background check came in this morning, for all the good it did you. Not that the guy had killer written all over him, but I was able to dig up a connection to Purity."

He looked up from his cards, searching my face, and I squirmed under the scrutiny. "What?"

"I was surprised to find the security cameras in the house were off. The case against that PTF psycho would be a whole lot easier with that footage."

"Kai asked me to turn the cameras off earlier that day. He needed to tell me something that he didn't want recorded."

David snorted. "Those cameras don't record sound."

"I know, but he wanted them off just the same, and I didn't see any harm." I shrugged and hid behind my cards. "I guess I forgot to turn them back on."

"Damn it, Alex!"

"I know, I know." In truth it had worked out well since I didn't want footage of Cat turning into a man finding its way to the PTF. We still had the outside footage of Johnson stunning me without provocation to prove I was acting in self-defense.

David's sudden laugh made me jump. "You are one lucky son of a bitch, you know that?"

"Yeah." I smiled. "I know."

His next comment was cut off by a knock at the door.

"Sorry to interrupt." Kai looked more awkward than I'd ever seen him.

"That's all right, Kai. I was hoping to see you before you left."

"Left?"

"Well, yeah. I figured you'd be headed back to the reservation."

"Ah, of course."

"This is my friend, David. David, this is Kai."

"So I gathered." David stood up, placing his cards face down on the table. "I think I'll head out. I'm sure you two have things to discuss." He leaned over to plant a kiss on my forehead, then turned to Kai. "She's done enough. Put her in danger again and you'll regret it."

To my surprise, Kai actually bowed. "I understand." He kept his eyes down until David left the room. When he looked up, his expression was pained. "I would have come sooner, but the police and an unpleasant man named O'Connell were questioning me."

"Yeah, I've had that pleasure. What did you tell them?"

The hint of a smile twitched his lips. "The truth, of course." Then his smile fell. "I'm sorry, Alex. I brought you into this mess, but I wasn't there when you needed me."

"You couldn't have known Johnson was the killer, or that he would show up at the house. Even if you'd been there, he was wearing anti-fae armor."

"Still, I'm sorry."

I waved off the apology.

"I took the liberty of collecting your discharge papers on the way in." He held out a stack of documents he must've magicked the nurses to get. "Unless you'd rather spend another night here?"

THE BUMPY ROAD made my ribs and thigh ache, but I was happy to be on my way home. Two long, dull days in the hospital were quite enough. Once we had some distance between us and any prying ears, I asked the question that had my stomach in knots for two days. "Did you get it?"

"Yes. I was surprised you left it in the open."

"Yeah, well, I didn't have a lot of options. What did you do with it?"

"Returned it to its rightful owner." He glanced sideways at me. "He was impressed with your work."

"I didn't do it for him."

"Nonetheless, you've pleased him. He hoped you would come in person, but I advised him you would not yet be safe at court."

"Safe?"

"There are many rules at court, and even small mistakes can be deadly. To that end, I've convinced my lord to let me remain here and tutor you in the customs of our people. When you're ready, I will take you to the Court of Enchantment."

I shook my head. Accepting that I was a halfer didn't mean I was ready to take the plunge into their world. "What makes you, or him, think I want to visit a fae court?"

"Now that you've been acknowledged, a meeting with my lord is inevitable."

"Well, if he wants to meet me, he can come here." I crossed my arms.

"The mortal authorities do not look favorably upon fae lords leaving the reservations. Besides, do you really want that particular connection coming to light?"

I bristled at the implication, but he was right. I couldn't afford to draw more attention from the PTF now that I'd opted not to register. Especially with O'Connell snooping around.

"I know this isn't what you had in mind, Alex, but you must realize your life can't go back to the way it was. Not entirely."

I nodded. I was a part of the paranatural world now, whether I liked it or not. I could either stick my head in the sand until the next crisis, or let Kai prepare me for it. "How long is your visa good for?"

"Three months."

I pursed my lips. "There would need to be a few changes if you're sticking around that long."

"Whatever you say."

My quiet life had been shattered, invaded by people who wanted to hurt me, or help me, or love me, or kill me. I wasn't quite sure where Kai fit yet, but it was worth finding out. Even if it meant making myself vulnerable.

"Did Gramps say what he intends to do with the box? Or how Johnson found out about it in the first place?"

"That's not something he would discuss with the likes of me. Perhaps when you see him, you can inquire for yourself."

"What happened to the other artifacts the PTF recovered?" Sol had called to tell me that working together, the police and PTF found several magic artifacts in Johnson's possession, including a small mirror that altered perception and a bracelet that ensured no trace of him was left at the crime scenes.

"I fear those must remain in mortal hands. The police require evidence."

We drove in companionable silence for a time, and I watched the world slip by. As we rolled up the winding road of Boulder Canyon, however, a new worry came to mind. "What about those fae we killed? I was right to kill Johnson, he admitted what he'd done and made it perfectly clear what he planned to do with me, but we were wrong about the fae."

"Yes, I'm afraid we were climbing up the wrong tree with them."

I cocked my head to the side, staring.

"You know." He waved a hand. "Chose the wrong course of action."

I rolled my eyes. "Barking up the wrong tree."

His brow creased. "How does one bark up a tree?"

I opened my mouth, closed it, and shook my head. "Never mind."

Kai patted my arm. "It's true those fae were not Aiden's killers, but neither were they innocent. They attacked first, which means we were acting in self-defense. Just as you did in your home."

"But we lured them there with the intention of confronting them, they just got to it first."

"Our intentions are irrelevant. The fact that they acted first is all that matters. In the eyes of the fae, you are guiltless."

If only human emotions were as clear-cut as fae laws. "I don't feel guiltless."

"Again, I apologize. It was my mistake. I should never have brought you to that meeting."

"It was our mistake. I thought they were guilty, too." It was strange to assuage a fae's conscience after the grudge I'd carried so long, but my experiences over the past few weeks had proven that monsters weren't necessarily evil, and good guys weren't always good. Fae, human, whatever, we all just did the best we could.

We lapsed into awkward silence until he made the turn up my driveway.

"Do you know if my cat is all right?"

Kai snorted. "Your cat will be fine."

"He was hurt pretty badly."

"He's a resilient breed." He pointed as we came over the hill in sight of my house. "See for yourself."

Perched at the edge of the porch was a tall man with a braid of silver that draped over his shoulder and fell to his waist. At least he was wearing clothes this time.

Kai opened the door to help me out like a perfect gentleman. Once I was steady on my feet he gestured toward the house and said, "I'll give you two some space."

Walking was difficult with the tight brace that held my leg straight. To ease the awkwardness as I hobbled toward the porch, I asked, "Aren't you worried about being caught on camera?"

"The security system is off." His voice was deep and rich, its smoothness like a balm after the harsh croak it had been the only other time I'd heard it.

"I'm glad you're all right." I bit my lip. "I need to thank—"

His hand shot out to cover my mouth before I could finish.

"Don't," he said.

I gently pulled his hand away. "I know I'm not supposed to, but you saved my life. I owe you for that."

Quirking his lips he said, "Then you can repay me now."

"What?" Had he been expecting a favor? Still, I could hardly take it back, and he had saved my life. "What do you want?"

"To continue living here, and for you to keep my presence and nature a secret."

"Why? I mean, what were you doing here in the first place?"

"I've been keeping an eye on things."

"Things? You mean me?"

He smiled. "When the killings started, my lord—Lord of the Shifters—believed you might be called into play by the Lord of Enchantment, as indeed you were. We are not currently at war, but the lord likes to stay informed of any interesting developments, and you are very interesting."

"So you were spying on me."

"Yes," he said blandly. "And aren't you glad? My orders were simply to observe, but I didn't see much point in watching you become a corpse."

"Well, I am grateful, but if you want to stay here we're going to have to set some boundaries."

"I'm a cat." He shrugged. "Boundaries don't apply."

I snorted. "That's another thing. I can't keep calling you Cat."

"Why not?"

"Well, you're a person," I reasoned, "you must have a name. What do you want me to call you?"

His smile exposed pointed teeth. "You may call me Chase."

"Great, Chase the cat," I laughed. The conversation felt surreal, but I pressed on. "I think some people may already know about you. It would explain why some of my guests acted so strangely when they saw you."

"I don't expect you to control the rest of the world, you must only promise not to knowingly reveal my presence to anyone."

"That I can do," I agreed. "Just to be clear, you want to stay as a cat, not a person, right?"

"That's correct."

"I suppose that's okay." Then I hesitated, thinking of all the embarrassing moments Cat had witnessed since I let him into my house. My cheeks grew hot.

"This should prove entertaining," he purred, and sauntered into the house.

A chilly breeze pushed me toward the open door, tugging at my clothes and pulling several strands of frizz loose from my ponytail to whip around my face. I breathed deep, the crisp air biting my lungs, and tugged the collar of my coat tight. Heavy clouds were rolling in over the mountains.

Kai joined me on the porch, following my gaze to the looming storm. "Winter's coming."

Want more?

Continue the series with

COURTING DARKNESS
Book 2 of The Magic Smith series.

Acknowledgements

This book has had a long journey from concept to shelf, and there are quite a lot of people who helped along the way.

First and foremost, I couldn't have done this without the tireless support and encouragement of my wonderful husband, David, and the friends and family who never stopped cheering me on no matter how many times their questions of, "How's the book?" were met with the same, "Still working on it."

Thanks to my first readers, who struggled through the book when it was 120,000 unedited words, and to my critique group for helping me trim it down. Thanks to Ella Marie and the Belcastro Agency for taking a chance on me, and Bell Bridge for buying not only this book, but the next two as well. A huge thanks to Debra Dixon, the amazing editor who helped me through the last stages of revision to create the book you now hold.

And finally, thank you, the reader, for making this book's journey complete.

About the Author

Born and raised in Colorado, L. R. BRADEN makes her home in the foothills of the Rocky Mountains with her wonderful husband, precocious daughter, and psychotic cat. With degrees in both English literature and metalsmithing, she splits her time between writing and art. *A Drop of Magic* is her first novel.